Praise for *Lost and Never Found*

'Superb series'
Joan Smith, *Sunday Times* (Best Crime Books of 2024 so far)

'As in all fine novels, it is the voice that grips you:
ironic, eloquent, but compassionate'
Nicholas Chee, *Bookbrunch*

'Better than Morse in its bite, pace, urgency and characterisation'
The Critic

'Class conflict and police corruption are at the heart
of the third novel in this superb series'
Sunday Times (Pick of the Month, Jan 2024)

Praise for *The Broken Afternoon*

'The detectives Ryan Wilkins and Ray Wilkins – no relation –
are back . . . Having established their relationship so vividly
last year in *A Killing in November*, Simon Mason spreads
his wings to show just how good a writer he is . . . a funny,
thrilling and life-affirming story'
The Times

'There is no one else like him!'
Mark Sanderson, *Sunday Times Crime Club*

'This pacy tale, with twists and raw emotion, is gripping'
The Sun

Praise for *A Killing in November*

'This is a terrific crime novel, with a startlingly
original protagonist we're going to see a lot more of.
Oxford's mean streets just got meaner'
Mick Herron

'It's a brave writer who sets a new crime series in Inspector
Morse's Oxford but Mason has come up trumps with chalk-and-
cheese cops DI Ryan Wilkins and DI Ray Wilkins . . . It's well
plotted and very funny'
***** *The Sun*

'This has a TV series written all over it'
Daily Mail

'Simon Mason has reformulated Inspector Morse for the 2020s'
Mark Sanderson, *The Times* (Best New Crime Fiction for Jan 2022)

Also by Simon Mason

A Killing in November
The Broken Afternoon

LOST AND NEVER FOUND

Simon Mason

riverrun

First published in Great Britain in 2024
This paperback edition first published in Great Britain in 2024 by

riverrun

An imprint of

Quercus Editions Limited
Carmelite House
50 Victoria Embankment
London EC4Y 0DZ

An Hachette UK company

A CIP catalogue record for this book is available
from the British Library

PB ISBN 978 1 52942 589 5
EBOOK ISBN 978 1 52942 587 1

1

Typeset by CC Book Production

Printed and bound in Great Britain by Clays Ltd, Elcograf S.p.A.

MIX
Paper | Supporting
responsible forestry
FSC
www.fsc.org   FSC® C104740

Papers used by riverrun are from well-managed forests and other responsible sources.

For Eluned

ONE

The illegal car wash on the southbound road out of Oxford is the cheapest in the city, a makeshift compound of oily puddles and streams, slick and black under dripping awnings. Here, hour after hour, cars shunt slowly across the concrete, while dozens of men and women in waterproofs and galoshes crowd round them with hoses and sponges, soaping, spraying, wiping, rinsing. Occasionally these people speak to each other, brief asides in a language that might be Russian or perhaps Albanian. Mostly they are quiet. They are tired, bending and reaching in unvarying routine as the cars creep past: the saloons, the four-by-fours, the station wagons, hatchbacks, minivans, coupés, sedans. They know them all, these cars, all the brands and models; they have seen them all many times.

But they have never seen a Rolls-Royce Phantom. Here it comes now, on this slush-coloured February morning, enormous and otherworldly, gliding on to the splintered, streaming forecourt, one hundred per cent out of place, a visitation from another dimension; and the men and women stop to look. They have never seen anything so strange, that huge boat-like hull, that unearthly colour – crystal over Salamanca blue – the whole flowing technology uncannily natural, like the movement of blossom in a breeze or waves on the surface of the sea. They are seeing these things for the first time, vividly, and will remember them later, when the police arrive to take their statements, as they will remember the driver, a woman of complete self-possession, who sits behind the wheel, ignoring everything, obliviously performing neck exercises. Though they never look at her directly, the car-wash men and women take in everything about her: her elfin face, ragged-chic blond hair, distant blue eyes, small pointed chin. A young face, though she is not young; she looks like a child left in charge of the family car. They watch her from the corners of their eyes when she gets out and walks slowly over to the picnic tables set up at the edge of the compound to wait while the interior cleaning is being done. She stands there in a pool of greasy water, wearing elegantly tight-fitting olive-green slacks and an expensively simple blue sweater, and a touch, here and there, of bespoke jewellery, slim, modest, remote, her eyes strangely vacant, as if her mind were fixed on something else entirely, as if she existed without any connection to the current moment; until, at last, a man detaches himself from a little group of workers and walks across the wet compound towards her.

TWO

That evening, in the famous auditorium of Oxford's town hall, the Thames Valley Police gala dinner was taking place. At ten o'clock it had been proceeding, in formal mode, for more than three hours, and now, in the unstructured gap between meal and speeches, it was starting to lose its shape. While the stage was being prepared for the award-giving, the diners, sitting twenty to a table under the intricately decorated ceiling, removed their jackets, undid their waistcoats, discreetly adjusted their ball-gowns and gave rise to an impressive babble. People wandered about; some had to go outside. Liqueurs were served; the room was warm and dimly lit and loud.

At a table almost in the middle of the crowded floor, DIs Ryan and Ray Wilkins (no relation) sat with their partners, trying to keep a conversation going with Detective Superintendent Dave 'Barko' Wallace. Wallace was a copper of the old school, a wide man with a thick neck, outspread thighs and a seal-like body not shaped for tuxedos. He sweated steadily from his shorn head down, his small eyes angry and vigilant, as if intent on catching someone out. He was a bore. Ryan noticed his apparent inability to blink and wondered if it was a Govan thing, like his gargling accent or intimidating silences.

Ryan was good at noticing things, he looked at them quickly along a jabbing length of bony nose and the details stuck to his eyes. He sat contentedly with a can of energy drink, which he'd had to bribe a waiter to bring him, idly scratching, noticing his girlfriend Carol's left thigh, suddenly pale and bare where her dress had fallen to one side, the result of a nervous restlessness. He noticed movement at the back of the stage, and nodded towards it.

'Wonder Woman flown in.'

Ray released his wife's hand and turned in his seat. Both he and Diane were London-Nigerian, highly educated and elegant with it; Ray in particular was a stylish dresser, wearing tonight a silk tuxedo with blue and maroon floral patterns and black satin lapels. He had one of those handsome faces in which all the features seem to come together in a common purpose: the boy-hero jaw, the shapely mouth, intelligent eyes. By contrast, Ryan looked like the trailer-park kid he was, badly finished off about the chin and ears. He had a sort of borrowed look about him. His suit – rented, of course – was slightly big, and itchy around the groin.

Barko said, unblinking, 'You referring to Deputy Chief Constable Lynch?'

On stage, there were two people. One was the Lord Lieutenant of Oxfordshire, a former banker, now carnivalised in eighteenth-century tunic, complete with cap, sash and ceremonial sword. The other was the guest speaker of the evening, a shortish,

4

powerful-looking woman dressed in a black leather jacket and jeans, strikingly at odds with the evening dresses on display everywhere else. She was listening, or perhaps not, to the Lord Lieutenant, her face impassive behind Aviators.

Barko said, 'Son, that lady's had more commendations than any other serving officer in this force. Big ones. Silver Medal, Bravery Award.'

'CBE,' Ray said.

Ryan shrugged, peered into his can, tilted it far back, swallowed, gave a little grimace.

Perhaps Barko would have said more; he leaned towards Ryan with sudden intent, but at that moment the on-stage microphone came to life with a screech, like a hideous malfunction of the pleasant hubbub, and everyone turned again, wincing, towards the stage and the legendary figure of Chester Lynch, standing there alone now, relaxed in the limelight of their attention. She was still wearing her Aviators. Ryan remembered then that Barko had long ago served with Lynch's unit, perhaps even before the creation of the Chester Lynch legend, when Lynch was not yet the gloried maverick she would become; and he wondered what their relationship had been like. Carol turned to him and, as she smiled with that dazzling mouth, he saw in her eyes something else, some strangeness – mild panic almost, or judgement. Then Lynch began her address.

'Didn't want to come here, do this.'

Her voice was the well-known gravel-chewing cockney drawl, her face the familiar carved oddity, all planes and angles, not so much handsome as riveting. Riveting was the quality she cultivated. Her skin was so black it was almost purple.

'Make a little speech, hand out an award. Didn't want to do it.'

She left long pauses between her sentences, silences which no one disturbed.

'They said, "Come on, Chester. You'll see all these beautiful people. The young men," they said. "The women. The whole force has got good-looking," they said. It's true, by the way. But that's not why I come.'

She shook her head slightly, looking down at them.

'They said, "It'll be a spectacle." *Spectacle*'s actually the word they used.' She snorted lightly. 'They talked about the meal, the braised beef cheek, sautéed whatevers, the canapés, the Krug . . . Don't know what else. Candied fruits, is it? Snuff? They said, "It'll be elegant." Do I look like I'm interested in elegant?'

She gestured slightly, contemptuously, at her clothes.

'They told me they'd make everything easy, send a limo. You know the sort of thing – champagne on ice in a little silver bucket; peanuts in one of them lead-crystal tumblers, weigh a tonne in your hand.'

She took off her Aviators, slowly folded them and put them carefully into the inside pocket of her jacket. 'Well. I didn't come for the ride. I didn't come for the nibbles. No.' She lowered her voice. 'I'll tell you why I come.'

She looked round the auditorium. Thirty seconds seemed to pass. No one breathed.

'I come because you're fucking brilliant people. My people. That's why I come.'

There was applause, then – a lot – and she stood, drenched in it.

'Alright, alright,' she said. 'Calm the fuck down.'

Laughter. The laughter of the willing.

'It's not about me,' she said. 'But they told me I got to say something about myself anyway. You know, by way of introduction. A few words. It's nonsense, I know that – stupid – you don't need to tell me. No one needs my story; you've all got your own. Still. They did ask. And I can do it in three minutes.'

She took a breath, looked around.

'Grew up in Walthamstow. Scholarship girl at the university here. Wanted to be a copper, became a copper. Came to serve here in, I think, early 2002, worked the beat four, five years. Did some training, got some skills. Same as you. Did a little time in Violent Crime, got moved on – some of you heard about that. Ups and downs. Had some ideas – about street crime, vagrancy and so on. Put them into action, got some results. Got kicked in the coccyx by austerity, like everyone else. Then they put me in charge of this National Uplift thing. Well, I'm a black woman, aren't I? See me on television, in between the sitcoms and the documentaries about endangered types of moth.'

She looked at them with what seemed like the purest anger.

'Best years of my life? No question: working the beat, up at Rose Hill. Learned all the important stuff then. Make the tough choices. Take the difficult decisions. Why? They're the ones get results. Don't matter what they call you, and I've been called some things – on the street, in the boardrooms – I know that, I got the nicknames. Don't matter. Don't even matter if there's truth in the nicknames. Results, that's the thing. That's what I'm about.'

She shrugged modestly, buttoned her leather jacket.

'End of speech.'

Her watch was a heavy metal thing, chunky on her wrist; it caught the light as she lifted it.

'Two and a half minutes. Result, right there.'

More laughter, a murmuring of appreciation.

'Anyway,' she said, picking up the trophy that had been at her feet and casually waving it to and fro, 'speaking of results, there's a young man here tonight . . .'

Ryan stopped listening, went back to noticing Carol, who sat vividly next to him in her evening dress of electric-blue silk. She'd relaxed a little. They'd been seeing each other only a few months and they were still in the first phase of their relationship: he was living in a state of constant sexual emergency. God, she was built. Nine years older than him, thirty-seven, with one ex-husband and two kids, sharp-faced, alarmingly erotic, shockingly straightforward. She liked to shock, in fact. It was part of her attraction. She'd grown up wild in Didcot and other places, messed about, missed a lot of school, but now she owned four florists and lived in a converted farmhouse on the edge of Kennington. She had the business smarts big time, and the things that go with it – organisation, toughness, energy, a little bit of aggression. All in all, Ryan wasn't at all sure why she'd picked him out. They'd met one morning outside the infant school, where he was waiting with little Ryan to pick up his niece, Mylee. He hadn't even given her some old chat, they just talked about the kids, and something clicked, some weird mechanism pulled them together, set them going, all the way from St Swithun's Primary School to the fifty-fourth Thames Valley Police gala at the town hall.

Chester Lynch was still talking, but Ray was getting to his

feet, which Ryan thought was pretty uncool, a very un-Ray-like thing to do in the middle of a speech; and it was a moment before he took in the general applause, noticed people at nearby tables congratulating him. As Ryan watched, Ray leaned over and kissed Diane, buttoned his shimmering tuxedo and began to make his way towards the stage.

Fuck me, Ryan thought in shock. *He's fucking well won something.* Perhaps he actually said it out loud, because Carol turned to him with that look of hers that he didn't yet understand, hard-eyed and startled, as if she too was transfixed by the action on the stage, by Chester Lynch greeting Ray with a fist bump. And the next moment he was on his feet, fingers in his mouth, whistling and stomping his boots on the floor, while Barko sat immobile, staring at him in scorn.

They drove back to Kennington in her Range Rover. His Peugeot was still in the garage. For a while she didn't say anything, and he watched her as they went quietly through the hush of Oxford at one o'clock in the morning, past the cathedral, down the long stretch of road where the college playing fields are laid out like artworks on the carefully curated green of the water meadows.

'Just taken by surprise is all,' he said at last.

She gave a brief smiling pout of disbelief, looking at the road ahead.

'Alright. Jealous, then. A bit.'

The smile played at the edges of her mouth.

The urge came on him, very strong, to kiss her, touch her, put out his hand and feel the thin silk of her dress slide over her leg; he almost groaned with the force of it. But it also seemed a truth-telling urge, and he said, 'A bit, I don't know, pissed off. I mean, I did actually do quite a lot of the legwork.'

She drove on.

'This was after your discharge,' she said, after a while. 'So you weren't actually a policeman.'

'Just suspended,' he said defensively. 'Working my way back, fast track.'

They drove past the Tesco.

'Fast-ish,' he said.

They went over the railway tracks and turned towards Kennington.

'What's your problem with the lady giving out the prizes?' she asked, in a different tone.

'Lynch? She's alright. Just, like, everything's exaggerated with her. Toughest cop ever. Smartest cop ever. Coolest cop. It's like this whole Chester Lynch legend.'

He looked at her sideways, her profile.

'People got a crush on her. Ray's got a crush. Maybe it's a black thing.'

'Not allowed to say that, Ryan.'

They drove on.

'What did she get her CBE for?'

'Street vagrancy policy, I think. Sort of a clean-up. Move them on, basically.'

'And she got results?'

'If you look at the stats, yeah. Crime down, antisocial down, drug trade down. But police complaints went up big time, and, if you talk to any of the homeless – fuck, they hate her. Call her the Mover.'

They drove under the bypass, quiet now.

'Got moved on herself from Violent Crime,' she said.'

'Yeah, all the way up to DCC.'

'But moved on, why?'

'Well, that's something else. Scandal, controversy, whatever. Shot some local gangster in a lock-up. Rumour was she just took him down, personal thing. Don't believe it. Maybe even put it about herself, for the, you know – what's the word?'

'Notoriety?'

'That's the one. Worse thing, I think's, stuff with the homeless. I mean, they might be losers, but still.'

He shifted uncomfortably in his seat; it wasn't clear if it was the thought of Chester Lynch or his scratchy dress trousers that chafed him.

'Know any homeless, Ryan?'

Briefly, he thought of his old schoolmate, Mick Dick. Homeless, then dead. He sighed. 'Not anymore.'

They went slowly up the long road with its street bumps until they came to Kenville Road, where Ryan lived with his sister, Jade. Little Ryan would be there, asleep in his bed in the room he shared with his father, and Ryan thought of his son with the total abandonment of love. He looked at his watch: going on one thirty.

Carol slowed, came to a stop, looked at him. There was a moment's silence between them. 'Do you want to come back to mine?' Her dress had fallen off her thigh again and he stared at it, mesmerised, and swallowed. She knew he didn't like missing breakfast with his son, especially not after missing bedtime reading the night before.

'He had a tummy upset,' Ryan said.

She nodded. 'I'll get you up early, drive you back in time for breakfast. Or maybe,' she said softly, 'I'll just keep you up all night.'

He looked at her. They drove on.

So Oxford settled into sleep. A small city, damp, unconscious under February cloud, its clustered monuments making their familiar iconic gestures against the dim sky – here, the Radcliffe Camera's fat dome; there, the sharp tack of St Mary's spire – their outlines crisp as cardboard cut-outs. And, in the shadows of these buildings, on pavements slick with condensation, the homeless lay, silently outlasting the cold in their bags and tents. In Blue Boar Street, in Cornmarket, at Blackfriars, St Aldate's, St Ebbe's, outside the Odeon in Gloucester Green and in other haunts, they crouched, hunched under fire escapes or in doorways. In the shadows of the great colleges, wrapped in layers, wearing scavenged boots that didn't fit, they lay prone on cardboard beds rimmed with the day's detritus, invisible under piles of clothing. They persisted, getting through the night, alone, or in twos or threes, or in larger groups, not sleeping but sometimes no longer conscious, left out in the open like so much litter, lost things. But, at the makeshift camp in the graveyard of St Thomas the Martyr, at three o'clock in the morning, there was no one. It was deserted. They'd vanished in haste, leaving everything behind them – their tents and boxes, rags and empties – abandoning the graveyard with its tilting tombstones and dripping yew, putting distance between themselves and silent, dirty Becket Street, darkest and dirtiest street in town, where a Rolls-Royce Phantom lay buckled and wedged in the entrance to the rail station car park.

THREE

Somewhere a phone was ringing. It nagged, thinning out his dreams, bringing the room back to him. He woke with a grunt, found the bed stuck in his face and rolled on to his back, groping around, eyes shut.

'What?'

A voice told him what.

'Yeah, but. Why not Traffic?'

The voice told him why not.

'Fuck it,' he said. 'It's four o'clock. What about the other Wilkins?'

But the voice had rung off.

He lay there a moment, preparing himself. Next to him, Carol lay, smelling faintly of sweat and perfume, and he longed to roll towards her, feel her warm body against his, but he turned the other way and hauled himself out of bed, and stood there in his underpants, skinny runt of the trailer park, with his bowed legs and bony shoulders. He remembered then that he had no clothes with him but his rented tuxedo.

'Fuck's sake.'

Carol, completely unmoving in the bed, said, 'Take my car. Just stop talking.'

Silently, he smelled his armpits, winced, began to get dressed.

He'd never seen such a thing before, not close up. It was enormous – so big and luxurious it didn't seem like a car somehow, more like a piece of real estate, a deluxe apartment crash-landed in grimy Becket Street, taking up almost the entire width of the road, its elegant frontage a little crumpled now, crudely stuck in the entrance to the rail station car park. The colour of it was weird. Dazzling, shimmering. He thought of peacocks – a slaughtered peacock dumped in someone's dirty backyard. He'd never seen a peacock, in fact. He knew a bit about dirty backyards.

Forensics were on their way. Bobbleheads were stringing tape across the road; they threw him glances, smirked.

'The fuck you looking at?'

They were serious again, bending to their task.

He straightened his tuxedo, felt out of place in his evening dress; a passer-by, not too observant, might even assume the car was his, that he'd crashed it. He looked around, sniffed the air, yawned. He went up close, felt the bonnet, made a call. 'Here, now. . . . Yeah, abandoned. No driver, no passengers. . . . I dunno, half an hour ago. Listen, why isn't this Traffic? . . . Yeah, it's a fucking big car, but it's still a car.'

An explanation was given. Emergency had received a call, at 03.10. A woman had said politely, 'This is Zara Fanshawe.' And then, 'Always lost and never found.' She had been going to

14

say something else, but was abruptly cut off. The message got passed along, where it puzzled the duty staff at St Aldates. As they were puzzling, a night officer called in an apparent traffic accident in Becket Street: a Rolls-Royce Phantom, damaged and abandoned. They checked the reg. It was Zara Fanshawe's car.

But there was no sign of Zara Fanshawe.

Ryan calmed down, got interested, started noticing details. Not much damage to the car. It had come down the street from the south, turned as it reached the car-park entrance and collided with the little booth just inside. He took a closer look: gashes in the gorgeously lacquered passenger-side flank, a headlight shattered, bits and pieces scattered around, the grille buckled – though the little statue of the Spirit of Ecstasy on the great blunt nose still fluttered jauntily above the damage. That's the thing about ecstasy, he thought – once you're in it, you're in it, even after you've crashed. He peered through the driver's window at the luxuriously appointed interior. More weirdness. It looked like a cross between a space-flight control desk and an antique drinks cabinet, impossibly high-tech and absurdly old-fashioned at the same time. The door opened when he tried it and he poked his nose inside, looking around. It was spotlessly clean, the model of a perfectly valeted Rolls-Royce – the walnut dash, the cream-coloured soft leather steering wheel, the sexy virgin thigh of the door's upholstery.

There was a cheap, well-thumbed paperback in the side pocket. He squinted at the title. *The Catholic Confessional and the Sacrament of Penance*. Nothing else: everything photo-perfect.

Withdrawing, he looked around. The narrow, gloomy road was sunk between the screen of spindly trees fronting the car park and a row of tall Victorian tenements used as guest houses and lodgings, the dirty brickwork of one still painted with the ancient words *Flory's Commercial Hotel*, a leftover sign for a leftover place. To the north was the great green ziggurat of the university's Saïd Business School, the snout of money lifted heavenwards. Opposite the car-park entrance was the little humped church of St Thomas the Martyr, its modest tower hidden among the darkness of trees.

He made a second call. 'Collision, yeah. . . . Just a wall. No signs of injury; don't think she was going very fast. Like she was trying to get into the car park and missed. Check out the hospitals, will you? No one else involved, far as I can tell. . . . Yeah, taking a look round now.'

Hitching up his loose dress trousers, he went into the car park, empty apart from half a dozen vehicles left overnight, and scanned around. No sign of anyone. Going back out, he went across the road and through the wooden gate into the church-yard. It was dark under the trees, dank, tombstones here and there blotted with wet. On the ground along the inside of the wooden fence was a mess of belongings: a two-man tent, some sleeping bags, cardboard sheets, blankets, newspaper – all the makeshift sleeping materials of the homeless. Scattered about were empties, litter, carrier bags. To one side stood a super-market shopping trolley filled with clothing; a fire in a shallow pit still gave off a dingy light. People had been here – recently, too – but they'd all gone.

He went back to the road. The car filled it. Despite the damage, it had a sort of perfection, the vast machine engineered to pre-cision, gorgeous as an artwork, gleamingly clean; it seemed to glow in the grubby darkness. He walked up and down, looking, thinking. Zara Fanshawe. He'd heard the name, could dimly bring to mind a face; he'd seen it recently somewhere, in the pages of one of Carol's lifestyle magazines perhaps.

Forensics arrived. The street was sealed, tapes up. Ryan talked to the guys. They were working quickly, trying to finish before the car park started to fill with the first of the commuters: a tow truck was on its way. The duty staff called back. No Zara Fanshawe at any of the hospitals.

'Who is she, by the way? Some sort of celeb? . . . Don't matter.' He glanced at his watch. 'Yeah, APW, in case she's staggering round town concussed. Try the hotels too – expensive ones, anyway. Probably she's just walked off, left the mess for someone else to sort out, gone for a lie down in the Randolph. . . . Forensics here now. Paps on their way, I bet. That's what's going to drive all this – front-page fuckery. . . . I'm going back to bed, but, yeah, give us a bell if you get anything.'

In Carol's Range Rover, he drove slowly along Oxpens, past the college of further education and the ice rink and the brick bulk of the Westgate. It wouldn't do to prang her car. He felt strange, sitting so high above the road for once – precarious. The Rover smelled strange too – feminine, perhaps. It was untidy, thickly littered with Carol's stuff, wrappers, crumbs, brochures from a bank stuffed in the side pockets, boxes of business cards advertising Carol's florists stacked on the back seat, copies of the *Oxford Mail* on top of everything else, the front page of one of them featuring DCC Chester Lynch, he noticed now, her weathered, forceful face a little bit more famous. He went down the Abingdon Road, past the park where he sometimes took little Ryan, and over the red-brick bridge into Kennington; and, as he went by Kenville Road, he instinctively slowed down, thinking of his son. He came to a halt, lost in his thoughts. At this time, little Ryan would be asleep, deeply unconscious under his tractor-themed duvet, small and chunky in the sleepsuit, his cheeks pink, his smooth hair hot to the touch; and Ryan felt something churn inside, some actual physical displacement, as if his liver and kidneys swooned a little. He started up again and drove away at walking pace, then slowly picked up speed and drove on to Carol's.

A few minutes later, he pulled on to her drive, turned off the engine and sat there in the cooling car. Half past four, still dark, freezing rain coming on again, scrappy bits of it flecking the windscreen. What had happened to Zara Fanshawe? Perhaps nothing much. Explanations were easy. She'd simply lost control of her car. She interrupted her call to Emergency because she was in pain, or preoccupied, or she dropped her phone. The homeless fled because they habitually avoid contact with the authorities, frightened of being 'moved on'. She wasn't in a hospital because she was in a hotel. Simple.

He didn't think so. Something niggled, something to do with the sheer spectacle of the Rolls-Royce Phantom lying smashed and abandoned in the narrow road. A question. What had Zara Fanshawe been doing, anyway, driving her exquisite Rolls-Royce down a dingy, dirty backstreet in Oxford at three o'clock in the morning?

He got out of the car and went through drizzle into the house.

★

Ryan was not the only young father awake. Six miles to the north, in a tastefully expanded terrace house in affluent Summertown, the 'other Wilkins', Ray, sat in his dressing gown on the floor of the spare room, feeding Felix, the younger of the twins, from a bottle. He looked down at the scrunched-shut face of his son and thought of his award. It was his first, the Queen's Commendation for Bravery, a silver leaf, and Chester Lynch had told him that evening it would not be his last. Ray had spent twenty minutes in conversation with the legendary Deputy Chief Constable and was aware that it had gone to his head, though he dwelled on it nevertheless, replaying highlights of it pleasingly exaggerated to match the soothing, surreal, but virtuous calm of four thirty on a dark February morning, with the tiny package of his oblivious son resting swaddled in his lap.

He could still feel the woman's presence, a sort of heat-glow on his skin. He remembered the way she'd looked at him, the intentness of her stare, the slight, dangerous pauses before she spoke. The most highly decorated black woman in the force's history. He felt it. 'I like you,' she'd said. 'You think when you need to think, but, when you need to get in the room, you get in the fucking room.' Ray had begun to mention Ryan and the work that he'd put in, but Lynch shook her head, shut him down. Holding the little silver leaf up to the light, where it gave off a dull expensive gleam, she said, 'This is about you, Ray; this is who you are. Rule number one: don't fuck with your biggest asset.' She leaned forward. 'I'm going to keep my eye on you.' For a wild moment, Ray thought she was going to embrace him, but then she turned abruptly away to someone else, her voice changing to a different sort of growl.

Ray was used to women looking at him with interest. This had been a different experience altogether, a kind of scrutiny, he thought, or a form of hypnotism. He shivered at the memory of it.

Lying in Ray's lap, Felix wriggled and grimaced, a shudder passing across his silky little face, before sinking back into the feeding trance. It was chilly in the house. Pulling together the kimono-style collars of his dressing gown – Egyptian cotton, Bown of London – he saw himself from the outside, a man with his six-month-old son, and felt suddenly both his responsibility and his accomplishment. He remembered the message which he had found on the house phone that night from his father, a prosperous man of blunt views and crude feelings, not always helpful, sometimes downright distressing, but tonight childishly uplifting. *Ray, my boy. You make me very proud. The first of many. Now you show them what you can do. Superintendent soon, not that fool Wallace.*

He thought briefly of Ryan. When Ray had got the call earlier about the incident in Becket Street, he'd asked them to cut him some slack and contact the other Wilkins. He reasoned that he was probably still over the limit, and Felix needed feeding, and, besides (he'd added charmingly), he was a prizewinner. Charm was still one of his things. Handsome Ray, hanging in there. High-ranking Ray next? He began to think again of Chester Lynch, the way she'd looked at him, but was roused from these thoughts almost immediately by movement in the nursery room next door. A moment later, Diane padded in carrying Oliver.

'Him as well?'

'I'll do it.'

20

She settled down at Ray's side with Oliver on her lap. It was quarter to five. Outside, a dark, still night. They said nothing, listening to rain against the window, a quiet stroking sound, and the whispering grunts of feeding babies. The city was not yet awake, north Oxford was hushed. Only in town, five miles away, were there people about, a few clubbers emerging into the pre-dawn darkness, the occasional rough sleeper dragging his bedding out of the rain and, in Becket Street, the high-vis guys working under floodlight as they manoeuvred a Rolls-Royce Phantom out of the car-park entrance and on to the back of a tow truck, while every few minutes another bike or car or van swerved alongside and yet more photographers ran into the road, unloading their kit in haste to join the feeding frenzy brought on by the glamorising name of Zara Fanshawe.

FOUR

'Who is she?' Ryan asked. 'Heard the name, but . . .'

Nadim Khan, Communications Intelligence, standing in front of the window in Barko's office next morning, a neat silhouette against the pale glare of an overcast sky, briefed them in her usual brisk manner. She was the department's information guru, close friend of Ray, touchingly tolerant of Ryan. Her eyes kept going to him as she spoke.

Since her youth, Zara Fanshawe had been a familiar figure in the media. Officially the Honourable Zara F., youngest daughter of 11th Viscount Fanshawe, she'd first made the news a month shy of her seventeenth birthday, representing Great Britain in showjumping at the Atlanta Olympics, fresh faced, well spoken, puckish and photogenic. After graduating from Oxford, she'd been romantically linked with a string of celebrity boyfriends – Prince, Meat Loaf, the youngest son of the Grand Duke of Luxembourg, etc. – with whom she was photographed on yachts, on red carpets, outside clubs in London, Berlin and Los Angeles. There were offers of marriage, some engagements, but also, quite quickly, hints of problems with recreational drugs, to all of which the media had responded with enthusiasm, taking particular care to be around to record mishaps and give oxygen to rumours, and introducing a new range of photos now more likely to show her outside A & E or in the back of a police car than displaying an engagement ring. They were equally delighted by her first stay in rehab when she was twenty-five, and in due course respectfully covered her big *Hello!*-style wedding to Lawrence Hobhouse, a man remarkable for nothing but extreme wealth – after which her partying became a little more extreme, her mishaps a little more frequent. Then, suddenly, in November, at the age of forty-two, there had come a great change in Zara Fanshawe's life. She'd vacated the celebrity-watch pages of the magazines and tabloids and disappeared into St Anne's Addiction Rehab Clinic in Oxfordshire. When she emerged at Christmas, it was to announce that she was terminating an unhappy marriage and launching herself on an addiction-free life. The grateful media, appreciative of variety, were delighted all over again. Here, they said, was a woman who had triumphantly taken back control of her life, damaged but sober, fragile but calm, a spokesperson for vulnerable women everywhere, and they were proud to support her. For a month or so, this was the new Zara Fanshawe.

'Now this,' Barko said.

Media outlets everywhere had bumped all other stories. Gone were the reports of a failing government, sexual misconduct allegations in Parliament, travel chaos at airports, unlawful behaviour of ministers who had better things to do than resign. The lead story was now the disappearance of 'troubled' celebrity Zara Fanshawe, supported by sensationally angled photographs of the damaged Phantom, alongside archival shots of Zara at celebrity parties and charity balls.

'Disappears. Like she just drops down a hole. Out crawl the lowlife, the bottom feeders with their Nikons. I don't like it. I want it over.'

Crammed into his uniform and wedged behind his desk, Barko stared at Ray and Ryan as if they were perhaps to blame. Ryan wore a puffa, silver trackies and yellow Reeboks; Ray, a black wool double-breasted peacoat over texture-knit sweater and long beige cable scarf. Both looked tired, but Ray would still have looked good in a 'Winter Outfits for Men' catalogue and Ryan wouldn't have looked out of place in a sociological piece on urban deprivation.

'Not turned up at the Randolph, then?'

Nadim shook her head. 'Or any other hotel. Or hospital. No sign of her at all.' Except, now, in the media.

'Lowlife,' Barko said again, out of his small and barely moving mouth.

They waited. Nadim waited. Like DCC Lynch, his mentor, Barko was a great user of silences; he liked to punctuate them with the sudden outbursts that were his trademark. Ryan started fidgeting.

'Scum turned up as the car was being loaded for removal. Suppose you were gone by then,' Barko said to Ray.

Ryan stopped picking his ear, frowned. 'Was me got the call.'

Barko looked at Ryan, looked back at Ray, small eyes getting smaller.

'I couldn't get out,' Ray said, after a moment. 'It got passed to Ryan.'

Barko considered him for a moment, said nothing, turned

back to Ryan.

'First impressions, son?'

Ryan gave Ray a quick sideways glance. 'Bends her car, gives Emergency a bit of philosophy about being lost and found, disappears. Interesting, I think.'

Barko grunted. 'Why isn't she in a hospital? Why isn't she in the Randolph? Why isn't she sitting on a bench in Bonn Square? Why is she fucking nowhere? I don't like it.'

Ryan shrugged; scratched. There was brief silence.

'Car's a piece of work,' he said conversationally. 'Looks like something that's never used – know what I mean? Kept for best. This weird gleaming colour. Open the door, get that little whiff of new leather. Inside's that clean, can't hardly believe anyone was actually driving it. No litter or nothing. Nothing in it at all,' he said, 'except for that little book about religion, in the side pocket.'

'She's Catholic,' Ray said. 'Comes from an old Catholic family. I checked it out.'

Barko glared at him. 'I come from an old Catholic family – least, there were lots of old Catholics in it – but I don't drive around in a quarter of a million pounds.' He looked at Ryan. 'Witnesses of the crash?'

He shrugged again. 'Homeless down there would have seen it, heard it at least, but they'd all fucked off by the time I got there, and they won't talk to us, anyway. Made me think, though. What's this sort of car doing in Becket Street, three o'clock in the morning? Poky little street, nothing there.'

After a moment, Ray said, 'Rail station car park's notorious for drug deals. And she's had a lot of issues in the past.'

'Yeah, but – come on. Drives a Roller. She wants a fix, got

to be home delivery only, right? Any case, thought she'd got off the drugs.'

'Talked to her ex, first thing. Lawrence Hobhouse. He was pretty cynical about that. He thinks she's started using again. In his view, she was probably off her head and lost control of the car. She's done it before, many times.'

Ryan frowned. 'If she was going to have a drugs relapse, why'd she come to Oxford to have it? She could've had it quite comfy at home, in Kensington.'

Ray ignored him. 'Hobhouse says she'll turn up in a couple of days. It's what usually happens.'

'And where was he yesterday?'

'London. Meetings in his office all day, business dinner all evening, in bed by ten. They're completely estranged, live apart. He's had zero contact with her since moving out of their home last June.'

'What about the call she made? That was weird, too. "Lost and found" palaver. She was about to say something else too, I think.'

Ray dismissed this. 'Most emergency calls are incoherent, odd tone – about a quarter of them get cut off, for a thousand different reasons. Let's not sweat the small stuff. The question is: where's she gone?'

Barko grunted. 'Aye. That's the question we're being asked.'

Ray said, 'I got the house-to-house going, and a search team for the rough ground beyond the railway line. Nadim's looking at the cameras in the car park. The DSs are calling round personal contacts. Lines are open for public calls. No sightings as yet. Likeliest thing, though, is she turns up in a few days, like her ex says.'

He spoke with the natural authority of a recent award-winner and waited for acknowledgment.

Ryan gave him a sneer instead. 'Busy little bee.'

'Up early,' Ray said.

'Not four o'clock early,' Ryan said.

Barko gave a grunt, turned glaring at the wall, as if trying to stare it down. 'I don't like it,' he said at last. 'We're in the fucking spotlight, here. Big-money car gets pranged, people notice, these bottom feeders get their Nikons out. Lady leaves a garbled message, does a runner, everyone's talking. Smelled bad from the word go, now we got the paps all over it.' He glared at the wall, daring it to contradict him. 'Okay, for all we know, there's nothing more criminal here than dangerous driving, but we're in the shop window, so we start serious and get it done.' He finished with the wall and turned back to Ryan and Ray. 'I want it over, understood? Both of you on it. Get the basics up and running, and sort it.'

Nadim gave Ryan the address of Zara Fanshawe's apartment.

'You'll have to drive,' he said to Ray, 'the Peugeot's still fucked.'

'Final thing,' Barko said.

They turned at the door.

'Ryan leads on this one.'

There was a moment, like a sudden jolt of something in the air. Ray's face tightened; Barko stared him out.

'Turn and turn about, son. Fair's fair. Last case you worked together, you got the gong. This time, you report to the other

27

Wilkins, we'll see what he can do. Get on to it. I want this done soon as, otherwise those paps are going to cause us grief, I can fucking feel it.'

FIVE

Ray drove in silence, keeping his eyes on the road. His car was tuned and clean; it made the smooth, reassuring noises cars in adverts make. In the back were two baby seats, serious items tilted upwards with intent, padded and buckled like the seats of astronauts.

When Ryan started to talk, he put music on: Bach's *Goldberg Variations*.

Ryan talked over the top of it, his voice irritatingly nasal.

'Got a cabinet, then?'

'What?'

'One of them trophy cabinets, put it in.'

Ray, who had actually spent some time designing a plaque on which to mount his silver leaf to its best advantage, said shortly, 'No.'

Ryan tsked. 'Make the most of it, mate. Can't hide your stuff under a bush.'

'Bushel.'

'What?'

'Hide your light under a bushel. Doesn't matter.'

'If I had it, I'd wear it, make sure everyone clocks it.'

'I'm sure you would.'

'Got a shell suit in silver, go with it really well.'

They motored up the ramp on to the M40. When Ryan looked as if he was going to speak again, Ray leaned forward and turned up the *Goldberg Variations*. Ryan turned it down, stared at him a moment.

'Come on, Ray. Raymond. Don't sulk.'

'I'm not sulking.'

'Got the award, didn't you? Picture in *Police*. Look smooth, too – something about the mouth, I don't know what. Kiss a baby, or something. And you got to shake hands with Supercop. What did I get?'

'You got back in.'

'Shouldn't never've let me go, mate. Travesty. Miscarriage of justice.'

'You tried to kill your father with a brick.'

Ryan sniffed, blew out his cheeks. 'Yeah, alright. Fair point.'

They drove on for a while, not listening to Bach. The long, insignificant escarpment of the Chilterns appeared, a ruck in the strewn blanket of the countryside.

'So, anyway, what was she like? Little chit-chat you were having there with her.'

'You mean the DCC?'

'Wonder Woman, yeah.'

'Just the usual. Congratulations, keep it up.'

They drove on. The sky became overcast, a drifting rain

obscured Christmas Common and Turville Heath. Some fields edged closer, some disappeared.

'She likes you. You can tell.'

'She was just there to hand out the award, Ryan, that's all.'

'Way she looked at you. Marked you out. Hot-stuff Raymond. That's the way it works with her lot. The Chester Lynch mob. Same with Barko, way back.'

'You're just fantasising now.'

'You watch. Mention her name, watch Barko's face – goes all sort of stiff. That's loyalty, that is. Way it works, Ray. Everyone's on someone's side.'

'Whose side are you on?'

Ryan thought about that, breathing loudly.

'Barko's?' Ray said. 'Thames Valley's? Mine?'

'Little Ryan's,' Ryan said at last, 'if I'm honest.'

Off Westway, they nosed into London traffic, through Bayswater and round the park, a vague impression of trees and sky soiled by drizzle. They came to Kensington, grace land of money, and went along South Carriage Drive, the park still accompanying them, but different now, more decorous, deferential, as they neared the luxury block of One Hyde Park, jutting out of the surrounding Victorian red brick like a high-tech shelving system, which, in a way, it was, neatly stowing a variety of multimillionaires where they could lie at the side of their airborne pools and watch the park turn pink in the sunset.

As they drew up, Ray received a call.

'Babe.'

Diane's voice said, 'Are you anywhere near a Tesco?'

'Not just now.'

She wanted disposable nappies, antiseptic cream, lavender oil. Also, there was something wrong with the Baby Dynamic pushchair. Also, he had forgotten to swap the baby seats over to her car. Also—

'Babe, I've got to go.'

'You've got to go *to Tesco*.'

'Later. Ryan and I need to get on.'

'Is Ryan there?'

'Hello, Diane.'

'Remind him to go to Tesco.'

Leaving the car on double yellows, they went across a large width of scrupulously clean pavement towards the entrance, Ray buttoning up his peacoat, Ryan hitching up his trackies.

'Diane alright, then?'

'She's fine. Tired. We're both tired.'

They went into the lobby, which appeared also to be a car showroom, with sports cars scattered here and there instead of sofas, and set off on the longish walk to reception.

'Was meaning to ask your advice. You're a relationships sort of guy.'

'What does that even mean?'

'Married. You live together.'

'So?'

'So, Carol's got this thing about me moving in with her. Least, I think she has. Hard to read, sometimes. What do you think?'

'Hasn't she noticed how irritating you are?'

They arrived at the desk and Ray did the talking. The receptionist was sympathetically aware of Ms Fanshawe's motor accident. Personally, she added, she hadn't seen her for a while.

'When was the last time?'

'Actually, maybe not for a couple of weeks.'

She was happy to let the two detectives go up to the apartment, though she had no authority to let them in if Ms Fanshawe wasn't there. Did they have authorisation themselves?

Ray looked at Ryan, raised his eyebrows.

'Overriding need for speed,' Ryan said to her. 'Safety of your resident at stake.'

She was sorry. 'I can't take that responsibility.'

'Alright,' Ryan said. 'Alright. No bother. We'll just put you down for the damage.'

She was silent.

'You seen it on TV, right? We don't even need one of those battering things. Why I brought this guy with me. Look at the size of him. He's a boxing blue from Oxford University. You heard of Oxford University, right? All them dining clubs, kicking the fuck out of restaurants and that. Kicking a door in's nothing to him, won't take a minute. Got your name, Sandra – cheers for that. We'll just put it in the system so everyone knows what happened, and get up there. Thanks for your time.'

The elevator rose like a slow, smooth exhalation of breath to the fourth floor. Outside, the park obligingly lowered itself to show them the tops of its attractive trees. Ryan juggled the key from hand to hand, and Ray watched him sourly.

'All you had to do was pick up the paperwork. That's literally all you had to do.'

'My advice to you, Ray? Don't sweat the small stuff.'

'If she reports you, you'll struggle. Especially with your record. Intimidation.'

'Middle-class manners didn't get us the key. Anyway, she'll not report me.'

'How do you know?'

'Basic psychology.'

The elevator doors opened. The landing was like an art gallery.

'Listen, Ray. What I was saying before about Carol. I really want to make it work. But, the thing is, little Ryan thinks he's – I don't know what – losing me, or something. He's proper upset. Does my head in.'

They walked between towering sculptures, towards Zara Fanshawe's apartment door.

'Not that it's not good with Carol and me. Better than good, if you know what I mean.' He tipped Ray a wink.

'You don't need to explain.'

'Permanent boner, mate.'

'Ryan, please.'

They arrived at the door.

'You remember, right? What it's like at first.'

'I don't want to hear about it.'

'I'm doing things I didn't do when I was sixteen. Have you ever done that—?'

'Ryan!'

Ray knocked on the apartment door.

'Louder. She might be in there, tripped out.'

'Why don't you knock?'

'I'm lead, here. Got you to do my knocking for me.'

Ray knocked again. They waited.

34

'Anyway, it's not just the fucking – we get on really well. She's smart. Got four shops, did I tell you? Flower shops. Her own business. Just the start, she says.'

'Tell me later, will you? She's not there; give me the key.'

They let themselves in, and stood there.

'Christ almighty,' Ryan said.

SIX

Meanwhile, in Oxford, Carol sat waiting in the lobby of the bank, briefcase in lap, staring at the opposite wall. She had her hard face on. Her appointment was overdue.

She had dressed with care, and wore a navy skirt suit, formal but tightish, over a white blouse and high-heel navy suede pumps; her A-line bob was non-nonsense chic. Though she did not need to, she was wearing glasses; she focused on the empty wall, unmoving and self-contained, rehearsing numbers, scenarios, arguments.

At last, her financial advisor appeared, not nearly so full of apologies as he should have been, and she waited a moment in disdain before following him into his office. Actually, he was only one of her advisors: she had others, long-standing, at various banks; and, in the last few weeks, had rapidly acquired more. She wondered why they were all men under thirty whose hair looked as if it was cut by their mothers.

Declining to sit directly opposite him, instead positioning her chair at an unsettling angle to his desk, she unloaded her laptop, fired it up and began to talk through her business plan – though, even as she did, she noticed his inattention. His eyes continually went to the door, his fingers buzzed in his lap. On his desk was a copy of a newspaper with a front-page story on Zara Fanshawe.

'Big news day,' he said.

She ignored him.

'I think it's the drugs, don't you?'

She went on with her description of the proposed equity breakdown for a few minutes more, as his attention drifted to his phone. She paused.

'D'you have to be somewhere?'

His name, she noticed now, was Darren, and she was angry suddenly that she was being seen by someone wearing a name badge.

He shook his head, made a casual gesture for her to continue.

She'd been with his bank for nearly ten years; it had been one of her first backers and, until recently, had been keen to lend to her: every year, someone used to get in touch to suggest fresh investment; she had to fend them off. No longer. The economy had wobbled, the market had gone soft. Geo-politics. Fuel crisis. Policy adjustments. Tax rises. Inflation. Florists, with their tiny margins and supply-chain issues, were among the first to be hit, and, for those overexposed from fast expansion, the situation had gone from worrying to desperate almost overnight.

Carol resumed her pitch, resentfully, daring him to stop her, knowing he would, as in fact he eventually did with a regretful but distracted air. Unfortunately, he had no authority, he said, to offer an extension on her loan.

'Whose authority do you need? Have I been talking to the wrong person, Darren?'

He rephrased: the bank could not, at the current time, verify that the necessary preconditions for further investment were in place.

All this, Carol had foreseen. Now, she purposely let her irritation show, before folding away her laptop. This was the risky moment she had been preparing for, and she began to talk it out, not too fast. She was sad, she said, not to see any more loyalty from them, expressing with intimidating firmness her disappointment that her earliest partner was turning down the opportunity to secure, on entirely favourable terms, a bigger share of the business's profits.

Just when she was about to get to her feet, he said, 'I'm glad you came in, though. I'm sure you noticed that the principal of the original loan is now overdue.'

Before returning to her shops, she sat in a cafe for a while, trying to think. However hard she tried, she could not get beyond the facts. The situation was simple enough. The principals of four separate loans were now overdue and when repayment was enforced she would lose her house. The businesses were underwater. Staff at two of her shops had already quit; with takings down more than sixty per cent, she'd been reduced to sending them into the centre of town to hand out cards to passers-by, a sign of desperation too obvious to be ignored.

She sat there with her second latte, staring blankly at the newspaper she'd bought, thinking of the farmhouse, which, over the years, she'd restored – the great glazed arch overlooking the paddock with its horse, the sweep of blond floorboards that ran from porch to kitchen, the long timbered attic where the children slept. She thought of the children, who had grown up, unlike her, in comfort. Of her ex, who would blame her. And, with a tenderness that surprised her, of Ryan, who knew so little about her. And at last she thought of someone else, someone she didn't want to think of at all. For several moments, she sat looking at her phone, fighting with herself. As always, fear made her aggressive. Then she dialled.

She heard someone breathing on the other end of the phone.

'Get my message or what?' she said.

There was no answer.

'I'm not scared of you,' she said. 'Never was.'

No answer.

'So don't be stupid,' she said, more harshly. 'I'm in trouble, you're in trouble. And if I lose, you lose. I'll make sure of it.'

SEVEN

'The fuck's that smell?' Ryan said.

They pushed their way past accumulated mail on the carpet and went cautiously into the apartment. *Apartment* was the wrong word. *Statement. Event. The psychodrama of money.* There was no right word. The gold walls of the curved hallway shone like mirrors as they followed it round to the main reception, where they stood for a moment, gazing into the enormous box of wealth. Opposite them: a twenty-metre-long window exhibiting the dignified Kensington brickwork and bay windows of a more modest age. Behind them: a gallery wall of artworks, stretching high above to a ceiling glamorised with a sheen of concealed lighting. In front of them: a showroom of frankly gigantic furniture, including an eighteen-seater sofa, supplementary sofa for ten, backless couch for an overflow of half a dozen more – all in the same plush, boxy style – and solid triangular coffee tables here and there among them, like vast wedges from a children's game, each precision-engineered out of what appeared to be half a hundredweight of gold. It would all have looked spectacular in a magazine, if it had been in pristine shape. But it was not. It was horribly soiled – liquid stains mapping the silken carpet, dried-up pools of stuff, spilt food, trails of dirt – and everywhere the mess of dirty crockery, cans and empties, cigarette butts.

'Twenty-two-million-pound apartment,' Ray said, 'and she's turned it into a drug den.'

They listened. There was a noise somewhere, water dropping, moving. And then there was that smell. Ryan sniffed cautiously.

'What the fuck is it, Ray?'

It wasn't coming from anything in the room. They went back out, along the hallway to the dining room, and found it similarly disarranged, the brushed-zinc table piled with takeaway cartons filled with rotting food. But the smell wasn't there either.

They exchanged glances. 'Got to tell you, I got a bad feeling about this.'

They went on down the hall, stepping over discarded clothing, empty bottles. The smell got worse; they covered their mouths and noses.

At last, they reached the kitchen, the smell overpowering now, and there, on the marble floor, lay the swollen bodies of two French bulldogs, bat-eared and wrinkly, resting on a thickened stain of their own making. Parts of them had split open; maggots writhed in the gaps.

They scrambled to open windows.

'Least it's not human remains,' Ryan said, when he could speak. He looked around at the general disarray.

Ray peered into the sink, half filled with bits of foil, burned spoons, tell-tale little plastic bags. 'Here's your drugs relapse, right here. The state everything's in, it looks like she's been using again for quite a while.'

Separately, they went round the flat, stooping, examining.

'You ought to look at these clothes!' Ryan called from inside the walk-in wardrobe in the master bedroom. 'Price tags still on some of them. Cost more than I earn in a year and not even Adidas.'

They nosed around. Ray splashed his way across the bathroom and turned off the gold taps.

After a while, Ryan remembered to call it in. Briefly giving directions for the forensics team, he carried on with his search. In the apartment's spa, he met up with Ray, and they stood together in the therapeutic hush. The long turquoise shimmer of the illuminated pool ran the full length of the room, screened by a floor-to-ceiling bronze-coloured blind. Ryan found the switch and they watched the blind rise, disappearing into itself at the ceiling high above them, revealing as it went the long view across Hyde Park, treetops receding delicately into mist, like a painting by a Royal Academy master expensively hung just outside the window: *Symphony in Dove Grey*. With Added Crows.

'Not bad,' Ray said.

Ryan said, 'Got a park near us in Kennington, mate. Does the same for nothing.'

In the daylight coming through the window, they saw the mess here too: cans floating in the pool, rubbish piled up along the edge, on the reclining loungers and polished floor, in the sauna and steam rooms. Scattered round the chairs were glossy lifestyle magazines, mixed together with books and brochures about health, leaflets offering spiritual guidance, catalogues advertising crystals, celery juice, herbs from India – the purifying comforts of the super-rich.

Ryan took a look at some of the books. 'You're educated, Ray. Some Julian guy from Norwich, Augustine of Hippos.'

'Spiritual leaders. Paths to self-enlightenment. Hippo, singular.'

'Right, got it. Hippos're pretty fucking big things; you wouldn't want more than one.' He waited. 'Come on, Ray, crack a smile.'

Ray didn't.

They went back to the kitchen. The mess was worse, there. 'Dogs gone to a different place. How long you reckon they been left?'

'Couple of weeks, at least. Forensics'll say. Hard to know whether she wasn't here, or here but too out of it to feed them.'

At last, Ryan stopped being larky; he fell quiet. He'd been suppressing the memories of his last days with Shel, but now he remembered the filth and detritus in the flat they'd shared, Shel's lack of interest in anything except her next fix, even the baby crying nearby on the floor. He remembered the way she'd lain on the couch, so lacking in shape that, in some sense, she wasn't there anymore. Nothing of her was left, in fact, not even in her face; it could have been anyone's grey skin, slack mouth, dead-fish eyes. And little Ryan, crying there on the floor, ignored. How long would she have left him there if Ryan hadn't come back? As long as Zara had left her pets?

'Ryan?'

'Be alright in a minute.' He gestured at the mess. 'Worse after a relapse. Shel went five months once, never touched a needle, but when she was back on it – chaos. Just went blank. You know, nothing in her eyes. Rubbish piled up round her, she never even noticed it.'

They went together through the bedrooms, where they found more drug paraphernalia of various kinds, in various states of use, piled in heaps next to the beds.

'Funny, though,' Ryan said. 'Shel just sort of shrank, took up less and less space. In the end, she never got off the couch. This Zara chick's spread it everywhere.'

'She's been living on her own for months. Nothing to stop her.'

'Then just wanders off. Made a mess, don't care. These millionaires, eh? Got to love them.'

Ryan got a call. Forensics on the way, ETA five minutes.

'Check the post before they get their hands on it?'

They went back to the apartment's front door, where a pile of unopened post lay on the carpet. Most were circulars: free magazines, brochures, charity appeals. Among them was a postcard, obviously hand-delivered.

'Gloves,' Ray said.

'Forgot them.'

'Christ, Ryan.' Ray handed over his rubbers.

On one side of the card was a picture of brightly coloured T-shirts hanging on a line, on the other a scrawled message in clumsy felt tip: *Bobby's in the kitchen. You know where I am.* It was signed with the letter *P*.

'Garble. Interesting, though.'

There was also a large padded envelope, obviously a purchase. It was covered in stickers containing import-duties information, and had been sent from a company called Safewear Laboratories Inc., based in Baton Rouge, Louisiana. Professionally sealed, it was harder to open, but at last Ryan got into it and pulled out a black rubberised tube, about six inches long. At one end was a screw cap, at the other a button and nozzle. Unscrewing the cap, he removed the canister inside. Along the side of it were printed the words *Advanced three-in-one formula, military-grade tear UV marking dye.*

Pepper spray, as used by the US army.

'Now, that's even more interesting,' Ryan said.

Forensics arrived. There was no more for Ray and Ryan to see in the apartment, and they went to talk to some of her neighbours.

In fact, they saw hardly any of them. Of the sixty-two apartments, fifty were currently unoccupied, the owners elsewhere and, in any case, anonymous. At ten of them, the staff who answered the door were unable to say when the principal residents would be at home, and steadfastly refused them entry. In one of the remaining apartments, the owner was unable to speak English; in the other, he had returned that morning from a six-month stay in Monaco and had never met Zara Fanshawe or indeed heard of her.

They went down to the offices of the maintenance staff, and there found Carlo, an overweight, unshaven former mechanic from Calabria. His little room was decorated with posters advertising operas from the mid twentieth century.

'You like the opera?' He had a florid face that bunched when he talked. 'Italian opera?'

'Hip-hop more my thing,' Ryan said. 'I like pizza, though.'

Yes, Carlo knew Zara Fanshawe. He liked her. Over the four

years or so that she'd been living there, he'd serviced her smart-home system, pet spa, movie parlour, the Wi-Fi in her gym; he'd fixed minor plumbing problems, even taken up packages. He hadn't seen her recently, he said, but she always took the trouble to say hello. Not like some. Of course, she had her ups and downs, he knew about all that, but he didn't judge people. He thought perhaps she'd been calmer since her husband moved out. Sometimes.

Ray said, 'Any unusual visitors?'

Carlo was uncertain.

Ryan said, 'Anyone coming round with treats?'

Carlo was baffled.

Ryan mimed popping pills, shooting a load.

Carlo winced, nodded. He didn't judge. She had money, she liked fun. But there was a guy who used to come regular, yes. Not a nice guy.

'Got a name?'

'Pablo.'

They looked at each other. 'Mr P, maybe.'

But Carlo couldn't tell them anything about him, except that he drove a black Range Rover with tinted windows.

'Course he does. Fun-boy hearse.' Ryan's face clouded. 'Fucking dealers.' He calmed himself. 'What about her ex, Hobhouse?'

Now, Carlo's face darkened and he unleashed a torrent of abuse, much of it in Italian. Lawrence Hobhouse was not a nice man; he was a man without love for his wife, a cold man, calculating, vindictive and jealous. Very English. 'Also, he never give tip.'

46

They gave him a card and asked him to get in touch if anything else occurred to him, and left him in his room full of opera memorabilia. Briefly, they went back to the receptionist, returned the key, asked her about Zara's visitors. Like Carlo, she said that, for several months, now, there had been far fewer than usual. No Hobhouse, no man in a black Range Rover.

'Everyone comes in the main door?'

Now, she hesitated. There were several other entrances to the building, in fact.

'So, someone could get up there without coming past reception at all?'

It was true. They would need to use a high-spec pass key, but of course a resident could arrange that.

Upstairs, Forensics were still at work, but there was nothing for Ray and Ryan to stay for. They asked the receptionist to send over a list of all Zara's callers since Hobhouse had moved out, footage from the cameras at all the exits, in the underground car park, etc. It was late afternoon, time to leave London.

They walked back across the huge lobby, and Ryan stopped.

'Know what we should do?'

'What?'

'Go see Hobhouse.'

'Sure. Livvy can set it up when we get back.'

Livvy Holmes was the DS supporting them on the case.

'I mean now. Out of the blue.'

'An appointment would be better.'

'Make him jump a bit.'

'That's why an appointment would be better. Less jumping, more sensible conversation.'

'See the man jump, see the man.'

'What does that even mean?'

'Anyway, I'm lead, right? Who knows, there might be a Tesco nearby – you can pick up that stuff for Diane.'

Ray made a gesture at once exasperated, resigned, scornful and aloof, and walked ahead, and Ryan swaggered behind, grinning.

EIGHT

On the way, Ryan read the Wikipedia page out loud. Lawrence Hobhouse's life had been a slowly accelerating ascent of five billion pounds. He'd grown up in the small Peak District town of Buxton, where as a boy he used to amuse himself by investing his pocket money in the stocks and shares of businesses his family had never heard of: shipping lines, feedstock manufacturers, petrochemical companies. He studied maths and economics at University College London, where he would get up at six thirty on Sunday mornings to log on to poker sites and pick off the drunks coming home late on Saturday night in Boston and New York. For a time, he worked as a trader for J. P. Morgan; soon, he set up a hedge fund, GoldRay Capital Management LLP, with a man in Dallas he'd met only twice, using pattern-detecting algorithms to spot trends in bonds and commodities. He was ultra cautious. Foreseeing the crash in 2008, he eliminated his entire holding of bank shares, took advantage of the resulting plunge in interest rates, and, two years later, GoldRay was Europe's third-largest hedge fund. He had eccentricities; he collected discredited saints' relics, which he housed in a museum in Jersey, where both he and his business were domiciled for tax purposes; he was secretive and, some said, on the spectrum, and he did not allow himself to be photographed.

Naturally, GoldRay's non-dom main office was not actually in Jersey, but in Knightsbridge, near the Tube station – four floors of marble, glass and chrome inside an Edwardian red-brick mansion opposite the Ecuadorian embassy. They left the car on double yellows and went up the stone steps into the immaculate lobby. If the receptionist was flustered by the unexpected appearance of two detectives, she didn't show it. Mr Hobhouse was in a meeting, she said; she had no idea if he would be available to see them without an appointment. Her expression, an ideal blank, suggested not. Ryan assertively put forward the opposite view, and, still very composed, she made a call, and they sat to wait.

All the walls around them seemed to be made of glass, fish tanks inside fish tanks, the lower panels milled to crystal obscurity, displaying only the winged company crest and, above, a glimpse of high ceilings and discreet lighting systems. There was a hush, enhanced, not broken, by the ceaseless polite murmur of the receptionist answering and redirecting calls. A few other people were waiting in the lobby too: a woman in an intensely sober business suit, and several men, dressed similarly, all silently engrossed in their phones; occasionally they were greeted, escorted away and were replaced by others just the same. There was a man wearing jeans and a T-shirt, who crept in shortly after they arrived, giving a package to the receptionist and sitting, waiting deferentially; other couriers came and went, observing the same hush. Conspicuously out of sync with all this, Ryan lay almost horizontal on his seat, enfolded in his massive puffa, picking loosely at the groin of his glow-up silver trackies, feet planted wide in screaming yellow Reeboks, sniffing loudly. He watched the others to catch their eye and stare them, embarrassed, back to their phones.

Ten minutes passed and he got up and ambled aggressively over to the receptionist; Ray was too slow to stop him.

'Not being funny, but does he have a short-term memory issue?'

Without looking at him, indeed with minimal recognition of his presence, she quietly passed on the message and Ryan sat down again. Ray got a call and went out into the corridor to answer it. Ryan sat there, fidgeting.

Ten more minutes passed.

This time, Ryan did not get up, but shouted across: 'You'd think he'd like to help, wouldn't you? I mean, police waiting to speak to him.'

The lobby underwent some slight psychic trauma. The startled receptionist, however, managed to avoid even acknowledging Ryan, and he got to his feet.

'Don't know much about finance, but I'm thinking this sort of thing's not great for the share price, right? Sort of thing you'd want to discuss nice and quiet, in private.'

Ray came back into the lobby at speed and got in front of Ryan at the receptionist's desk, talking to her cajolingly, while Ryan continued to speak loudly to the room. 'Course, it's not fraud, not embezzlement, what have you. Just that his wife's gone missing, suspicious circumstances. Maybe he's not bothered who knows about it.'

The inoffensive-looking man in jeans and a T-shirt, who had been sitting with them in the lobby, appeared unobtrusively behind them; they didn't see him at first. Looking up briefly from his phone without making eye contact, he said mildly to the receptionist, as he went past, 'Let them through now, Stef. Rockingham Suite,' to which she replied, 'Of course, Mr Hobhouse.' Then they were in a corridor, following him past more fish-tank offices.

Ray glared at Ryan. Ryan shrugged, pointed at Hobhouse, mouthed the word *cocksucker*.

Hobhouse barely looked up from his phone. He continued ahead of them along the corridor in the same unconcerned manner – limping slightly, they noticed – neat and childlike in jeans, fat white sneakers and bright tee, so at odds with all the suits around him. The wealth generator's prerogative. On his right wrist was an oversized Mickey Mouse watch with a Day-Glo pink strap. As they passed one of the offices – with a door tagged *Hobhouse* – they were silently joined by a large, impressive-looking man wearing a double-breasted suit in charcoal grey, recognised at once by Ray as a William Westmancott, from Savile Row's most expensive bespoke tailor. This man did not look at them either, or say anything, but simply fell into step with Hobhouse, walking with him to the end of the corridor and into a boardroom, where not only the walls but all the furniture in it seemed to be made of glass. Attached to these walls were large rectangular touchscreens and down the middle of the room was a long empty table, at the head of which Hobhouse and his companion took their places. As if of their own accord, the glass walls darkened. While Ray and Ryan seated themselves,

Hobhouse continued to look at his phone with the innocent absorption of a child. Finally, he spoke, not so much to them as to the room, which presumably he was used to addressing, in a voice that was both careful and colourless.

'This is Guy, my lawyer. I can give you –' he glanced at Mickey Mouse – 'ten minutes. Then NASDAQ will be opening.'

'Do better than that down the station, if you want to try it,' Ryan said.

Ray said quickly, 'But, seeing as we're here, a brief conversation will be fine. Thank you.' He placed his phone on the glass table top. 'Do you mind if we record it?'

'Everything in this room is automatically recorded,' Hobhouse said. 'Nine and a half,' he added, after a pause.

LOCATION: Rockingham Suite, GoldRay.

INTERVIEWERS: DI Wilkins (Raymond; dress sense very presentable) and DI Wilkins (Ryan; dress sense very dubious).

INTERVIEWEE: Lawrence Hobhouse, billionaire (dress sense childish).

OTHER ATTENDEE: Guy Beaumont, lawyer (dress sense impeccable).

WILKINS (RAYMOND): We spoke earlier, if you remember, on the telephone. And I want to say again that we know how very difficult this must—

WILKINS (RYAN): Ray, mate. Nine and a half.

WILKINS (RAYMOND): Obviously, you'll be anxious about her.

HOBHOUSE: Not really, no. We've been separated for some time. In any case, I know that the time for anxiety comes later, once she reappears. Then there'll be aggrieved people to compensate or placate, hoteliers who want to know why she left without paying her bill, local police forces who were called out to rescue her, that sort of thing. Now, this is no longer my concern.

WILKINS (RAYMOND): This time, she seems to have been involved in an accident.

HOBHOUSE: An accident's usually involved.

WILKINS (RAYMOND): What do you think happened?

HOBHOUSE: As I told you this morning, I expect she was under the influence of narcotic substances and lost control of her car. It's the usual thing.

BEAUMONT: Seven minutes, gentlemen.

WILKINS (RYAN): Come on, Ray.

WILKINS (RAYMOND): If you don't mind, we have just a few more—

WILKINS (RYAN): Let's speed things up. Last time you saw her?

HOBHOUSE: June, last year.

WILKINS (RYAN): Contact since?

HOBHOUSE: No contact.

WILKINS (RYAN): None at all?

HOBHOUSE: As I've just said, none whatsoever.

BEAUMONT: Can you keep your tone a little less confrontational?

WILKINS (RAYMOND): Yes, of—

WILKINS (RYAN): What about the day of her murder? Where were you?

HOBHOUSE: I've already told your colleague.

WILKINS (RYAN): Haven't told us what you did after dinner. Ended before ten, right? Plenty of time to get to Oxford.

HOBHOUSE: I went home. I went to bed.

WILKINS (RYAN): Anyone corroborate that?

BEAUMONT: Once again, I must ask you to—

WILKINS (RAYMOND): Perhaps I can—

WILKINS (RYAN): Bought herself some pepper spray. Why would she do that?

HOBHOUSE: I've no idea.

WILKINS (RYAN): Scared of someone.

HOBHOUSE: If you say so.

WILKINS (RYAN): You?

HOBHOUSE: Of course not.

BEAUMONT: Please, gentlemen! A little more care.

WILKINS (RAYMOND): Apologies. Can we ask, however, if you're aware of any threats she might have received?

HOBHOUSE: I'm not.

WILKINS (RAYMOND): And, just to confirm, no one's been in touch with you about your wife's disappearance?

HOBHOUSE: What do you mean?

WILKINS (RAYMOND): You've had no demands for money, for instance?

HOBHOUSE: You think she's been abducted?

WILKINS (RAYMOND): We have to consider every possibility.

HOBHOUSE: It's hardly likely a kidnapper would be so

financially illiterate as to wait till we'd separated before making a ransom demand.

BEAUMONT: Three minutes remaining.

WILKINS (RYAN): Do you mind not doing that? It's putting us off.

WILKINS (RAYMOND): We found some correspondence in her apartment. Do you know someone called Bobby?

HOBHOUSE: No. She always had her own circle of friends. I didn't have much to do with them.

WILKINS (RYAN): What about Pablo?

HOBHOUSE: Pablo. [Silence] Yes.

WILKINS (RAYMOND): Her supplier?

HOBHOUSE: I believe so. I never met him. But it makes sense.

WILKINS (RYAN): What d'you mean?

HOBHOUSE: He's Oxford-based.

WILKINS (RYAN): Interesting. What do you know about this Pablo?

HOBHOUSE: Nothing at all. I don't imagine he's the sort of person Zara would have wanted to introduce to me.

WILKINS (RYAN): She ever mention Becket Street to you?

HOBHOUSE: No.

WILKINS (RAYMOND): If she was going to stay in Oxford, where might she have gone?

HOBHOUSE: The Randolph, perhaps. The Old Parsonage. We stayed there once or twice.

WILKINS (RAYMOND): She's not there. No reservations made in her name.

HOBHOUSE: I can't help you, then. But, look, all these questions are really off the point. Pepper spray, ransom demands – all that's nonsense. I'm familiar with the situation. In a few days' time, she'll reappear, having recovered from whatever excesses she was indulging in.

BEAUMONT: And now, gentlemen—

WILKINS (RYAN): What about you? Got places of your own in Oxford she could stay?

HOBHOUSE: No. Well, I have a property portfolio as part of my investments, of course. [Pause] In fact, Polstead Road rings a bell. North Oxford, I think. My personal fund manager can give you the details. But almost certainly it's leased, like the other properties. Anyway, it's very unlikely Zara would have been aware of it. She was only interested in the few homes we used ourselves – Kensington, the one in Mustique, Cannes, and the country house in the Yorkshire Dales.

As he spoke, looking at his watch, he turned to acknowledge other people entering the room, who took no notice of Ray or Ryan as they filed in and sat at the table. On the glass walls, screens lit up: graphs and charts; a feed to a woman on the floor of a stock exchange; a financial news channel. Hobhouse was looking at his phone again, the lawyer Beaumont nodded to dismiss them, and, as the meeting began, they got up and left the room.

They went bumper-to-bumper along Westway, out into the trickling dusk of Buckinghamshire, and joined the trail of car lights looping towards Oxford. What little colour there had been in the

February fields had leached away and the sky was charcoal grey.

The radio was filled with speculation about Zara Fanshawe, stories of the 'missing socialite', the usual fever-mix of clichés and speculation. No more reports of twenty-mile tailbacks of lorries at the ports, billions of pounds of contracts fraudulently handed out to the chums of ministers, the desperate collapse of foreign military misadventures, of dishonesty, corruption and incompetence and all the disheartening evidence of a country that had lost its way. Here, lost instead, was Zara Fanshawe, disappeared, dead of injuries sustained in her crash, perhaps, or incapacitated by a breakdown or amnesia, or abducted, or involved in some criminality, or – this by far the favourite line – victim of a drugs relapse, holed up somewhere, out of it. Underlying most of these stories were two assumptions: that her disappearance was sensational, and that the police were idle or incompetent or both.

For a weary country, it was a welcome break from reality.

Ryan turned off the radio.

'Useful visit to Money Nuts, though.'

'You might have been a little less disruptive.'

'Only way to deal with some of these people. Five minutes, gentlemen! Silver-spoon mouth-breather.'

Ray rolled his eyes, drove on in silence.

'Pablo,' Ryan said, after a while. 'Oxford-based – got something right there to pull on.'

'Doesn't change the basic picture, though. What Hobhouse said about her sounds right, to me. Likeliest thing is she pranged her car because she was off her head. After picking up a bad one from Pablo, maybe.'

'Yeah.'

They drove on.

'Maybe.'

They sped smoothly past High Wycombe, hidden behind its hill, on into the gathering darkness.

'Pepper spray, though. Heavy duty. Who's she scared of? Not Pablo; he's her regular.'

'Scared of everyone, perhaps. Drugs will do that for you.'

'Course.' Ryan looked out of the window. They drove on.

Ray glanced at him. 'Pablo's the one we want to talk to. Got Livvy on it?'

'Course – do it in a minute. What about Bobby?'

'Don't know. He's in the kitchen, cooking it up? Anyway, Pablo knows him. The way forward's through Pablo.'

'I know that. Don't need to worry. I know dealers. Scum of the fucking earth.'

Ryan talked to Livvy. They drove through the Chiltern Gap and down across Milton Common. Night had fallen. Up ahead, a faint glow of Oxford, like a rind of smouldering ashes dropped on the dark ground.

'Just can't help feeling the pepper spray came too late for something,' Ryan said.

They drove on in silence.

As they reached the city, Nadim called. Barko was going up the wall, she said. Certain media outlets seemed to have decided that there was something suspicious about Zara's prolonged disappearance, something nefarious – criminal, even – which the police were failing to uncover. He'd asked her to pass this on to them, by way of encouragement. They did not feel encouraged.

She also had an update for them: a couple of things. First, she'd sourced details of Zara's various credit cards and found no activity on any of them for two weeks. Nothing. Second, something Livvy had asked her to tell them: although there was still no trace of Zara, there had been, finally, a sighting of her in Oxford, on the afternoon before her accident.

'The manager of the Oxfam bookshop in St Giles' saw her when he went out for lunch that day. She was outside Blackfriars, just down from Oxfam.'

'Blackfriars. College of some sort?'

'Theological college, yes.'

'I know it. Archway, railings, funny old-fashioned lamp posts. There's always some homeless guy sat on a bit of cardboard outside, asking for money. What was she doing?'

'According to the bookshop manager, she was sat on the pavement, on a bit of cardboard.'

Silence for a moment.

'Begging?'

'Apparently.'

'Is he sure?'

'He's a very sure sort of person. He identified her immediately from the photograph. She'd made a vivid impression. Well, she would. Expensively dressed, he said – olive-green slacks, blue sweater, some tasteful jewellery. Very composed, just sitting there on the pavement next to a bundle of blankets and a sign saying *Homeless Please Help*. It wasn't what he expected. He didn't know who she was, but he said hello. She didn't say anything, smiled at him nicely. So, he walked on. When he came back to the shop, she wasn't there.'

More silence.

'Ryan?'

'The day she crashed?'

'That's it.'

'Off her head,' Ray said.

Ryan said, 'Anything more recent?'

'Nothing.'

'No witnesses of the crash?'

'No.'

'City cameras? What about the Roller? Not like it's . . . What's the word?'

'Inconspicuous,' Ray said.

'Yeah, that.'

'All we've got so far are images of it heading towards Becket Street shortly before three on the night of her disappearance. No sign of it anywhere else in the city.'

He blew out his cheeks. 'Poser. Hang on, I'll ask my driver what he thinks.'

'Don't push it, Ryan.'

'He's busy, Nadim. Cheers for the update. See you tomorrow.'

'Aren't you giving the press conference later?'

He hesitated. 'Don't think so. Barko'll do it, won't he? Anyway, I've got to be home for Ry's bedtime.'

They went slowly round the ring road.

'You can drop me off by Redbridge, driver. I'll walk up.'

Ray made no reply.

'Cheers,' Ryan said. 'Obliged to you. Take the rest of the day off.'

NINE

He walked under the bypass and up the long strip of Kennington's main street, daydreaming. He thought about Shel, how she was before she got really ill, that look she used to give him, a softening of the eyes, a ragamuffin smile; he'd see it cross her face sometimes, even in the last days. He thought about Zara Fanshawe's luxury flat, the bulldogs bloated on the kitchen floor, the outrageous squalor, Zara sitting on a square of cardboard on the pavement outside Blackfriars: *Homeless Please Help*. Drugs can do that, of course – chase you out of your posh home onto the street, crash your car for you, kick your beautiful face in, make everything else disappear, even your own baby. Still. There's a bit of you that stays you, always. That was the bit to look for now in Zara Fanshawe. She came to Oxford for a meet-up with Pablo. That was a theory. Or she came to Oxford to meet someone she was scared of. Another theory, also interesting.

He walked past bungalows and semis, bald grass verges and cheap brick walls, vans and taxis and pickups, and began to daydream of his son. For several days, now, he'd missed bath time and bedtime with him, and he was disgruntled and his son was distressed. He daydreamed his son lying with him on the narrow bed as they read together a book about a mole and a mouse, which they had read before, perhaps fifty or sixty times. Little Ryan thought Ray was the mole and Ryan and little Ryan together were the mouse. Little Ryan would be drinking a beaker of warm juice, gradually he would grow sleepy, his cheeks would become flushed, his eyelids would close, slowly, slowly, and then he would be asleep, and Ryan would hold his breath and there would be no sound in the little room except the moth-like flutter of his son's breathing.

He came to Kenville Road. Tonight, at least, he was home in time for bath and bed, and even for half an hour in the swing park first.

Little Ryan was three and a half years old. Standing twenty inches tall in his favoured tartan trousers with the elasticated waist and his tractor-themed jumper, weighing thirty pounds, much of which seemed to be concentrated in his sizeable but delicate head, he was a startling blond with a round face, pert mouth and piping voice. He loved above all things conversations, and, because he had just started going to nursery, he had an enormous fund of things to talk about and new words with which to talk about them. Ryan told people in a joking voice that his son was going to be prime minister; he was not joking, however.

King Georges Field Play Area wasn't in a field but on a narrow strip of concrete between the main road and the community centre. On a wet, dark February evening, it was deserted and little Ryan had his pick of the equipment. Light fell across the playground from the windows of the centre, creating stripes of wet shine and plunging darkness, through which little Ryan revolved as he sat on the roundabout.

He began a conversation.

'Daddy?'

'Yeah.'

'Are you here now?'

'Well, I'm not anywhere else.'

'But are you *here* now?'

Little Ryan often posed questions which seemed to Ryan a sort of philosophy.

'Yeah. What do you mean?' he added.

'But are you going?'

Ryan belatedly realised what he was getting at. 'Oh,' he said. 'No, not tonight. I'm staying home with you.'

'Will we have a bath and bed and *Mouse and Mole*?'

'That's it.'

Little Ryan examined his father's face intently, as if to locate the truth in it.

'Promise.'

Ryan asked him about his tummy.

'It's partly nice and a bit not nice, but only a bit. It's not hot,' he said in a cool, evaluating voice, already thinking of a new topic of conversation into which he could put newly learned words.

'Daddy?'

'Yeah?'

'Why mustn't you rip string?'

Ryan considered the question.

'What d'you mean?' he said at last.

'Why mustn't you rip it?'

'You mean cut it, like in that story we—'

'*No*, Daddy, *rip* it.'

He was stumped.

'Why not?' little Ryan persisted.

'*Rip* it? I don't know what you mean, Ry.'

'Daddy! I'm talking about string.'

'Yeah?'

'In different countries, different types of string, different *phases* of string.'

'Skin?'

'String!' He looked with bland interest at his father. He sighed theatrically. 'Doesn't matter,' he said.

He went round and round on the roundabout, the high gloss of his hair defying the darkness, while Ryan watched him, smoking a cigarette. Kid's a genius, he thought.

'Shouldn't smoke, Daddy,' he said as he sailed past.

'Giving up tomorrow.'

The roundabout slowed to standstill, and Ryan helped him off.

'I've heard that before,' little Ryan said, as they set off home through the wet darkness. On the way, little Ryan developed the theory that he had a camera in his head. 'When I do this,' he said, rubbing the side of his right eye with his right forefinger, 'it takes a photograph. It goes into my ear and then I can take another photograph.'

'Nice,' Ryan said.

They held hands, crossing the road. Little Ryan developed another theory, that he could see much better in the dark than he could in daylight.

'Funny stuff, light,' Ryan said, to keep the conversation going.

Little Ryan began next to talk about budgerigars, about which he knew an astonishing amount. He was the conversationalist from hell and Ryan wished him to go on talking forever.

They reached Kenville Road.

Little Ryan said, 'Will we have bath and bed and *Mouse and Mole* now?'

'That's it.'

Then Ryan's phone rang.

Livvy told him that she'd picked up the keys to Hobhouse's Polstead Road property. As it happened, it wasn't leased: it had been sitting empty for two years, on the market, waiting for prices to peak.

'Empty?'

'Empty, shut up, power off.'

'Probably nothing to do, then. Hobhouse said she didn't even know about the place.'

Livvy was silent.

'Even if she knew about it, even if she went up there, how would she get in?'

Still Livvy said nothing.

'And what would she be doing in an empty house?'

Silence.

Ryan could imagine Livvy in the office, sitting with the phone. DS Livvy Holmes, thirty-seven years old, single mother of three, fifteen years in the service without much advancement, a woman with knowledge of the world, of people, a shrewd understanding of young men who can't seem to behave properly, who say the wrong thing, can't make up their minds, make excuses for not putting in an extra hour in the evening to get a job done properly.

She said, in an even, non-judgemental voice, 'Would you like me to go and check it out?'

Ryan stood there on the corner of Kenville Road, looking up at his house, looking down at his son, who was waiting for his bedtime read.

'Fuck it,' he said at last. 'I'll do it.'

Walking up to the house, he tried to explain to his son.

'But, Daddy, you promised.'

'I'll be back really quick. I'll come in and give you a kiss after you've gone to bed.'

Little Ryan regarded him solemnly without speaking, then turned and went into the house, where Ryan's sister, Jade, was waiting for him, and Ryan stood there on the empty driveway. It was only then he remembered the Peugeot was still in the garage. He called Ray, but Ray didn't pick up. He called Carol, and she told him she was in Wallingford, at a supplier's, and at last he called an Uber and walked down to meet it.

In Grove Street, Ray and Diane were eating an early dinner. They sat at their dining table with bowls of Tuscan white bean pasta and glasses of Dolcetto, looking a little ragged. Ray had changed into a turtleneck pullover. He was moody. He had been talking for about twenty minutes and now he stopped, though not because he had finished what he wanted to say, and they sat for a moment in distracted silence, listening to the burpy, rustling noises coming from the baby monitor set up on the table between them.

When Ryan called, Ray just glanced at his phone and ignored it.

'Oliver was in such pain today,' Diane said. 'I think he has colic.'

Ray didn't respond. After a moment, he went on, as if unaware of what she had just said: 'I can't actually believe it. You couldn't make it up. Literally the day after I'm given a national award. Literally the day after.'

Diane, who had heard this already, got up to clear away the empty bowls.

'Just personal, that's what it is. Nakedly personal.'

Diane murmured sympathy.

'Wouldn't be surprised if there's something else as well.'

'What do you mean?'

'You know what I mean. Natural order of things resumed. That's Wallace. He might as well start calling me Man Friday.'

'He spoke very highly to me of the DCC.'

Ray muttered to himself.

'I hope it's not affecting your relationship with Ryan,' she said mildly.

Ray snorted. 'Ryan! Ryan loves it. Finds it funny.'

'Perhaps he's embarrassed.'

'*Ryan?* Ryan wouldn't know what embarrassment was if it reared up in front of him and bit off his nose.'

Whimpers came from the baby monitor, whispery bleatings.

Diane came back to the table. 'Oliver,' she said. 'I told you.'

'He'll settle down.'

The crying started immediately, miniature gales of pain, surprising for being so piercing.

'Ray?'

He sat, brooding. 'Absolutely loves it, Ryan. Little digs all the time. Ray, do this; Ray, do that.'

'Will you see to him?'

He glared at the wall – talking to it, in fact. 'It's a joke,' he said. 'He doesn't have the skills, doesn't even have the basics. Not to lead. He's not across the detail, doesn't organise a search, the phones, a warrant, doesn't have his gloves, forgets to call things in, can't handle Wallace. But he's behaving as if—'

'*Ray!*'

He turned to her, startled.

'Ollie,' she said.

Bitterly, he stood, face clenched. He seemed about to say something else, then he turned for the stairs.

Diane called after him, 'By the way, your father called. There's a message on the answerphone.'

In the spare room, he paced up and down with Oliver draped over his shoulder, as if the little boy had just fallen on to him from the ceiling. Whenever he stopped moving, his son set up a thin shriek and he set off again. His thoughts ran obsessively on themes of injustice, and, though he knew this was unhelpful, he found it hard to stop.

'I've got to move on,' he said in a whisper to his son.

Half an hour passed and he became tired. At last, Oliver slept, and Ray sat on the carpet with him in his lap, not calm, but emotionally numb; and finally, despite himself, his thoughts turned to Zara Fanshawe. He knew rich girls. He thought of all the Zaras he'd met at Balliol, all the Beatrices, Ianthes, Alexandras. He remembered their bright enjoyments, their gilded entitlement, childish innocence, intelligence. They had poise, style – that was their great defining feature; they knew how to behave, even when their lives were in turmoil, even when they'd fallen foul of drugs (and he'd seen that more than once), when they were unpredictable, high or upset or desperate. Or scared – scared enough to arm themselves with pepper spray, say. Even as they sat begging on the pavement, they would smile nicely at passers-by. Sitting in their crashed car, they would speak calmly to Emergency. It did not mean that they were calm. Or nice.

It was seven o'clock. Diane had gone to bed to get some sleep before another broken night. He put Oliver back in his crib and went downstairs to get a drink. In the back room, he felt strong enough to play his father's message on the phone – a lengthy and nearly unintelligible account of family involvement in Nigerian politics, ending with his intention to come to Oxford to see his grandchildren and his son, the 'future commissioner'. He said he wanted to know what things were like at work, now that Ray was the recipient of the Queen's Commendation for Bravery.

Ray wished he hadn't played it. He was filled again with all the queasy pain of his disappointment. His father had ended his message by asking him to call back as soon as possible, but instead Ray stood there, doing nothing, finishing his drink. Another call came in from Ryan and he petulantly cut it, and went upstairs.

And now it began to rain, a fine drizzle billowing in the breeze, soaking the stone fronts of the buildings, darkening the pavements. In the Westgate shopping centre, along the front of Blackfriars, in Cornmarket and Bonn Square and Little Clarendon Street, rough sleepers shifted under whatever cover was to hand, tucked their heads into their chests, folded into themselves. A sort of hard stillness settled in. But there was movement at St Ebbe's. Out of the flickering darkness, a man staggered down the hill towards the church. He was wrapped in layers of mixed clothing fastened with a cracked belt, his head thickly and crustily bandaged, and he shoved a supermarket trolley in front of him as he came, limping wildly in ill-fitting boots. In St Ebbe's churchyard, under a sign saying *No Litter No Alcohol No Dogs*, a small group of people stirred uneasily, hearing the clatter and scrape of the trolley wheels. They began to mutter. But it was too late; he was suddenly among them, lashing out, roaring, causing panic.

They cringed away from him or scrambled to their feet, screaming insults; they pushed and shoved and fell again. It was not immediately clear what he wanted, perhaps only the drama of the violence, but soon they realised that he was shouting at them about stolen things, a bag. Money. He was surprisingly energetic for someone so old.

'Fuckers got my bag! Fuckers wait till I'm gone, come creeping to my skip. Who's got it? Who?'

He slashed at them with wire coat hangers grabbed out of his trolley. One of them fell heavily against a tombstone; others, having screamed, moved away resentfully into the shadows. Still he did not stop. His trolley overturned and he seized someone and fell with her to the ground, struggling and shouting, shaking her with his mittened hands as she lay there, until suddenly he was exhausted and fell back in a heap next to her, and there was only the sound of the woman's sobbing.

'You *fuck*!' she suddenly screamed, and lay back again, crying.

71

'Waitrose, you absolute fuck,' she said, more quietly, between her sobs.

'Who's got it, Lena?' he said. 'Tell me.'

'How the—'

'I'll fucking gut them. Lena, tell them. I want my money back,' he said loudly. Spittle glistened yellow in his beard. His bandage had come loose and his tangled grey hair fell to pieces around his gristly face.

'You know what?' she said. 'There's something wrong with you. You need help.'

'I'll have all the help I need, thank you, when I get my money back.'

'You haven't got any money, Waitrose.'

'I got it!' he said fiercely.

'Where'd you get it?'

He fell silent. He made frightened, mumbling movements with this mouth. 'I have to get out,' he went on, in a desperate voice. 'Do you fucking well understand? I have to get out, now. I need that money.'

'Why? What you done?'

His eyes went slantwise round the graveyard. 'The Mover's coming,' he said. He bellowed it louder – 'The Mover!' – an Old Testament prophet in his wilderness, all rags and spittle, looking round with satisfaction to see the effect on the figures cringing in the dark. 'You get me my money back,' he said quietly to the woman.

He hauled himself to his feet.

'What you done, you have to get out?' Lena said.

He ignored her.

'What you done, Waitrose?' she shouted, but he went without reply, pushing his trolley, limping furiously into the wet darkness until there was only the creak of the trolley wheels, and soon that was gone.

TEN

At last, Ryan reached Polstead Road. It was late, now. Unable to get a ride from the station, where he had picked up the estate agent's keys, he'd walked in the soft drizzle all the way through town and up the Woodstock Road, thinking about his son and cursing the weather, Ray and Zara Fanshawe. And now, his clothes spongy with damp, he stood in the hush of north Oxford. Polstead Road was a quiet avenue of large red-brick villas, graceful sycamores and weathered brick walls, a stage set of Edwardian England, home through the years to professors of divinity, minor baronets, suffragettes. Even the evening darkness here seemed refined. At one end of the street, in the same worn red brick, was a pleasant pub and, conveniently next to it, a working men's institute originally intended to keep men from drink. Number 1A, at the other end, where Ryan was loitering, was a tall, comfortable house keeping a polite distance between itself and the road behind a wall, privet hedge and iron gates. No lights on; it was completely dark.

Ryan pushed open the gates, noticing the overgrown garden,

and went up the mossed-over path to the front door. A blue plaque on the wall informed him that a man he had never heard of, responsible for a chemical process he had never heard of, had spent his boyhood there between 1890 and 1905, years he knew nothing about. Of course. This was Oxford, land of the utterly obscure famous. In the darkness, he went along the side of the house and down some steps into the back garden, a long plot of scratched earth, dumped weeds and a wet pelt of lawn running down to a low-slung garden cottage at the bottom, all dim in the darkness of overhanging willows. Crossing a small patio, he found a door into the lower ground floor and saw that the glass panes in it had been broken and the door recently opened, and he stood there a while, thinking about that, then retraced his steps to the front door.

He let himself in and stood in the hallway, listening. There was no sound, only the hush of emptiness, a stillness of damp plaster and dusty floorboards. On the floor by his feet was a heap of circulars – months, if not years old. It was pitch dark, the lights didn't come on when he tried the switch, and he went into the front room and stood there in the weak lamplight coming in from outside through the curtainless window. There was no furniture, no carpet. He took out his phone and called Ray again, the fourth time in the last half-hour. As before, the call went through to voicemail and he left another message.

'Fuck's sake, Ray, what you up to? I'm in the Polstead Road place. There's a broken window, and, I got to tell you, I got a bad feeling.'

Then he went out to the stairs and climbed slowly to the first floor, hearing the boards creak, listening out for sounds from above, though there was nothing, less than nothing, a thickening of the silence, and he felt the hairs go up on the back of his neck. When his phone rang, he started so violently, he almost overbalanced.

'Will you fucking well work on your timing, Ray? I nearly fell down the stairs.'

A familiar squeaky voice said, 'Daddy!'

'Ry! Mate.'

'You shouldn't swear, Daddy.'

He stood there, exposed, on the stairs.

'Sorry. You got me at a—'

'You promised me a kiss.'

'Yeah, I know, it's just—'

'You *promised*!'

'Yeah.'

He could hear the distress in his son's voice.

'But you're not *there*, Daddy.'

He looked round, puzzled, as if to try to find himself. 'Yeah, I am.'

'Here,' little Ryan corrected himself.

'No, I'm not there,' Ryan said.

This was more of the mind-bending philosophy his son seemed able to effortlessly prompt.

'But why, Daddy?'

Ryan began to explain that things were taking him longer than he'd thought.

'Did you get lost?'

'No, it's just . . . Listen, I'm sorry.' He looked at his watch, squinting in the darkness. 'Fuck, shouldn't you be in bed?'

'*Daddy!*'

'Sorry.' There was a pause. 'How's your tummy?'

This was a desperate gambit. Little Ryan was uninterested in it. 'You said you'd be *here* for a kiss.'

'I'll be home soon. Promise, Ry. Thing is, I'm in this house.'

'What house?'

At last, little Ryan was distracted.

'Big, old house. Funny, really – like a ghost house. No one lives here, see. All the rooms are empty, nothing in them at all – no chairs or tables, nothing like that. Better keep my voice down.'

'Why?'

'In case the ghosts hear me.'

There was silence as little Ryan absorbed this.

'Only kidding. But it's creepy alright. Listen, I'm going into one of the bedrooms now. Yeah. Nothing here, just the fireplace and a sort of old cupboard, great big thing, built into the wall. The ceiling's really high, there's a big old light hanging from it, but it don't work. Nothing works here. I'm going to go upstairs now. Can you hear that? That's the floorboards creaking. Scary, isn't it?'

He could hear his son breathing at the other end as he listened, and he went on up the stairs, peering around in the darkness, talking softly.

'There's more rooms up here. One of them's a bathroom; it's got this old bath in it, standing in the middle of the floor, with great big taps; I reckon you'd have to be strong just to turn them on.'

'Will you turn them on?' his son whispered.

'Not now. Maybe later. I'm just going to go into these last few rooms. Here's another bedroom, smaller this time. Just one more.'

He went to the end of the corridor and pushed open the door. Under the window, in the faint lamplight, was a camp bed, a simple, low, old-fashioned thing, canvas and metal rods, and sprawled on it was the body of a woman, warped and twisted in the rictus of death.

'Daddy? Are you there, Daddy?'

He cleared his throat. 'Tell you what, Ry. Call you back, alright?'

He went up close to make sure it was Zara Fanshawe. It was. She was lying convulsed on her back, a broken doll flung on to the camp bed, legs akimbo, arms splayed over the sides of the cot, hands stretched out, fingers spread wide and crooked as if to grasp something beyond her reach. Her head was turned sharply, unnaturally, the other way. Chic blond hair framed a face gone ugly, the skin of her cheeks shrunken, lips curled back from her teeth, eyes huge and desperate, lumpy bruises, purple and yellow, wrapped around her throat. As if not just dead, but still trapped in the jolting moment of death. Ryan hunkered down and took a long look at her. She was wearing an expensive sweater and olive-green slacks, nice jewellery, but, in that inhuman pose, in that desolate attic, she seemed stripped of everything, poor as a street beggar, nothing left but a body twisted into an attitude of pain.

Lost. A lost thing.

He rose and looked around. The little attic room was a mess. There was a handbag, a holdall upended in a corner, things strewn across the wooden floorboards – clothes, toiletries, shoes. She'd been camping here for a while. He thought about that as he looked around. The end of big money, squatting in a deserted house like a vagrant, a woman stripped of everything, without the protection of money or education, vulnerable, almost as if she was making it easy for someone to come and shake and wrench and twist her to death, and dump her on a camp bed and leave her there, like rubbish.

And again he thought of Shel lying on the carpet, her bloated face, her blue skin, not Shel anymore, a dying woman, a body; and he felt all the anger again too, standing there clenched, waiting for it to pass.

He called it in, at last. 'Number 1A, that's it. Upstairs, fifth bedroom, on a little fold-up bed. Looks like she's been camped here. . . . Not much, the whole house is empty.'

He listened.

'No, it's not. No.' He winced. ''Cause I know what an overdose looks like, right? Neck's been broken. . . . Yeah, alright.'

He called Ray again, and this time he answered. He could hear a baby crying in the background.

'Where've you been? Fuck's sake, I been calling all evening. Anyway, big news this end – just found her. . . . No, she's not. The opposite. . . . Yeah, bad. You'll see when you get here. . . . In a minute, then.'

He looked round, frowning. He'd remembered his gloves and he put them on and went over to the handbag lying at the floor and began to poke around in it. The usual stuff, mainly: keys, packet of tissues, wallet, packet of mints, pens, lipstick, phone charger. No phone – that was interesting. But nothing else, just a business card. He glanced at it and frowned.

'That's weird,' he said out loud.

*

79

It was midnight when Ryan got to Carol's. Little Ryan had already been asleep when he got home, and Jade had prohibited Ryan from disturbing him.

'Saw the presser just now on the television,' Carol said. 'Thought you might have been in it.'

'Barko's a better man for that sort of thing.'

'Do you want to have a look?'

She found the clip and played it again. Superintendent Wallace, filling the screen. They watched him read out a statement to the effect that a body had been found, subsequently identified as the missing woman Zara Fanshawe, and that, as a result, Thames Valley Police had opened an investigation into her murder. He gave a brief item of information – that a lead was being pursued – and made an equally brief appeal for anyone with information to contact them. He continued economically with a pithy expression of horror at the nature of the crime, made various sentimental comments about family at this sad time, their need for privacy, the proper outrage and grief of the wider community, and, his lips slightly out of sync with his voice, concluded by saying time-honoured words to the effect that justice would be done. Then the clip ended and a newscaster began a thirty-second summary of Zara's interesting life. Carol turned the television off.

They sat in silence.

'You found her, right?'

'Yeah.'

'Was it bad?'

'Yeah.'

He glanced at her, found her looking at him – that look he didn't understand yet, hard-eyed, slightly panic-stricken.

'Following a lead?' she said.

'Can't talk about it, you know that.'

'Real, though, is it?'

'Don't know. Maybe.'

'But . . . you got a suspect in mind?'

He didn't reply, looked away. He said in a quiet voice, 'Soon as I saw the broken window, I had this thought I was going to find her there. But, got to be honest, I was expecting an overdose. And the thought of it scared me. Would've brought it all back, you know, finding Shel that night. It did a bit, anyway.' He breathed out. 'Course, soon as I saw her, I knew it wasn't an overdose.'

Carol's face was pale.

'Oh, yeah. Someone put a lot of effort into killing her.' He fell silent, shook his head. 'Funny. Big old house – mansion, really – but nothing in it, no furniture, no curtains even, nothing. Damp, electricity off, more like a squat – and there she is, little posh girl, dressed very nice, and very dead.'

He looked at her fully then, and this time she turned away.

'Small,' he said. 'Really small. Like a child, really. You know, sort of breakable.'

He left a pause.

'Do you know much about her?' he asked, after a moment. The tone of his voice had changed, she caught it at once and turned back to face him.

'Only what I've read in the papers. Why?'

'Don't suppose you ever met her?'

'Met Zara Fanshawe? Why do you ask?'

''Cause there was one of your cards in her handbag.'

81

She didn't seem to know what to do. She got to her feet, sat down again, staring at him. 'One of my cards?'

'Bit weird, isn't it?'

She hadn't taken her eyes off him. It was like she was forcing herself to keep looking at him. She said, 'She must have taken it from one of my girls. Told you, they've been handing them out all week.'

Ryan nodded. 'Okay. Useful. We can have a chat with them, then; maybe get a sighting of her from town cameras. Where were they?'

She took out her phone and sent him a note of the locations. There were four or five of them, all in the centre of town.

'My card,' Carol said, 'in a dead woman's bag.'

She went to the sink to get a glass of water.

'Odd, though,' Ryan called after her. 'What would she want flowers for, in an empty house?'

ELEVEN

There was only one story, next morning. In death, Zara Fanshawe completed her journey from the lifestyle sections and
gossip columns to the front pages, and was seen everywhere –
generally aged seventeen, pertly fresh-faced on the back of an
Olympic horse, as if her murder had rejuvenated her, restored
her innocence and made her worthy of our grief. The dramas
of her life were rehearsed, with special emphasis placed on her
final few months of sobriety, her willingness to own her story
and to speak on behalf of vulnerable women everywhere. There
were few details of the circumstances of her death; the police
had declined to release them. Lawrence Hobhouse, who had
identified the body, had also made no statement. In certain
uninhibited areas of the Internet, the gap was filled by persistent
rumours of narcotic misadventures.

Nadim and Livvy joined Ryan and Ray in Barko's office for
the morning briefing. Nadim relayed the key findings of the
forensics report. Zara Fanshawe had been killed thirty or so
hours earlier, almost certainly in the Polstead Road house, on

the night of her disappearance. Death was caused by multiple catastrophic fractures of the neck: someone had taken hold of it and twisted and wrenched it until they had broken it. It was murder – violent, deliberate and full of rage.

'Toxicology?'

'No trace of any chemicals in her system.'

'Interesting. What about the broken window?'

Livvy took over. The forced entry at the back of the house had been recent, perhaps the same night as her murder. There was something else too. Recent boot prints in the dust of the floor around the window and elsewhere in the house. Not Zara's. Size six, not size three.

'Distinctive tread,' Nadim said. 'Identified as Magnum Panther.'

'I know Magnums,' Barko said. 'Worn them myself. Outdoorsy.'

'Yes. Coppers on the beat wear them. Warehouse staff, ground crew at airports, anyone on their feet all day.'

'Dealers,' Ray said. 'Someone out there in the rail station car park, waiting for a punter at three in the morning.'

They thought about that.

'Other details?'

There was the business card from Carol's shop. Livvy was already checking the sites in the town centre where Carol's staff had been handing them out.

Ryan said, 'Don't know, but Ray's right – scumbag Pablo's still the only real thing we got to pull on, right now. We need to get a grip on him pronto. Could be she went down there to meet him, something went wrong, little rich girl trying to do a street deal, winds up with some fucking murderous scum instead. Bit weird she ends up at Polstead Road, though. And, if he took her there to kill her, why didn't he nab her jewellery while he was at it?'

'Or did she walk back to Polstead Road and the perp follow her?'

'Could be.'

'What's she doing in an empty house, anyway?'

Barko said, 'Suppose there's nothing useful yet from the neighbourhood?'

Livvy reported. Officers had been doing the door-to-door in Polstead Road: neighbours knew nothing, had seen nothing. So far as they knew, the house was empty. No one had seen anything of Zara.

'Money make you blind? Reckon she'd been camping there a couple of weeks. Someone must have caught a glimpse of her.'

'It's a private sort of place. Discreet.'

Barko said, 'We need to know more about her movements round Oxford in the days leading up to her murder. Much more. If she was camping in Polstead Road, where was her car? Put it another way: what was she up to?'

But, as Ryan had said, their focus should be on tracing Pablo. They discussed tactics. Livvy and Nadim got loaded with basics, and they prepared to go.

'This case,' Barko said. 'Knew it smelled bad. Wasn't even a crime at the beginning and the paps were all over it. Now, it's a great big shiny murder.' He looked at Ray and Ryan narrowly. 'And it's like you two are just watching it grow.' He reminded them both that they were in the spotlight, now, until they found Zara's killer. 'Only way to get ourselves off the front pages is to get it done,' he said. 'So, move to it. And keep moving.'

They filed out.

'Ryan,' Barko said. 'You stay.'

He closed the door and stood there waiting, while Barko went to the window and looked out, arranging himself in front of it, a compressed shape of uniform, dark and abstract against the light. For several minutes, he didn't turn round. A bad sign. He didn't say anything either. Another bad sign. But Ryan, who had grown up with much worse, stood relaxed, idly scratching. In his experience, there was little point in jumping until you knew where the kick was coming from.

Finally, Barko spoke: 'Do you want to talk me through your evening, son? After you found her.'

Ryan stopped being relaxed, saw where the kick was coming from. 'Did you want me at the presser?'

Barko turned, his expression shadowy and unstable. 'Oh, the penny's dropped, has it, bright boy? Twelve hours too late. Yes, I wanted you at the presser. No, you weren't there. Yes, I'm wondering if I made a mistake giving you the lead. Comment?'

Ryan shook his head in a passable imitation of remorse. He opened his mouth.

'Save it,' Barko said. 'Listen to me.' He came up close and lowered his voice. 'You need a win, understand? There are people here, influential people, who've expressed qualms about you being back onside. I took a risk for you, son. Personally. So, this is how it's going to work. You're going to step up. You're going to be a big boy and do all the big boy things. Including press conferences, answering questions, being polite.'

'Got it.'

'Nightly reports on my desk until this is done.'

'Sir.'

Barko scrutinised him with small, malevolent eyes. A slight jerk of the chin indicated that he was free to go.

Some of the photos that had been appearing in the media were pinned to the crazy wall in the office shared by Ryan and Ray. Also, photos of Becket Street, the massive twisted car, the trashed living room in the apartment at One Hyde Park, the doorstep at Polstead Road with its pile of circulars, the attic with its horrifying body, and little Ryan, mouth open, having a conversation. Ryan was a half-hearted and wayward user of crazy walls.

Ray looked up and raised his eyebrows as Ryan came in.

'Barko? Nothing much.' Ryan waved a hand dismissively. 'Just, you know, congratulations, keep it up sort of thing.'

'Was he angry you missed the presser?'

'Well, you could have reminded me.'

'I was only there to do the driving.'

Ryan screwed up his face. 'Hope you're making a start on scumbag Pablo. Can't afford to hang about, Raymond. Got to work the lists, liaise with Narcotics, have a word with Violent Crime, all that. Takes time. Best get on it.'

Ray was about to make a retort when he got a call.

At the door, Ryan said, 'I'm just going to have a chat with Nadim, so I'll have to leave you unsupervised for a bit, but, don't worry, I'll be back in a couple of minutes.'

Ray showed him the finger.

Nadim had pulled out more information about Zara Fanshawe from a variety of sources, and she went through it with Ryan.

They had new personal information, things that had not been aired in the media: a damaging parental divorce during her privileged childhood, for example; loneliness at a string of Catholic boarding schools, eating disorders, a promising academic start at Oxford abruptly cut short when she left the university without taking her degree. There were statements she'd made recently during meetings at Families Anonymous, her hopes and consolations, her determination to remain clean, her vulnerability and, like a little grace note of disquiet, her constant fear of a relapse.

'What about a fear of other people?' Ryan mentioned the pepper spray. 'Pick up any disputes, anyone threatening her?'

Nadim shook her head. 'But we didn't find any devices at the apartment. No laptop, no phone. Nothing at Polstead Road either; it looks like the perp took her phone. It's slow trawling without them. On the contrary, though, she seems to have had a lot of friends. Well liked.'

He thought about that.

Nadim waited. She said, 'When are you going to bring your adorable son into the station again?' She was a big fan of little Ryan.

'What, expose him to Barko and Ray? How about never? Never good for you?'

'When did you get so mean, Ryan?'

'When they started getting shouty and sulky.'

She sighed.

He went back to Zara. 'What about a police record? Disturbances, obstruction of justice, drunk and disorderly, that sort of thing.'

'Nothing, actually.'

He was surprised. 'Really? With her lifestyle? All that went on? No charges, no helping with enquiries? Nothing to do with drugs?'

'Nothing at all, except a single driving ticket, from years ago.' Nadim brought up the ancient ticket on her laptop and Ryan peered at it. She went on, 'You'd think from the media she regularly spent nights in a police cell. But then, obviously, women in newspapers are not usually real women.'

'Any mention of a Pablo?'

Nadim shook her head. Something had come in recently, though – a new piece of information from One Hyde Park. As she talked, Ray arrived in some haste and stood there impatiently waiting to speak, while Nadim explained that new CCTV footage from the underground car park showed the Rolls-Royce Phantom leaving, two weeks earlier, driven by Zara, and not returning. 'So, she's probably been away from home for a fortnight. Makes sense, with the state you say her dogs were in. She could well have been in Oxford all that time, though of course there's no sign of the car in the city yet.'

As she finished, Ray said, 'Got something—' but Ryan, his attention still snagged on the image of the old driving ticket, held up a hand. 'Hang on, this is interesting.'

'Ryan, it's important.'

'Yeah, but look at this. Funny or what? She was stopped in Godstow Road, two in the morning, New Year's Eve 2005. Dangerous driving.'

Nadim and Ray both looked at it, looked at him.

'She'd been to a New Year's Eve party. So?'

'So, look who booked her.' He grinned.

They peered at the name of the active officer. Police Constable C. Lynch.

'Your hero,' he said to Ray. 'The legendary. Seventeen years ago, working the beat on New Year's Eve. Dedication, that is.'

Ray said, 'Very interesting. Look, I've just had a call—'

'I think it's interesting. You could put it in a museum, couldn't you?' He carried on grinning. 'Sloppy done, mind. See? Didn't even breathalyse her.'

'For Christ's sake, give it a rest, Ryan.'

'Humble beginnings, mate. Gives hope to us all. Mention it next time you have a cosy little chat with her: "Saw your early work – bit shit, but like the effort." So,' he said at last, turning to Ray, 'what you got? Anything on that scumbag dealer of hers? Like I said, we can't afford to hang about, here.'

'We're meeting him in twenty minutes.'

Ryan stared a little. 'Straight up?'

'Grand Café in the High. Suit you?'

Ryan grinned. 'Fuck, Ray. My man. I was only gone, like, two minutes. You know, there's a lot of people here, influential people, say to me, "That Ray, is he really as good as, you know?" And I'm going to tell them, man, "You want a coffee with a drug dealer fixed up, he's like, *slick*." So, what happened? How d'you get hold of him?'

He hadn't. Pablo had called in, simple as that. He'd heard the news, he wanted to talk to someone about Zara Fanshawe.

'Did he say anything on the phone?'

'Nothing.'

'Changes the picture, though, right?'

'We'll have to wait till we hear what he's got to say.'

'Course. Bet it changes the picture, though. Dealers not that keen to talk, usually.'

'We'll see.'

'Fair enough. Let's go, then. Don't want to keep the scumbag waiting.'

TWELVE

They walked together, Ray all swishing coat and Ryan all saunter and slouch. It was grey and damp, and the High Street gleamed like pewter in the weak winter sunlight.

'Don't like the sound of him, myself,' Ryan said.

'You don't like dealers, full stop.'

'You wouldn't, if they killed your girlfriend.'

'Alright, but you didn't even talk to him.'

They walked on.

'Grand Café? What's that about? Why aren't we meeting on some street corner in the Leys?'

'It's just a place, Ryan.'

'What's he even come forward for? Makes no sense.'

'Relax. All we have to do is talk to him calmly.'

They walked past patisseries and boutiques. At the corner of King Edward Street, a man was sitting on a bit of plastic with a dog next to him and, balanced on the dog's back, a cat, and, on the cat's back, a rat, which kept slipping off. His sign said, *We Are Hungry Thank You.*

'Never seen that before,' Ryan said as they passed. 'Homeless guys getting inventive. Listen, tell you what, why don't we mix it up this time? I'll be the smooth posh one and you can be the one with the bad manners and irritating face. What about that, Ray?'

Ray said, 'Take a look at yourself as we walk past this shop window.'

Ryan looked, sniffed, said no more.

When they arrived at the cafe, they found a forty-year-old, floppy-haired blond waiting for them, elegantly bohemian in a burgundy corduroy jacket, red drainpipes and long cashmere scarf, brilliantly yellow. He came across and greeted Ray effusively with a double handshake.

'Recognise you from your picture at the awards dinner. So good to meet. I've ordered a pot of Earl Grey.'

He ignored Ryan, seeming to assume that he'd wandered in independently, and began to talk at once about the woman he called, 'Truly, madly, deeply, my soulmate.'

Ray tried to interrupt him, but he talked on.

'When I say we were close, I don't mean *close*, I mean *inseparable*, I mean *joined at the brain*, as if we felt the same things at the same time, actually had the *same feelings*.'

Ray tried again, but there was no stopping the man's verbal flow, his speech fluent, his vocabulary rich, his accent impeccably upper-middle-class, his user's sniff as elegantly casual as a Gucci accessory.

'Sometimes we had the same dreams,' he said. 'And don't even get me started on our shared love of Mantovani. It was Zara who—'

Ryan stepped up very close and clicked his fingers in his face, and he finally stopped talking.

'You Pablo?'

In bewilderment, the man looked to Ray for support and found none.

'Well, it's Justin, actually. Justin Darling. Pablo's an old nickname. I studied Spanish at university, and so—'

'You're the guy what phoned us just now? About Zara Fanshawe?'

He nodded. 'Yes, that's me.'

Ryan's expression seemed to drain him of further words and he fell silent.

'Sit,' Ryan said, not in a friendly way. 'Sit there, so I can keep my fucking eye on you.'

LOCATION: Grand Café, High Street, Oxford, oldest coffee shop in England, a gilded cabinet of polished marble and mirrors, filled with elegant, uncomfortable coffee-house chairs, the light hubbub of genteel chatter and obligatory aroma of roasting coffee beans.

INTERVIEWERS: DI Wilkins (Raymond; firm-featured), in black jeans, matching sweatshirt and Brando black leather coat, and DI Wilkins (Ryan; loose-faced, irritable), wearing Adidas trackies, Loop jacket and baseball cap.

INTERVIEWEE: Justin Darling, dressed like a young theatre impresario of the early 1960s.

WILKINS (RAYMOND): Detective Inspector Raymond Wilkins. My colleague, Detective Inspector Ryan Wilkins. No relation. Obviously. So. Call you Justin?

DARLING: Absolutely.

WILKINS (RAYMOND): What do you want to tell us?

DARLING: Well, it's not so much wanting to tell you something as wanting to make myself as useful as possible. I'm just devastated. I knew her for twenty years, I was one of her oldest friends. In fact, I think I'm right, we first met here, in this cafe, perhaps actually at this table, in Michaelmas of our first year, when she was at LMH and I was—

WILKINS (RYAN): Seriously?

DARLING: [silence]

WILKINS (RYAN): You come here to tell us the history of your beautiful friendship? Don't look at him, look at me; I'm the unstable one here. We got questions. When you've answered the questions, if he's any free time, my colleague here will listen to your confessions of supplying the rich and famous with drugs. Alright? First question. When did you last see her?

DARLING: A fortnight ago. I was in London, jogging through Thurloe Place, and I saw her standing on the pavement, just along from the Brompton Oratory.

WILKINS (RAYMOND): Speak to her?

DARLING: Just gave a little wave.

WILKINS (RYAN): Last time you saw her?

DARLING: Yes.

WILKINS (RYAN): You weren't with her in a house in Polstead Road, two nights ago?

DARLING: No.

WILKINS (RYAN): You didn't meet her in Becket Street at three in the morning, same night?

95

DARLING: Becket Street? No, horrid little street.

WILKINS (RAYMOND): The rail station car park's often used for deals.

DARLING: Oh, I never deal in car parks. That's really not my style.

WILKINS (RYAN): Can I just quickly check something here? You are a drug dealer, right? Not like you been supplying her with stationery or something?

DARLING: Strictly recreational. And reliably sourced.

WILKINS (RYAN): And fucking illegal, is my point.

DARLING: Oh! I assumed . . . I'm so sorry, I assumed, if I were assisting, this would be off the record, or whatever the phrase is. I mean, you do want my help? I'm not sure I could say anything useful, if you were to put me under caution.

WILKINS (RYAN): Well, isn't that lovely? Alright, another question, if you don't mind assisting with an answer. *You know where I am.* What's that about?

DARLING: I know where you are? I don't understand. You're right here.

WILKINS (RYAN): You know what, you should get in touch with the university, ask for your money back. *You know where I am.* What you said to her.

DARLING: Did I?

WILKINS (RYAN): Ray, mate, just letting you know, you might have to restrain me.

WILKINS (RAYMOND): We found a card from you in Zara's apartment. Hand-delivered. A card with a picture of T-shirts on it?

DARLING: Oh, wait, that's right. I hadn't been seeing so much of her as usual, so I dropped round a card.

WILKINS (RAYMOND): *You know where I am* is what you wrote on it. What did you mean?

DARLING: Just, here I am, if you need me.

WILKINS (RYAN): If you need a fix.

DARLING: No, no. No. You don't understand. Zara had been clean for months. I thought everyone knew that. That's what the card's *about*: clean T-shirts on a washing line. She did incredibly well, I was so proud of her. But it *was* a struggle, that's true, and sometimes she just needed someone to be with – you know, someone to cherish her, help her through her periods of temptation.

WILKINS (RYAN): What, like her drug dealer?

WILKINS (RAYMOND): How do you know she'd been clean?

DARLING: Because, in all those months, she hadn't asked me for a single thing. And she'd never go to anyone else. It's all about trust and loyalty, in our end of the business. And discretion.

WILKINS (RAYMOND): But you hadn't been seeing her so much recently.

DARLING: Well, no. I thought she needed space.

WILKINS (RAYMOND): Or she'd become reclusive, secretive, paranoid. That's what her ex-husband thinks.

DARLING: Don't believe anything that man says. Seriously. Jealous and vindictive doesn't even begin to cover it. Their separation was acrimonious in the extreme. There were hints of violence, threats.

WILKINS (RYAN): Zara scared of him?

DARLING: Absolutely. He hired someone to follow her. She'd look behind her, there'd be this menacing guy there; she could tell from the way he moved he'd been trained. Some ex-Special-Forces animal. Hobhouse even pursued her himself.

WILKINS (RAYMOND): He told us he'd had no contact with her since last June.

DARLING: Well, I happen to know that's not true, because I saw him myself in November, at St Anne's, when I was visiting her in rehab. The staff couldn't keep him away.

WILKINS (RYAN): What was he up to?

DARLING: He hated losing her, couldn't bear it. He's unbelievably possessive. She didn't need him anymore; she was rediscovering herself, growing away from him. Spiritually.

WILKINS (RYAN): Tell you that?

DARLING: Not exactly. Male intuition.

WILKINS (RYAN): Christ. We're in trouble, now.

DARLING: Listen a minute. She'd developed new tastes and dislikes, new sensitivities, the way you do when under the influence of something new.

WILKINS (RYAN): Example?

DARLING: She said strange things sometimes, things I'd never heard her say before. She asked me if I believed in lost things. I mean, where to start?

WILKINS (RYAN): Interesting.

DARLING: You see. I told her I'd lost a pair of brogues once and never got over it, and she said they were only lost to

98

me. 'Nothing's really ever lost,' she said, 'that's what's so terrifying.' Anyway, bottom line: she was changing her life and Hobhouse couldn't stand it. But, to me – to me, it was beautiful to behold. It's true, I only popped round to her place once or twice to spend a little down-time with her – late autumn, it must have been – but the transformation was remarkable. I think it's fair to say that, before rehab, she had some quite serious issues around self-respect. But, since rehab . . . She looked fabulous, her apartment looked fabulous; she'd fallen in love with life all over again.

WILKINS (RYAN): Brace yourself.

DARLING: What do you mean?

WILKINS (RAYMOND): We visited her apartment yesterday. There are unmistakable signs of drug abuse.

WILKINS (RYAN): Like a fucking drug den is what he means. Totally trashed. Couple of dead dogs in the kitchen.

DARLING: Not . . . the twins . . . ? Not Castor and Pollux? [Noises of distress, long silence] I can't believe it.

WILKINS (RYAN): Fair enough. But our question is: if you weren't supplying her, who was? Bobby?

DARLING: Bobby?

WILKINS (RYAN): Give you a clue, he's in the kitchen.

DARLING: Kitchen? Oh, yes! [Laughs] Bobby's not a person – it's a silk screen by Robert Rauschenberg. A picture. Limited edition. Beautiful piece – photographic montage of a bat and some public urinals in Vegas. Not familiar with his work?

WILKINS (RYAN): Only the early stuff: bogs in Littlemore,

shithouses in Rose Hill. Why were you writing to Zara about it?

DARLING: She sold it to me. I'd fancied it for such a long time, I didn't think she'd ever let it go, but, one day in the New Year, she suddenly said I could have it, if I paid cash. Five grand, but worth at least twice that.

WILKINS (RYAN): Cash?

DARLING: Don't tell the taxman. The rich, eh?

WILKINS (RYAN): Oh, yeah, thank fuck for the rich.

DARLING: Actually, she never really had much money of her own. Apart from an inheritance when she was in her twenties, which seemed to disappear, it was only with her divorce settlement that she was finally going to get some financial independence. Half a bill is what I heard.

WILKINS (RAYMOND): Can we keep the focus on the drugs?

DARLING: It's just so hard to believe. I know she was afraid of a relapse, I know that. You say the apartment was trashed, but . . . Perhaps she had guests, or house-sitters, or . . . She knows these people at the yacht club – they have friends, you know, people on the street, it's like their thing – perhaps they . . . I really don't want to believe it. Also, candidly, I feel a little put out she didn't come to me. I can't understand that.

WILKINS (RYAN): Course you can't. You don't understand shame. For most people, I think it's pretty fucking obvious.

WILKINS (RAYMOND): Listen, Justin, what would Zara do

if she needed a hit and didn't want to come to you? If she was desperate. You say she never used any other regular dealer. So, where would she go?

DARLING: [long hesitation] The street, I suppose.

WILKINS (RYAN): Like the rail station car park on Becket Street.

DARLING: Not the right thing to do. Not the sensible thing. She wouldn't have known how to handle it. But I suppose . . . she may not have been thinking properly.

Justin Darling, aka Pablo, Oxford alumnus, high net worth individual and supplier of recreational pick-me-ups to high society, couldn't bear to talk about it anymore. He sat there vacantly. That hollow, furtive look came into his face, making him look depraved.

Ryan said, 'Question, off the record. Just 'cause I'm uneducated. You went to Oxford, got a degree. How come you turned out a dealer?'

Justin shook his head as if he didn't understand it himself. 'Well,' he said, 'it's true what they say: it's a very good place for the right sort of contacts. I've got a place in Great Tew, a nice little flat in Kraków. I play squash with the local MP and I'm great friends with the director of Glyndebourne, which is handy for tickets, and my neighbour's on the Supreme Court and always happy to give me good advice, and I usually do what I want through the summer.'

'Nice.'

'Yes, it is.'

'Still a fucking scumbag, aren't you?'

101

Justin didn't take offence. Too well mannered. Besides, he'd been shaken by Zara's death. He rose, dabbing his lips, and they saw how old he was, despite his blond hair and frivolous clothes. There was something about his eyes, a look of weariness or uncertainty, as if he'd seen a lot and not quite taken it in.

'Last question, before you go,' Ryan said. 'Zara friends with any homeless people?'

'Homeless people?' Justin was shocked. 'The Honourable Zara Fanshawe? Don't be ridiculous.'

Without saying goodbye, he turned and left the elegant room, a diminished figure, a middle-aged man in a sadly comical outfit, looking as though he had lost his bearings, and Ray and Ryan sat there a moment longer, watching the baristas in black-and-white uniforms shuttling from side to side behind the long amber-coloured counter, tending to the machines.

Ryan said, 'Did you meet these types at uni? Is that what they were like? I'm beginning to think you're not so weird, after all.'

As they walked up the High, Ryan put through a call to a friend in Narcotics and asked him to see what he could do about putting Justin Darling away.

They came to King Edward Street. The man with the rat on the cat on the dog was still at his post, and the rat was still slipping off. Ray gave him some change.

'You do that, do you? Give money to people on the street?'

'I do.'

'Conscience thing, is it?'

'It's not about me, Ryan.'

'He's only going to spend it on stuff he shouldn't. Like rat care products.'

They went on towards Carfax.

Ray said, 'Do you believe him? About not supplying her?'

'Yes.'

'Me too.'

'Tell you one thing, we need another chat with the ex.'

When they came to Carfax, without speaking about it, they crossed over, away from the police station, and went through the crowds of shoppers in Queen Street.

'Think she got the cash so she could score some drugs on the street?'

'Why would she want cash otherwise? She doesn't care about tax on such small amounts.'

They crossed in front of the Westgate and down New Road, past the castle mound, that useless lump of grass, with the green ziggurat of the Saïd Business School rising ahead of them over the staid cottagey bulk of Nuffield College.

'Pepper spray for the same reason?'

'Could be.'

'Or because of the goon Hobhouse had hired to follow her?'

'Could be that too.'

They walked past the fast-food outlets that always seem to accumulate near rail stations and came at last to Becket Street and the rail station car park. Even in daylight, the street looked dim and dirty, trees in the graveyard of St Thomas the Martyr throwing the road into shadow.

Ryan sighed. 'All a bit confusing, though. She was clean when she crashed, right? So . . . what? She's on her way to score some drugs in Becket Street, bends the car, never makes it, ends up with a broken neck, a mile away, in north Oxford? No less odd than it was before. Odder. Odd she came to Oxford in the first place. Wasn't to see Pablo.'

'Shake off Hobhouse's guy, maybe.'

'Bottom line, she was down here to meet someone. Who?'

'Working hypothesis: a street dealer. We need to grill the local traders.'

Ryan sighed. He hawked, stretched his neck, spat, and stood for a moment contemplating the slash of spittle on the paving stone, while Ray looked at him with disgust.

'Got a bee in her punnet about things being lost.'

'Bonnet.'

'Yeah.' Ryan gazed at his spittle as if in a trance. '*Always lost and never found*. What's that about? She was lost. Did someone find her?'

'Someone found her out?'

'That's an interesting idea.'

The police tape round the entrance to the car park had largely gone, but a few pieces remained, strewn on the pavement like the sad remnants of a party. Loose rubble from the damaged wall still lay where it had fallen. There were tyre marks on the asphalt, a faint double flourish in black rubber, like a hasty signature.

This is Zara Fanshawe.

Always lost and never found.

Ryan said, 'Definitely odd. She wasn't off her head. Cautious driver, only one driving ticket all her life. So why crash?'

Ray shrugged. 'Avoid another car?' He corrected himself.

'No. Nadim checked the nearest CCTV. There was no other car coming into the area.'

'Someone stepped out in front of her? Dealer from the car park?'

They looked across the road towards St Thomas's churchyard, where the homeless camp was. 'Witnesses is what we want. Is that smoke?'

It wasn't. The camp was still deserted. They went through the gateway into the lonely company of ivy-clad sycamores and tilting green tombstones. It was dark under the trees, a permanent daytime shadow over tents and blankets, litter and cardboard, the trodden mud and crisped drift of last year's leaves and cold embers, but it was easy to see that there was no one about. They had slipped away and not come back.

'By the way, remind me to take Ry to see his mother at St Leonard's; I keep forgetting, and I think he's getting the idea it's Carol's fault somehow.'

Before they headed back to the station, Ryan asked Ray to hang on a minute.

'Can't you wait till you get back?'

'That strange tea, Earl of Whatsit. Gone straight through me.' He jogged behind the tower end of the church – and almost immediately there was shouting, muffled yells, a scream. Before Ray could get there, Ryan reappeared holding a woman by the arm. She beat her free hand against his face, complaining fiercely, though she soon grew tired and sullenly let herself be propelled across the graveyard to the tents of the homeless camp, where she pulled free and sank to the ground. They regarded her as she tightened her collar around her throat and modestly put a hand up to her tangled hair. She had a wide, bony face, hollowed out by hard living, a loose neck and jutting chin. Once, perhaps not long ago, she had been beautiful. Her hair was the colour of old rusted metal. Her coat was far too large for her and, when the sleeves fell back, her arms were all wrist.

She was frightened. 'Wasn't doing anything,' she said. 'What was I doing?'

'All we want to do is ask you some questions. Alright?'

'Not been moved on,' she said. 'No one said nothing about moving on.'

'Forget all that.'

She said nothing else, staring at the ground, motionless, as if, by sitting still, she could make them lose interest and go away.

'Alright?'

She glanced up at them and away, licked her lips. 'Got anything for me?'

'It's not like that. That's not the deal, here. What's your name?'

She muttered something.

'What?'

'Lena.'

'Lena, were you here two nights ago?'

She did not move her eyes from the ground or speak.

'Not last night, Lena. The night before that.'

Still she said nothing.

'There was a car, in the night, crashed into the wall, just over there. All we want is to talk to someone who might have seen it.'

She shook her head. 'Wasn't here,' she said at last, her voice a crackle of phlegm.

'Where were you? O'Hanlon?'

She muttered something else.

'St Ebbe's? In the graveyard up there?'

'Weren't doing nothing. No one came moved us on.'

'Don't worry about that. But you ought to get into the hostel, Lena, keep out of the rain. Do you know anyone who was down here that night?'

She shook her head.

Ray took out a photograph of Zara. 'Have you seen this woman, Lena?'

She put out a hand and touched it, and looked at it for a long time. 'Goldy hair,' she murmured after a while.

They looked at each other. 'Do you know her?'

Lena bent her head over it, though it was not clear if she was actually looking at it anymore. At last, she shook her head. It seemed to cost her a great effort.

'Sure? Haven't seen her?'

'No.'

'Have you ever seen her? Up St Giles', say? On the pavement where the street beggars sit.'

She shook her head again. 'Who is she?'

They sighed and exchanged looks.

'She was driving the car that crashed. Great big car, Lena. Enormous, like a fucking boat. You'd remember it.'

She shook her head stubbornly.

'We're trying to understand why she crashed. Maybe someone stepped into the road. Some guy from the car park over there, maybe. Maybe she swerved to avoid them. Maybe she even hit them.'

'Who?' she said at once.

'We don't know. That's what we're trying to find out.'

Ray said, 'Take another look at the photograph, Lena. Has anybody you know been talking about a woman like this? Has anyone been seen with such a woman? Here, or at St Ebbe's, or up outside Blackfriars, there on St Giles', round the homeless camps?'

'Like who?' she said, quickly again.

'We don't know. That's why we're asking these questions.'

She peered at them from under her brows. 'Was it a man? Man with a trolley?'

'Man with a trolley?' They looked at her. 'Why do you say that?'

She opened her mouth, shut it again. 'Don't know.'

'What man, Lena?'

She shook her head and would say nothing else, despite their efforts, and at last they left her there.

They walked down Becket Street, towards the rail station.

'Who knows what she's talking about,' Ray said.

'Scared. They're all scared. Scared of being moved on. That's your Wonder Woman for you. Any witnesses not going to speak to us, fuck's sake. Man with a trolley? What's that about?'

Ray shook his head.

Outside Domino's, they stood a moment, talking.

'Interesting, though, isn't it? Luxury car, dirty street. Rich woman, street dealer. What they call a pattern.'

Ray shrugged. Zara had been away from her apartment for maybe two weeks, maybe in Oxford, maybe looking for a dealer. Maybe looking for someone else. Too many maybes.

'We don't really know what she was doing. Only the mad Blackfriars thing.'

Ryan looked down Becket Street, remembering the sight of the enormous car skewed across it, shining in the darkness. That spotless paintwork, that pristine leather interior. He said, 'Wait. It's just come to me. We know one other thing she did.'

'What?'

'Got her car cleaned.'

Ray looked at him.

'If you'd've got yourself out of bed, you'd've seen it, mate. Paintwork gleaming. Insides too. Drive Carol's car, it's like driving her fucking handbag. Zara's a drugs mess, but there's nothing in the Roller at all, car's completely zen. End of a drizzly day in February? Someone just done it for her.'

'Private valet service?'

'Get someone up from London. That's the way they do it, isn't it? Ship them in from Paris to adjust the hem of their dress, fly them over from Brazil for a quick waxing. We can get Livvy and Nadim on to it, find out who her regular is.'

They began the walk back to the police station, Ryan jaunty again, throwing sidelong glances at Ray.

'What about you?'

'What do you mean?'

'Looking stylish. Get your jackets flown in from Milan?'

Ray ignored him.

'Come on, Ray, crack a smile. It's just getting interesting.'

Ray did not crack a smile.

THIRTEEN

But it wasn't a private valet service Zara had used. It took several hours for Nadim and Livvy to locate the car wash – last on their list and scarcely believable – and it was late afternoon by the time Ray and Ryan pulled into the Tesco car park next to it.

Ryan said, 'Diane asked you to pick up anything?' and Ray ignored him. Ryan fancied popping in to get a sandwich, and Ray still ignored him. They went together to the car-wash forecourt, where they were both ignored. For a moment, they just watched. Men and women, lit up in the winter darkness, were milling around the cars, some with power hoses, some with flannels and sponges. They worked fast and relentlessly, keeping the line of vehicles moving, gesturing at the drivers: *come forward, stop there, come forward*. The forecourt was black with water; streams of suds moved on the surface, swirling slowly towards grates. Beyond the awnings, a few cars were parked to one side, all their doors wide open, other men and women delving inside, spraying, wiping, polishing with the slightly desperate energy and concentration of jugglers. Gold Standard Service was a tenner for the outside; Platinum was fifteen for in and out. Cash only. The whole process took five minutes, start to finish.

'*This* is the place she come to? In a Roller? Really?'

A boy came over. He looked about twelve, but seemed to be in charge. He had the language skills.

'Yes, boss.'

Ray showed his badge and the photograph of Zara, and they went together into a shipping container set up at the entrance of the compound as an office.

The boy looked at them without interest. While they spoke, he wrote a name on a pad of paper and gave it to them. Ryan began to raise his voice and Ray put a hand on his arm.

'We know Mr Koroveshi. Currently in breach of a notice to close the business. But we're not interested in that, we don't need to speak to him.' He explained again what they were interested in, and the boy listened in silence and without expression, then went outside. When he returned, he had an older man with him, who stood in the corner of the container, as far away from them as possible, dividing his silent, anxious attention between the boy and the floor.

The boy explained that the man had helped wash the car they had described. He spoke no English, but the boy would act as interpreter.

They told the man they had a few simple questions which they would like him to answer. The boy spoke briefly and the man came suddenly to life, delivering a long, rapid and argumentative monologue, accompanied by many hand gestures and dramatic expressions.

'He agree,' the boy said laconically.

So it went, in short, droll asides and long, passionate out-bursts.

'He remember,' the boy said. 'Big, like boat.'

What about the woman?

The monologue resumed, fluent and intense.

'Yes, he remember. Very beautiful. Hair . . . like gold.'

'What was she doing? How did she behave?'

A longer, even more passionate outburst, accompanied, it seemed, by weeping.

'She sit. In the car.'

'That all? Did she appear anxious? Frightened? Anything strange about her?'

'Ah.' He asked, listened, nodded, thinking how to translate what he had heard. 'She look . . . like she . . . do *salah*. You understand?'

'Salad?' Ryan said.

Ray said, '*Salah*. Prayer?'

The boy nodded.

'As if she was praying?'

Now, the boy equivocated, shook his head. He frowned, made his face still, passed his hand in front of his unmoving eyes.

'I'd have said *stoned*,' Ray said. 'Except we know she wasn't.'

'In some sort of state of mind. Frightened, maybe.'

The man began to speak again, and the boy hushed him.

'What's he saying now?'

'Nothing. But.'

'Tell us.'

'There was other man with him . . . say he see the car other time.'

'He'd seen the car before? What man's this?'

The boy became reluctant to talk. He relieved his feelings by shouting suddenly at the man, who touched his forehead apologetically and moved away, creeping out in the same cowed manner as he had arrived. Gradually, they got the information out of the boy. This other man, Kreshik, had talked to the woman when she got out of the car, while they cleaned the inside. He had boasted to the others that he knew her. The boy did not believe it. No one there believed it. How could he? The man was a liar.

They'd like to speak to him, nevertheless.

But he had not returned to work the day afterwards. In fact, he was not wanted there. He had only been employed a few weeks; the boy thought perhaps he was a cousin of a friend of Mr Koroveshi. No one liked him; he was not a good man.

What did that mean?

The boy mimed smoking, sniffing, handling money.

Weed? Coke?

The boy nodded with distaste. Ray and Ryan looked at each other.

Where was this Kreshik now?

The boy shrugged. He had been living in a room somewhere, on his own. He didn't have any friends.

Where was the room?

The boy checked his phone, scrolled through his contacts, sighing to himself. He held out the phone and they leaned forward.

The address on the screen was Becket Street.

*

Carol's converted farmhouse was on Bagley Wood Road, not far from the Montessori nursery school, which her children had briefly attended in earlier years. Their photographs faced her on the desk where she sat now: Jasmine, aged nine, and Frank, aged seven, both dark-haired like their father, with the freckles and rabbity front teeth of childhood. Through the window was the winter darkness of the paddock, where their pony grazed, then the woods, beech and elm, and, beyond that, the Kennington Memorial Field, with its football pitches and play area. It was a quiet place of warblers, occasional rabbits and the munching pony. But Carol was not looking out of the window, or at the pictures of her children. She was at her laptop, looking at the news – *Murder of a Celebrity* – and brooding. On her desk was a letter from a bank informing her that a time period in her debt agreement had now expired without the expected financial resolution, and that, as a result, a legal process was underway to secure the value of her borrowings against the value of her property. It was the third letter of this sort that she had received in the past week. As she took it up again, she heard a van pull on to the gravel forecourt below, and went down to greet Jasmine and Frank, being returned by her ex.

Gary was a thickset, round-shouldered man of forty-three, with a meaty face darkened by heavy stubble. He was a painter and decorator by trade, a regular guy; he liked beer, football and cars. That evening, he'd collected the children straight from work and had not yet had time to change out of his overalls or boots, and he came noisily into the hall and crossed the spacious expanse of refurbished floorboards to the old fireplace, where he began to speak to his ex-wife without looking at her, relaying messages from school about the children, who had immediately gone over to the kitchen area and were delving in the fridge. Carol watched him. She had no complaints about him, as an ex. As an actual husband, he'd been useful but never ideal.

He came to the end of his messages and waited for a reaction.

'Do you want a beer?'

He shook his head. He had to go; he was picking up his girlfriend's kids from after-school club. But he stayed where he was. Frank and Jasmine took their snacks upstairs to the television room, leaving their parents alone in the big renovated space.

'What is it, Gary?'

'I want to know what's going on.'

'Don't know what you mean.'

One of the teachers had mentioned bad behaviour by Frank, and had wanted to know if things were okay at home.

'Teacher can fuck off. Things are fine at home.'

'Hey,' he said sharply, in the tone of someone bringing a dog to heel, 'this is important.'

She shrugged. 'No more to say. You don't want a beer, I got things to do.'

His face flushed and, when he spoke, his voice was deeper and rougher. 'You've not been straight with me.' He paused. 'I had a talk with your Heather.'

Heather was the former manager of one of Carol's shops, let go a fortnight earlier. She'd told Gary that the business was shot, heavily in debt, certain to close. Worse, much worse, she'd seen a letter from a bank suggesting that the farmhouse was collateral.

'You told me you never put it up.'

She said nothing.

He lost his temper. 'Christ! This is the kids' home. Think of that?'

'You've got a nerve. The kids are my life and you know it.'

He moved restlessly away from the fireplace. 'Course you didn't think of it. Just money with you, isn't it? Always money. All you ever fucking think about.'

'I'm not going to apologise for making money, Gary. Money gave the kids a home. Money pays for their holidays and their horse riding. Money keeps them safe and clean and happy, and all the obvious little things you take for granted.'

He began to argue.

'Listen to me,' she said. 'There's zero chance of losing the house. Not happening, understand? Not letting it happen. I got plenty of options.'

He ignored her, walking round the room, glaring, talking angrily, while she stood there, watching him. At last, he fell silent.

'Get out,' she said.

He took a step towards her, thought better of it.

He nodded bitterly. 'So, now you need more money. You know what, you can always go back to what you were doing before I took you on.'

After he'd left, she stayed there a long time, gazing at the empty room, not seeing it, hearing the children's voices upstairs. For a while, she looked at her phone. Then she dialled. The person on the other end said nothing.

She spoke carefully. 'I need help. Now. And, if I need help, you need help. Don't know about you, but I'm a survivor. So, I'm going to tell you where and I'm going to tell you when, and then you're going to make it happen.'

For a minute longer, she stood in the silence of the room. Then she went to the stairs and called the children down for tea.

In the Oxford rush hour, the city shrinks to half a dozen blocked medieval roads and bridges. Ray and Ryan sat in a jam under a low ceiling of night sky, watching white fumes rising from exhaust pipes through the streaky red reflections of tail lights.

'Why would she take her Roller to a place like that to have it cleaned?' Ryan said. 'Acting weird in the car, like a zombie. Not drugs. Some sort of psycho wobble. Scared, could be.'

They crept across Folly Bridge.

'But, anyway,' Ryan said at last, 'seeing as we got a bit of time, what I was saying about me and Carol—'

'Please, Ryan.'

'Seriously, do you think it could work?'

'I think you're capable of making a mess of just about anything.'

'Yeah. It's weird we're even together, to be honest. Why would she pick me out?'

'I literally don't understand it.'

'Me neither. But it's Ry I'm thinking about. Don't want to lose me, he says. Does his sad face.' Ryan contorted his face and Ray looked away. Ryan began to talk about his son. Little Ryan knew everything about the natural habitats, diet and mating habits of budgerigars, he could count up to a hundred, he was interested in light and time. He corrected his father whenever Ryan misread a passage in *Mouse and Mole*.

'I said to him the other day, "What gets me, Ry, is why mouse likes mole at all. Don't you think mole's a bit up himself?" And he looked at me with this look he's got, like he really thinks about this stuff, and he says, "Daddy, they're friends, Daddy." Kid's a fucking genius.'

He sat there grinning, and for a while they went without further conversation along the long, unlovely stretch of Oxpens, past redevelopments and unreclaimed spaces, towards the ice rink and pop-up overflow car park.

Then he said, 'But what if he grows up, realises what I'm really like? Pretty big let-down for him, if I'm all he's got.'

Ray said nothing to that. They crept as far as the post office.

'Oh. Another thing about the car.'

'What?'

'What she get it cleaned for? So she can go down dirty old Becket Street and score some drugs from car-wash man? Makes no sense.'

In silence, they arrived at last in the dirty old street, dimly lit in the February afternoon dark. The room Kreshik rented was in the house with the old *Flory's Commercial Hotel* sign painted on the brickwork, near the Domino's Pizza place on the corner. It was only twenty metres from the car-park entrance where the Rolls-Royce had crashed.

'By the way, I'm still starving. Don't want to share a pizza, do you?'

Ignoring him, Ray crossed the road and went up the steps to the front door, Ryan trailing behind. A young woman was coming out and Ray described Kreshik, and she looked at him suspiciously and told him the top floor.

'See him around much?'

'Why would I?'

'Last time you saw him?'

'What are you, police?'

Ray showed his badge. 'Last time?'

'How about never?'

'Helpful,' Ryan said. 'Public spirited.'

They went up two narrow flights of stairs, everything around them creaking, as if the whole building might suddenly give up and fall down, and came to a door. No answer. They went creaking down again, knocking on other doors. No answer from them either. Outside, Ryan called Nadim and gave her the details, asked her to start running the checks. They'd be back at the station soon – or not, if the traffic remained bad. But first, he said to Ray, he was popping into Domino's.

'For Christ's sake, Ryan, can't you wait? We've got to get back.'

But he'd already gone, and Ray stood disgruntled by his car. Closing his eyes, he listened to the quiet shunt of queuing cars in the Botley Road, the sloshing noise of a train going past, like the crash and fold and disappearance of a wave. He opened his eyes. Becket Street was dark and deserted; it lay in front of him like a dim smear, a streak of dirt, a nothing. Here I am, he thought. This is me. winner of the Queen's Commendation for Bravery and Ryan's driver, waiting while he orders pizza.

His phone rang. Number withheld. Most likely a cold call from the Indian subcontinent offering to repair his desktop or telling him that the subscription he did not have was about to run out. He shouldn't answer, but there was always the chance it was family from Nigeria, so he always did. There was the usual delay in connection, then another few moments of irritating silence. A cold call for sure.

'Yes?' Ray said impatiently. 'What do you want?'

An unexpected voice said, 'Not just smooth, then.'

'Who the fuck is this?' he said, registering too late the gravelly drawl.

'Chester Lynch. But you can call me Deputy Chief Constable.'

Ray was no longer in Becket Street, but in some more painful region of the mind. An expression he didn't dare visualise had taken over his face, he could feel the grip of it. He struggled to free his voice and began at last to apologise.

'Not interested. Listen, Ray, I want to fix up a time to talk. Alright with you?'

'Yes. Of course. Absolutely.'

'Heard about the dead celeb. Good one for you to handle, I think – tough, crappy media and that. Pressers going alright?'

'Actually, Ryan's going to be doing the pressers.'

A pause. 'The other Wilkins? Why?'

'Well. He's . . . he's leading on this one.'

A longer pause. Chester Lynch said, 'I'll send you a time,' and rang off.

Ray stood there, cursing. Cursing Ryan, cursing himself, cursing stupid, grubby Becket Street, down which a man came walking, a shadow out of darkness. He wore a hooded top and moved awkwardly, as if in pain, hands in pockets. As he came to Flory's Commercial Hotel, he threw away his cigarette and climbed the steps to the front door.

'Kreshik!' Ray shouted experimentally, and the man turned.

Ray went across the street, badge held in front of him like an icon, and Kreshik hesitated, then leaped from the steps and set off down the street. He ran badly, holding his side, and Ray caught up with him by the church, but Kreshik flung off his arm and scrambled into the churchyard, stumbling across the still-deserted homeless camp, where Ray caught up with him again.

'Kreshik,' he said, and Kreshik turned and hit him in the face. Ray felt his nose split. He grappled with Kreshik and they went down together on to the mess of cardboard and blankets, and Kreshik stuck his knee into Ray's groin and got to his feet, kicking Ray in the shoulder. He ran towards the other side of the graveyard, but he was struggling to move and Ray got after him, catching him by the wicket gate and tackling him to the ground. They rolled together, struggling in the darkness. From the street, Ray heard Ryan calling.

'Ray! Pizza if you want it, Ray!'

Ray croaked something back – it might have been 'Here!' or 'Help!' – it was hard to tell. He rolled with Kreshik on the ground, trying to subdue him, but the man was stubborn. He clawed Ray's face, butted him – then suddenly disappeared. When Ray sat up, Kreshik was lying on the ground and Ryan was standing there with a pizza in one hand and a half brick in the other.

They looked at each other.

Ryan said, grumbling, 'Queued for ages for double cheese, and then, 'cause of this palaver, nearly drop the fucking thing.'

Ray stared at him in fury.

In a few minutes, Kreshik was conscious. He sat on the grass, weeping; all the fight had gone out of him and he was no longer a hard man but a frightened one – as, in fact, he had been all along. He was older than he'd seemed, already middle-aged, with greying hair cropped short and a narrow face pinched with exhaustion. He looked at them in such fear, it was as if they could see his life in his eyes – a forgettable past, a hopeless future. He gingerly held his side.

Ryan looked at Ray. 'Take him in? What do you think? Once he gets a lawyer, we'll not get anything out of him.'

'We have to. We'll need an interpreter.'

'Good point.'

Kreshik said, 'I speak English.'

They looked at each other. Ray handed Kreshik the photograph of Zara, lit it up with his phone torch.

'Yes. She came to the car wash.'

'But you'd seen her before.'

He nodded. The night before, looking out of the window of his room, he'd seen the car in the street. It had of course caught his attention, a car like that.

'What was she doing?'

Nothing. The car was parked on the pavement opposite. It was dark, one o'clock in the morning, and she was just sitting in it, not doing anything, staring out of the window towards the church. He watched her for several minutes and she did nothing at all, just sat there. When he looked again, she was gone. But then, the next day, equally shocking, she appeared in her extraordinary car at the car wash, behaving in just the same way, disengaged, almost zombie-like, standing by the picnic tables, staring at nothing. He felt strange, under the spell of the coincidence: no one else at the car wash had seen her before, only him. These moments of strangeness are to be seized. He left his job and crossed the forecourt and went up to her. She

122

was beautiful. Even more beautiful close up. But also, like the car, not quite real.

'What do you mean?'

Kreshik thought. 'Her face. Her eyes.' He made a wiping gesture across his own eyes. 'She did not see me. I was only there.'

Ray said, 'What did you say to her?'

'I told her I had seen her in the night.'

'What did she say?'

'Nothing.'

Ryan said, 'Did you offer her drugs?'

He shook his head. 'I could see in her face she did not need any. I went away again.'

'So, that was it?'

'No. I saw her again, a last time.'

It was in the middle of the night, at the end of that day. He had been woken by the noise outside – the unsubtle, unmistakable bang of a car crashing – and he went to the window.

'Anyone with you?'

He nodded. A girl, she lived downstairs. She would confirm what he told them was the truth. At the window, he saw the car for the third time, but now slewed across the road, wedged in the entrance to the car park. For a moment, he watched, then he pulled on his trousers and ran down, across the road, but, by the time he got there, the car was empty; there was no one in sight, no one in the street, and the homeless at the camp in the graveyard opposite had all fled.

'Sure it was her driving?'

He nodded.

'Anyone else in the car?'

123

He shook his head.

'See anything else?'

He nodded again. 'Yes. There was a man.'

'Now we're getting somewhere.'

The man had appeared from the other side of the car, on the pavement, hobbling towards the driver's door. And that was when Kreshik left the window to run down.

They asked him to describe the man.

It was dark, Kreshik had just woken up, he had seen very little. The man seemed to be in pain, limping, as he'd said, but moving with surprising speed and energy. Bundled up in a coat, perhaps a hat, too – he couldn't be sure. He'd shouted something at the car.

'What?'

Kreshik shook his head. Noise, angry noise.

'Could he have come out of the car park?'

Yes, perhaps.

'Think the guy was a dealer?'

It was possible. Kreshik had seen them at work there.

He was still holding his side, looking at them fearfully.

Ryan said, 'By the way, how d'you hurt yourself? Not hit by a car, were you?'

Kreshik's eyes went sideways, furtive.

'Ray, here, do it to you? Looks cute, but he's an animal.'

He shook his head. 'I am not well,' he said, with a sort of forlorn dignity.

He had nothing else to tell them. They left him there and walked back to Ray's car.

Ryan said, chewing, 'That was interesting. Limping man.

Maybe the man she was down here to meet. Maybe she drove into him. But here's the problem.' He swallowed noisily. 'My pizza's gone cold, now. I'm going to have to ask you to time your brawls with suspects better, DI Wilkins.'

He laughed, mouth open, and Ray sat behind the wheel with his sore nose between his fingers, wincing. There was blood on his hands and down his Brando coat, new that season. He could hear Ryan chewing and felt his irritation growing into rage. It had been building slowly over days, but now it happened in a rush.

'He wasn't exactly young,' Ryan said. 'And not well. Surprised you let him take you.'

Ray took a breath, two breaths, tried to control himself.

Ryan swallowed, wiped his nose with a finger, looked for somewhere in the car to wipe his finger. 'Come on then, driver, let's get going.'

The noise Ray made was a shock to both of them; it burst out of him, a harsh, angry and desperate sound. 'Stop! Stop it! Will you *fucking* stop!'

Ryan stared at him, mouth open, semi-chewed pizza visible. He wasn't sure he'd heard Ray swear before. 'What?'

'*Enough!*' Less a word than an outburst of pain.

'Enough of what?'

Ray panted for a moment, as if getting his breath back. 'This! All this! These stupid, immature, pathetic, ignorant comments. Ray, do this; Ray, do that.'

'Fuck's sake, Ray, mate – it's just a bit of banter.'

'Is it? Or are you just hiding the fact that you have no idea what you're doing?'

Ryan pulled a face.

Ray spoke in a rush: 'It's true – look at yourself – no one can believe you're leading on this, no one. You're out of your depth. You're the most irresponsible person I've ever met. You don't take anything seriously, you stop for a sandwich, stop for pizza, threaten to kick doors in, neglect the basics, don't do the paperwork. You forget the pressers.' He ran out of breath and sat there, twisted, panting.

Ryan said mildly, 'Only forgot it the once, to be fair.'

Ray groaned, as if in agony.

Nadim's number came up on Ryan's phone – a welcome relief. He put her on speaker.

'Where are you?' she said. 'Presser in five. Did you forget? Barko's doing his nut.'

Ray groaned once more.

Ryan winced. But he recovered, as he always did. 'Yeah, alright. No need to shout.'

'You better get here, Ryan.'

He looked at Ray. Ray gritted his teeth, swung the car away from the kerb. The remains of the pizza slid into Ryan's lap.

FOURTEEN

At the long podium, they sat together, but not side by side, Ryan fidgeting at one end and Detective Superintendent Wallace sitting stiff and frankly furious at the other, occasionally moving his eyes sideways to give Ryan an intimidating look. As usual, Barko wore full uniform. Ryan had taken off his jacket (stained with Ray's blood) to reveal an oversized T-shirt in bright orange (stained with pizza). There had been no time to change. No time for any conversation with Barko either, except for the Super to express his displeasure at Ryan's appearance and tell him to make sure he made a good impression with his comments.

Facing the crowded room, Ryan felt uneasy. Making a good impression with comments wasn't his best skill. Nor was making a good impression at all. The journalists were interested in him, they watched him curiously, their faces clever and intent, keen to hear what he would say and how he would say it.

Worst of all, he was missing little Ryan's bedtime.

Barko tapped the head of a microphone with his forefinger. Apologising for the late start, he regretted he didn't have more time to give to them. He appreciated that there was public interest in Zara Fanshawe's murder. On the other hand, as they would surely understand, the force declined to give a running commentary on the progress of such a sensitive investigation. Although they had no further information, he could assure them that they were making headway, with the expectation of imminent results. Thank you. He would permit a few questions.

They came in a rush. Were they looking at any suspicious persons of interest? Was Lawrence Hobhouse one of them? Were Zara Fanshawe's previous problems with addiction in any way relevant? Barko's answers were authoritative, assured, cleverly to-the-point and ideally uninformative. Ryan's spirits sank further; he could see the journalists waiting to turn their attention to him, to demand the same clever, evasive answers. Uneasily, he remembered all the things Ray had told him in the car. Glancing at his watch, he pursed his lips. Jade would have put little Ryan to bed by now. He thought guiltily of his son, and guiltily of Carol, who had texted him several times in the last half-hour without him replying. In front of the journalists, he felt exposed. When his name was mentioned, he looked up and scanned the rows of faces until, a moment later, the question was repeated.

'Thoughts from the operational end, DI Wilkins?'

He glanced sideways at Wallace, whose eyes had grown very small. He sniffed, tried to relax, found himself scratching his groin, tried to stop scratching.

With angry eyes, Barko indicated the microphone. Ryan leaned forward. 'Not really.' Something caught in his throat and he brought up a little mucus. 'Like what the Super said,' he added, when he could. After that, there was a pause, which, it seemed, everyone in the crowded room was waiting for him to fill. 'Stuff ongoing,' he said, with a shrug, and shut his mouth.

A small murmur of something seemed to pass through the journalists and, after a moment, he realised it was amusement. It made him feel better: now he knew where he stood with them – where he had stood so many times before, called to face hostile teachers, social workers, disciplinary committees, to answer for his misdemeanours. As usual, it made him cocky. He sneered a little at the front row.

Someone asked if, given the extensive police questioning of the Polstead Road residents, any of them were under suspicion.

'Got nothing to say about that.' His sneer grew broader.

A journalist at the far end of the back row embarked on a long, multi-part question concerning a complaint made in the last hour by the office of GoldRay Capital Management LLP about irregular police tactics.

Ryan interrupted: 'We'll be going back there soon, so we'll see what they say next time.'

Barko quickly spoke across him. 'No truth in any allegations. I'm sure everyone appreciates the need for us to work rapidly and without fear or favour.'

He glowered at Ryan.

Someone asked a question about a similar complaint made by the management of One Hyde Park.

Before Ryan could say anything at all, Barko intervened to say that all police guidelines were being followed at all times. Thank you. Next question. Ryan felt the glare of Barko's critical scrutiny against the side of his face: it made him angrier still. It occurred to him that his problem was not that he didn't know

129

how to lead an investigation, as Ray had said, but that other people wouldn't let him do it.

A journalist in the back row stood, as if to formalise his involvement, and began to ask a question about Ryan's own disciplinary record. Ryan leaned forward abruptly towards his microphone, but Wallace was quicker; he put his hand over it, gave a sort of savage smile at the auditorium and said, 'Questions about the investigation only, thank you. Just time for one more. Yes, at the back.'

Ryan stared in fury – first at the journalist, then at Barko.

The final question concerned the reported but inconceivable sighting of Zara apparently begging on the pavement outside Blackfriars. Ryan began to answer, but Wallace cut across him again: 'Being pursued in the usual manner.' Ignoring Ryan, he began to sum up, stressing once more the seriousness and pro-fessionalism with which they were conducting their inquiry, but the journalist persisted, interrupting him to ask if the homeless community was providing the police with information and, if not, why not?

''Cause they all hate us,' Ryan blurted out.

There was a moment's silence. The journalist asked if he was referring to the controversial clearance policy implemented by Deputy Chief Constable Chester Lynch.

'No,' Barko said.

'What do you think?' Ryan said simultaneously.

Barko stood abruptly, face aquiver. 'Thank you,' he said. 'Nothing further to say.' His mouth was so small and tight that nothing more would have been physically possible.

Apparently there was still a lot the journalists wanted to ask, but Wallace took Ryan by the arm, lifted him and turned him towards the door.

On the long walk from the conference room to Wallace's office, Ryan calmed down quickly, as usual, and had a chance to run through his options. He could ride it out, contrite or indifferent, as the situation merited. He could fight it, defiant or indignant. Or he could go for distraction.

In his lair, Barko got himself in front of the window, where his bulky figure loomed dark and solid against the over-bright but insubstantial reflection of the illuminated office, short legs wide apart, meaty hands clenched. Dramatic. He paused a good, long, undermining moment and at last opened his mouth.

Ryan said, 'Interesting, though. Putting herself in danger like that.'

Barko hesitated.

'Pepper spray don't get to her in time, she comes to Oxford anyway. Why? Big moment. Not expecting to go back. Wrecks her apartment, don't care. Squatting in an empty house. No more private valet service for the Roller, not bothered. Come here checking out the homeless hang-outs. Afternoon at St Giles', two nights on the trot down Becket Street. Looking for someone.'

'Who?' Barko said, before he could stop himself. 'A dealer?'

'Don't think so. Someone what's going to change her life. Big risk, though, 'cause could be it's the same person she's scared of.'

'And?'

'Goes wrong.'

'How?'

'Crashes her car. Maybe knocks someone down.'

'What someone?' Barko said, again not meaning to. 'Same, different?'

Ryan shrugged again. 'Someone knows, though – some street beggar with a pitch outside Blackfriars, maybe, or someone at the homeless camp in Becket Street. Man with a trolley, I'd like to talk to. Call it spiritual growth,' he added nonchalantly.

Barko struggled to swallow all this and at the same time hang on to his fury with Ryan. He opened his mouth again.

Ryan said, 'I know, I know. Hold my hands up. Not good, the presser. Piss poor. Naïve. Get irritated, give away too much. Stuff about DCC Lynch inexcusable. Watched you, saw what you did. Little masterclass. Got it. Learn fast, that's me. Won't happen again. Sir.'

Barko seemed to think about that while Ryan absorbed his scrutiny, scruffy in stained jacket and T-shirt, vulnerable, penitent, willing, dutiful, as he hoped he appeared.

Barko's voice was theatrically low: 'Think you can bend me, don't you?'

Ryan shook his head. 'Stupid, but not that stupid.'

Barko regarded him. 'You won't know this, but I actually served with DCC Lynch.'

Ryan could've referenced the dates, but he kept his mouth shut.

'Inspirational's too weak a word. I was transferred before all the moving-on stuff, but I will not, repeat *not*, take kindly to any loose remarks about the Deputy Chief Constable – not on camera, not in private either. Understood?'

'Got it. Glad to get it.'

'Get this, too. These complaints about irregular behaviour. No more.'

'Got it.'

'And this whole Zara Fanshawe circus, I want it over. She's in town to meet someone? I want to know who, why and when. She's been murdered, for Christ's sake, and we haven't got a clue who did it or why.' He eyed Ryan for a while longer, and indicated at last that he was free to go.

FIFTEEN

Ray turned off the TV with the remote and there was a moment's silence.

His father said, 'This is the man? *This?* This man replaced *you?*'

He sat large and stern in the chair, dressed as usual in the bright corduroys and chequered tweeds favoured by the English upper classes. He was sixty years old, and over the years his body had gradually overflowed itself. His voice was deep, physical – it created significant sound waves. His skin was smoothly, densely black and his massive head was shiny: when he frowned, it was a dramatic event. With a big, pale-palmed hand, he waved away Diane's offer of another drink.

'Please, Ray. I can judge character. This man – he's not a police detective.' He made a dismissive gesture. 'He's lowlife. Everyone can see it.'

Ray's father had arrived, as threatened, out of the blue, with gifts for his grandchildren, miniature football kits in the colours of the Nigerian national team. Next time, he said, he would bring the English strip. Patriotically Nigerian, he was an enthusiastic Englishman by adoption, and, since his arrival in the country twenty-five years earlier, had been at pains to absorb English manners and customs, and for his only son to grow up with them already in place. For the first twenty years of his working life, he had been a group manager for the Nigerian National Petroleum Corporation in Lagos; for the next twenty-five, a retired man of leisure in London, with a modest investment portfolio, season tickets to Lord's and Stamford Bridge, and an increasingly angry view of the future. His name was Chidozie, but in England he called himself Henry. His pride in his son was as fierce, demanding and unstable as his pride in himself.

'How did it happen?' he said. 'Tell me, I want to know.'

'It doesn't matter.'

Henry Wilkins' face put on a performance of outrage.

'*Baba*, please.'

He began to count on his fingers. 'Head boy at St Benedict's. Exhibitioner at Balliol College, Oxford. Boxing blue. First-class honours degree. National Police Award for Bravery. For what? To be assistant to this lowlife? Ray, he should be cleaning water closets somewhere.'

Diane said, 'I think the journalists were picking on him.'

Ray's father continued as if she hadn't spoken: 'I know what it is. That fool, Wallace. Scottish – what do you expect? Leave him, for God's sake. Come to London, Ray. They need you in London.'

'We like Oxford,' Diane said, and was again ignored.

He began to talk of the metropolitan crime figures, the gangs, the litter in the street, the decline of cricket – sad developments in which he himself seemed helplessly and tragically implicated. It was, as Diane liked to describe it, the 'Lamentation of the Last Englishman', and Ray had heard it many times. 'This country,' his father said, with all the conviction of originality, 'is going to the dogs. The *dogs*, Ray.'

Drifting, Ray thought of the phone call he'd received from Chester Lynch earlier. She hadn't been in touch since. It felt like a chance of something snatched back before it had been properly made, as if, hearing about his subordinate position on the case, she had re-evaluated and backed away. He wondered if she'd seen the press conference and what she might have made of it and how it might change her view of him, knowing that he was now Ryan's assistant.

Ollie was making noises upstairs and Diane left to see to him. Ray's father talked on. Ray checked his phone: no messages. Briefly, but only briefly, he wondered what Ryan was doing after his disastrous press conference; then, he let his father's diatribe wash over him.

Ryan was outside his house when Carol called again. He stood in the evening quiet, listening to her voice.

'You're late. You coming?'

A pause. 'Yeah, course. Just checking on Ry. You alright?'

'All good. How did the press thing go?'

Another pause. 'Could've went better, to be honest.'

'You okay?'

'Yeah. It's only noise.'

'What about the case?'

'Well, can't say. But I got a funny feeling about it.'

'What do you mean?' She spoke quickly.

He sighed again. 'Wish I knew.'

'What do you think happened?' Her voice had risen an octave, and he frowned.

'Don't matter. Talk later. See you in twenty.'

His sister, Jade, met him in the hall. She was shorter than her brother, but just as pointy in the face, with the Wilkins nose and blond hair scraped back. Like Ryan, she'd weathered a difficult childhood and her manner was difficult to match; and she stood there now, very solid, in a short pink towelling dressing gown, staring at him in a way he recognised as problematic.

'Watched it, did you?' he asked uneasily. 'Nothing to worry about.'

'Calling out the Deputy Chief Constable on national television, Ryan?'

'She'll get over it.'

'Do you want to go back to working nights as security for cowboys paying half the minimum wage?'

'Don't worry. Won't happen again,' he added.

'I am worried. You got that look on your face, Ryan. That look you get when you get away with something once and you think you can get away with it again. Know what I call that look, Ryan?'

'Yeah.'

'What?'

'The knobhead look.'

'Right. Sort of look knobheads get.'

'Alright. Point taken. You're a lot harder to deal with than the Super,' he said. 'Listen. Know that girl you used to do bowling with, worked at Grendon, psych unit?'

'Rebekah.'

'Yeah, Rebekah. Didn't she leave Grendon, go work in that rehab place out near Burford? St Anne's.'

'So?'

'Got her number?'

While she passed it over, he asked her about little Ryan.

'How's his tummy?'

'Not what you should be worrying about, with Ry.'

Little Ryan, she said, had refused to let her read his bedtime story.

'That's not like him; he loves stories.'

But little Ryan had just shaken his head and turned away from her, and when she was leaving the room had said solemnly to the wall, 'My daddy's got lost. But he still loves me, so that makes me happy.'

'Fuck.' Ryan looked stricken.

'And you promised to take him to see the grave, right?'

'Going to. It's just . . .'

Jade said, 'Work to do there, Ryan, eh? He don't like you not being at home. Thinks he's lost his daddy. Make it up to him at breakfast. If you're staying here, that is.'

She saw the look on his face and sighed.

Ryan said, 'I'll just go up and have a look at him.'

'Don't wake him, then; you know what he's like if his sleep's broken.'

Ryan sat on a tiny plastic blue chair next to the bed, listening to little Ryan's breathing making a faint whisper in the quiet room dimly lit by the night light – a mesmerising sound, as hushed and steady as light rain. One cheek was visible, hectically flushed, and a swathe of close-fitting, new-looking blond hair. At times like these, Ryan doubted his son belonged to him – the boy seemed on loan – and a terror overcame him that he'd be taken away again. But the hush of the room gradually lulled him, slowing everything down; the busy details of the day fell away and at last he grew calm.

When his phone rang, the noise was so sudden and fast in the slow room, he almost fell off the chair. He seemed to have been asleep. By the time he had seen it was Carol again, little Ryan was awake, lying in bed unmoving, watching him. He cut the call.

'Ry –' a whisper – 'are you awake?'

The boy regarded him steadily.

'It's Daddy,' Ryan said unnecessarily.

Still unmoving and unblinking, his son said, 'Did you come back?'

Only when his father touched him did he seem to believe it. Ryan fished under the bed for their copy of *Mouse and Mole*, but it wasn't there.

'Are you alright?'

'I'm very sad.'

'Oh. Did you have a bad dream?'

'Auntie Jade said you didn't come back.'

'Yeah. Working late, had to stay, talk to this bunch of total . . . But I come back now.'

'Why?'

'See you, mate.'

'Why?'

'Well. See how you are. How's your tummy?'

Disregarding this as a distraction, little Ryan maintained his solemnly regretful expression.

'So,' Ryan said, flustered. 'It's been too long, I know. I've really missed you. Shall we have a conversation?'

Little Ryan said nothing. He was curiously still and unblinking, as if fixing all his powers of concentration on his father. Ryan's phone rang again. Again, it was Carol. He cut it.

'You know, a conversation, like we do. What d'you think? Something you want to talk about?'

Little Ryan considered this. 'I don't know,' he said.

'Not like you.'

'I don't know what's she called.'

Ryan stirred uneasily. 'You mean Carol?'

Little Ryan regarded him with dispassionate interest, waiting.

'Yeah, well. Funny you should ask about her, 'cause I was going to talk to you about her when I had a chance. She's a nice lady, Ry. She likes you.'

He began to talk about Carol, hesitant at first, then repetitious, becoming strained, a gabble, an untrustworthy voice running on in the honest room. He found himself sweating. 'She's really smart and good with kids, and she's got this big house, and everyone likes her. And she thinks it would be a good idea if we went to live with her.'

Little Ryan said nothing to this.

Ryan became desperate. 'Thing is, Ry, listen to me. She's . . . she's better than me. You know what I mean? Better . . . at stuff. Speaks better and that. You'll have better conversations with her.'

Silence from little Ryan.

140

'What do you think? Come on, Ry, say something. You like conversations. This is a conversation.'

'No, it isn't.' His little voice was suddenly sharp.

'Well. What is it, then?'

There was a long pause. 'It's a lump of despair.' And he finally burst into tears.

Jade put her head round the door. 'You're *such* a knobhead,' she said, and withdrew.

It was nearly ten by the time little Ryan had settled back to sleep. Ryan called Carol and explained. It was too late to see her, and he'd promised to be at breakfast with little Ryan.

'You alright?' he asked.

'Absolutely. Just be nice to have you here, is all. It's nights like this,' she said, 'when it'd be good to be living together. Don't you think? Not just for us. Nice for little Ryan too, not having to be worried that you were going to be somewhere else.'

'Yeah. Yeah, I know.'

'You don't sound that sure.'

'No, it's just . . . Talk later.'

'Alright. See you, then.'

For an hour, he lay on his bed awake, thinking. At last, he got up and stood at the window. Across the street, in dim lamplight, were houses just like Jade's – pebble-dash semis with rain-slick front gardens, vans and bins on the verges gleaming. It was eleven o'clock, a dark night under a sopping sky.

He got a call. Rebekah Bowen, phoning from St Anne's Addiction Rehab Clinic. She'd just come off her shift. Yes, she could answer some questions. Yes, she remembered Zara Fanshawe, remembered what had happened that night. How could she forget it? Yes, she could identify Lawrence Hobhouse. But she hoped she never saw him again.

'That's interesting,' Ryan said.

She talked for twenty minutes and, when she finished, Ryan continued to stand there at the window, staring at his reflection. He wouldn't sleep now for a while. He put on his headphones, cranked up the music until he felt it fill him. He looked at himself. Thin face, big nose, shiny smear of scar tissue under his eye. Skinny kid from nowhere. He put his hood up and his face fell into shadow. Slowly at first, then faster, he began to move to the music, throw some shapes, comic moves, a circus vibe, his thoughts going their own way, throwing their own shapes, directed not by him but by the noise in his ears, going at random to disparate things – a canister of pepper spray, a woman searching for someone dangerous at the homeless hang-outs. And a vindictive ex-husband, telling lies.

SIXTEEN

Out of dark clouds, the day dawned late on the small, wet city. The murder of Zara Fanshawe was still the lead news item, a story seen in pictures of the living Zara, but haunted by the unseen image of her murdered body, bereft and alone, in an abandoned house. Emotion ran outside the usual channels of sympathy and regret. There was a general conviction that something unusually bad had happened – though, because no one knew anything for sure, a result no doubt of police sloth and mismanagement, the news vacuum was filled by speculation. At the edges of stories of a woman wronged and abused, the victim of violence, lurid tales of Zara's former life were still currency, particularly if they could be given a dark connection with her murder; they frothed up in new and entertaining configurations. She'd become dependent on a psychiatric nurse during a long-ago stay in a private hospital in rural west Hampshire. She'd fallen in with a criminal network during a drugs binge in Ibiza. She'd committed some appalling act of irresponsibility and joined a Buddhist sangha in Plymouth, where she had inspired murderous resentment.

There were anonymous reports from all these places, and also from Casablanca, the Cayman Islands, the Meatpacking District of Manhattan and elsewhere. All these stories were the old story of the fall from grace. They were heavy on pictures, headlines and captions, and light on information; and people commuting into the city, sitting in cars or trains or on buses, read the stories on their phones and wondered idly what new stories of foolery a life of such cartoonish chaos would throw up next. Naturally, there was also specific, if not sensible, speculation about the identity of the murderer, though no mention of anyone from the homeless community or Justin Darling, who were obviously lacking the striking qualities the papers were looking for. The favoured potential killers included a well-known movie star Zara had dated before her marriage, a deranged minor royal from Lithuania, a number of high-profile members of the drugs world and, in some outlets, her ex-husband, a jealous man with the financial means to make anything happen, to whose offices Ryan now returned, solo, at speed, crossing the lobby in an angry flap of lime-green polyester, nodding at the open-mouthed recep-tionist, pulling in behind a suited member of staff as they went through the security door and accelerating past her, down the glassed-in corridor, leaving behind him a thin wail of protest.

Turning without slowing into the suite marked *Hobhouse*, where the man himself sat behind a glass desk, also open-mouthed, Ryan began to speak in a voice in keeping with his alarming appearance.

'Hello again. Can't say I'm not pissed off, having to do it over, but, if you're going to lie to us, not like I got much choice. Sit down, then?'

Hobhouse was operating on a slight delay. He sat there, frozen.

Still standing, Ryan went on, loudly, 'Told us you hadn't seen her since June. Told us you hadn't had no contact with her. Turns out it's just a lie, misleading a police investigation. Dear oh dear – fancy a perp-walk out your offices to the meat wagon, do you?'

Guy Beaumont, the lawyer, impeccably dressed as before, made a belated, hasty entrance into the office and began at once to bluster in an agitated baritone.

Ryan didn't look at him. He said to Hobhouse, 'Tell Brooks Brothers, here, to piss off and close the door on his way out.'

Beaumont was already on the phone, fruitily announcing that he was making immediate contact with the Police Federation, when Hobhouse finally came to life.

'It's alright, Guy.'

'Lawrence?'

'You can leave us. Don't worry, it's okay.'

'I—'

'It's fine. But . . .' He hesitated. 'Better close the door, as he says.'

Beaumont withdrew, the door closed. The room seemed to catch its breath, become still again. Hobhouse once more seemed childlike – and, if not lost, then defenceless.

Ryan finally sat and they faced each other. 'No point in looking at me like that, I'm not the sensitive one, he's not here today. I'm the one thinks you ought to answer questions truthfully. Went to St Anne's, didn't you? November. Three times, was it?'

'Twice.'

'Twice. After that, you was banned, right?'

'Discouraged from returning.'

'Fight in a corridor, I heard. Attacked her. Nurses had to break it up. Talked to one of them myself. Want to explain?'

Hobhouse's expression went out of focus, as if he were entirely preoccupied with remembering something very painful. He sat there silently for a while, breathing, face congested.

'Yes,' he said, at last. It was a different voice, less certain, less clear. 'I do want to explain. But where to begin?'

'How about the beginning?'

He thought about that. 'Yes, alright. Chronology. Can't understand anything without it. Transactions, balance sheets, the tax system. Relationships. The thing is, I'm not very good with people.'

Hobhouse sighed once or twice, and began.

He had separated from Zara in June, moving out of the apartment in Kensington. He'd asked her for a divorce, which she refused, but from that moment they lived apart, didn't see each other. Then, at the beginning of November, he got word that something had happened, that she couldn't cope anymore.

'You had her followed.'

'I'd hired someone to keep an eye on her.'

'Ex-Special Forces, we heard.'

He frowned. 'Nothing of the sort. A care worker. Someone who could recognise the signs.'

With Zara, a crisis always began the same way: she withdrew, shut down, went into a zombie-like state; and then she would, usually spectacularly, lose all self-control. Early November, she was like a zombie. Midway through the month, she took an overdose, a serious one, much more serious than any before.

Hobhouse got word, he got her into hospital and, some time after that, to St Anne's. There were a couple of weeks of calm, the crisis seemed to have passed.

'Then, one night at the end of the month, I got a call asking me to go down urgently. There was an incident, they said, ongoing. On the phone, they wouldn't tell me what it was. When I got there, it was about two in the morning. Zara was up on the roof. She was in great distress, threatening to kill herself. I wasn't allowed to go to her. The hospital's chaplain was up there – he'd crawled out of a window and along the ledge to sit with her and talk. Finally, she allowed him to bring her down. But, as soon as she saw me in the corridor, she went berserk.'

He sat, head bowed, for nearly a minute.

'She didn't know what she was doing.'

He sat silently again.

'Neither did I,' he added.

He had to leave, of course. But, a fortnight later, he got another call, this time from Zara herself. She had to see him. After talking to the director, he went down again and this time found a very different Zara, calm now – strangely so, in fact – and, at the same time, it seemed to Hobhouse, fearful. Noises outside the room where they sat continually alarmed her; she shrank into her chair when she heard footsteps in the corridor. But she told Hobhouse that she'd done a lot of thinking and knew now what she needed to do. She'd called him down to tell him that she agreed to the divorce, so that he was now, as she put it, 'free' of her.

'An odd thing to say. But there was something odder. She wouldn't accept anything in the settlement. Nothing. No property, no possessions.'

147

'That's interesting.'

'I didn't understand. She knew the power of money as well as I do.' He made a gesture. 'Money creates, money buys the future.' He shrugged. 'But she was very insistent, fierce about it.'

'So, absolutely nothing?'

He hesitated. 'Nothing of value. She wanted, I don't know why, something quite valueless from my collection.'

'What?'

'A half shekel the monks at Hailes Abbey used to claim was one of the thirty pieces of silver Judas received for betraying Christ. A poor modern forgery, in fact.' He gave a little grimace. 'I assumed she was making a point about our relationship. Anyway, I sent it to her straight away, and she sent me a message saying that, as far as she was concerned, we were now divorced.'

'And then?'

'I never saw her again.'

Ryan thought about all this. He said, 'What do you think happened up on that roof?'

Hobhouse had spoken to the chaplain later. Zara had talked endlessly about wanting to die – 'Kill me now, bag me up' – but without any explanation.

'Why would she want to die?'

Hobhouse shook his head. 'I'm the last person you should ask. I never understood her. Our marriage . . .' He made a gesture of helplessness. 'Zara was the most exciting person I'd ever met. Also, the most chaotic. She seemed not to be able to live without chaos. I can't cope with anything even slightly disordered. We were stuck. I couldn't live with her, but I couldn't stop . . .'

He fell silent again.

'Couldn't stop loving her,' he said at last. 'You think she was frightened of someone. At St Anne's, I thought she was fearful. But I cannot think of a single person who didn't like Zara. She was almost certainly the most-loved person I've known. She just wasn't . . . in control of herself.'

A minute or two passed.

Ryan said, 'What happened at the beginning of November? What was the thing that triggered her?'

He shook his head. 'I have no idea. Only that it must have been something very shocking to her.'

Ryan nodded at last, got up. Hobhouse didn't even look at him; he was lost in his own thoughts.

At the door, Ryan turned back. He said, 'Did she know any homeless people?'

Now Hobhouse looked up. 'What a strange thing to say. No, of course not. She grew up on a country estate, she lived very comfortably all her life. To be honest, I'm not at all sure she knew homeless people even existed.'

Falling silent, he returned his attention to the table, and Ryan went out then and left him there, sitting in his glassed-in silence.

As Ryan left Kensington, Ray was being shown into the drawing room of Fanshawe Hall, a modest country house in north Oxfordshire with not more than twenty bedrooms, seat of the old Catholic family for generations, where the Viscountess was waiting for him by the elaborate fireplace in the parlour. She was a tiny hunched figure, sunk in an overlarge armchair, still and fragile as Wedgwood porcelain in her immaculate powder-blue white-trimmed skirt and jacket, hands folded in her lap – a figure

149

of fortitude, the bereaved mother of a murdered daughter. Ray had spoken to her earlier on the phone to introduce himself, and the dignified old lady before him now was exactly as he had imagined. Her face was finely creased, her hair a cloud of purest white, and, when she spoke, her voice had the clear, tuning-fork tone of the very refined.

Ray again offered his sympathy and she faintly smiled.

'I know, in a sense, it's only a courtesy call, but it's appreciated, thank you.'

He said that he would be happy to try to answer any questions she might have, and she regarded him steadily before she asked him about the manner of Zara's death.

'You mustn't be afraid of my inability to take it,' she said. 'In our class, we're bred to disregard pain.'

Ray described, as delicately as he could, Zara's murder, while she watched him, and, when he finished, she simply nodded and turned away slightly, as if to examine a painting on the far wall.

Ray hesitated. 'I wonder if I might also ask you one or two questions as well. It won't take long.'

'Questions?'

It would help, Ray explained, to know a little more about Zara as a person, and, more specifically, about any recent conversations they'd had, anything Zara might have told her, anything that struck her as unusual.

Her gaze was mild but authoritative; it seemed to pass through him like X-ray waves, as if in search of some other part of the house where, perhaps, her memories resided. 'One wonders how well one knows one's daughter. I daresay our lifestyle isn't very conducive to intimacy between parents and children. She went off to boarding school when she was seven, as we all did. And, once she moved to London, I read about her life in the papers more than I heard about it from Zara herself. Still,' she said, after a moment, 'I was very surprised to read that she had crashed her car.'

'Why?'

'She was such a very careful driver. Extremely so. I should say it was one of her defining characteristics, despite the continual insinuations of the press.' Lady Fanshawe sat for a moment, remembering. She put a slow, careful hand up and fractionally adjusted her hair. 'Perhaps, when she was very young, she was a little reckless. But, when she was still at college, or perhaps it was afterwards, at New Year, I think, she received a notice for careless driving. It affected her very badly. I think perhaps it made her superstitious. At any rate, after that, she was a fearful, overcautious driver. Almost as if it put a shadow in her mind, as if she felt she was fated to have a really serious accident one day.' After a moment, she added, 'I suppose, now, that in a sense she was right.'

Tea arrived and they sat drinking it quietly. Ray noticed the mementos of Zara in the room: photographs, riding trophies and medals. There seemed to be nothing of her as an adult. The Viscountess continued to reminisce. Zara had been a carefree girl, happy and popular. Very determined. Her horse-riding talent was a thrill for the whole family. Remarkably, her success had never become a pressure, not even during the Olympics; Zara seemed to carry it all off without a worry.

'It was Oxford that made her sensitive and morbid,' Lady Fanshawe said. 'Dreadful place.'

'Which college?'

'Lady Margaret Hall. Debs' college, at least it was when I was there, after the war. Do you know the university?'

'I went to Balliol.'

'Ah. One of the clever ones. Did PPE, I suppose.'

Ray admitted it. Rather less economics and philosophy, and rather more politics.

'I'm surprised you're not prime minister. We could do with one. Though perhaps we'd be better not having another from that place.'

Ray asked what Zara had studied.

'Anthropology and ancient archaeology. Dead-end subject, but she was passionate about it. What she couldn't cope with were the parties.' Because of her fame at the Olympics, Zara had been a celebrity upon arrival at university and was instantly in demand. Garden parties, country-house weekends, punting picnics, the usual Oxford entertainments, half bunfight, half historical pantomime. 'Drugs everywhere, of course. All so innocent, so carefree. As you doubtless know, many people can take drugs just occasionally, keep it casual, but there are some who can't – addictive personalities, I suppose we must call them – those who have no natural defence against the toxins, who can't ever leave them alone. Zara was one of those. And it started at Oxford. As if she fell down a hole. A sort of party-going hysteria crept into her life, and also – what can I say? – a sort of darkness. Highs and lows. You know she left university without taking her degree?'

Ray said that he did.

'So disappointing. There was an unpleasant incident. Punting, one afternoon. A boy drowned. Misadventure. They had, of course, been taking something – cocaine was her drug of choice at the time. Zara left at the end of that term. She fell apart. I knew then that she was always going to be fragile.' She gave a little snort. 'Different from the rest of us; we're all tough as old boots. No sentiment in us at all. Barbarians with added refinement, as Zara's father used to say. Not that he had much in the way of refinement.'

Ray said that Zara had found strength at the end of her life to break her addiction. He reiterated that there were no signs she had taken any narcotics in the period before her death.

Lady Fanshawe acknowledged it in silence and took a tissue out from the sleeve of her jacket.

'It's my belief,' she said, 'that drugs weren't the major problem in Zara's life. Men were,' she said. 'As so often, a toxic presence in the bloodstream, if you take my meaning.' The first time Zara had sought psychiatric treatment had been at least as much to do with men as actual narcotics. 'Although, of course, it was reported in the press as rehabilitation.'

Ray asked about Zara's relationships.

'I would say that she scored high on quantity, low on quality. I very rarely liked her boyfriends. And, indeed, there were so many, it's impossible to remember them all. Actors, financiers, minor royals. There was one absolute disaster just before the breakdown I mentioned, though I don't recall his name, and my impression was that he was a complete nonentity. Like so many of your sex.'

'What about Lawrence Hobhouse?'

'Strange choice, I thought. Father figure, perhaps. Her own

father buggered off with the nanny when she was eight, as I'm sure you know.'

Ray left a small pause. 'Do you know if she'd been seeing anyone since separating from her husband?'

She leaned forward. 'Well, you will think me an odd fish, but as it happens I did wonder. She called me, quite a rare event, just a few days ago, and I thought I hadn't heard her sounding so cheerful in years. Or perhaps not cheerful exactly. Calm. Or . . . relieved. No, not quite that either. Determined. Yes, that's it. As if she had decided to do something about herself finally, and a great weight had been lifted from her. And I thought to myself, Has she found someone decent at last? But, before you ask, no, she didn't say anything directly about it. Not a word.'

Ray finished his tea.

'I'm sorry to ask you this, but, given the terrible circumstances, I have to: do you know of anyone who might have wanted to cause Zara harm?'

She shook her head. 'Oh, no. Everyone loved her. Even when she got into scrapes. Perhaps especially then.'

'It's possible her former addiction issues might have brought her into contact with criminal elements.'

'You mean drug dealers, I suppose. I don't think so. She never said this, but my impression was that she relied on an old Oxford friend, Justin, a very civilised young man. Although,' she added, 'a moron.'

Ray nodded. 'We've talked to Justin. He thought Zara had changed in the last few months too. Perhaps you're right – perhaps it was the result of meeting someone new.'

They sat for a moment in silence.

154

'This will sound strange,' Ray said, 'but did she have any contact with anyone sleeping on the street?'

'You mean charity work?'

'No. A personal relationship.'

She shook her head in bewilderment. 'No, never. The very thought is fantastical.'

He got up to go and she extended her hand as lady dowagers do in old films. As he bent towards her, he smelled violets, slightly stale.

For a moment, she held tightly on to his hand, and he thought she might start to cry, but instead she said, in her thin, clear voice, 'You asked at the beginning if I might remember anything unusual that Zara said to me recently. Nothing significant, I'm afraid. But there's something trivial that sticks in my mind. When we finished our last telephone call, she said, "God bless." That's all, just that. But I hadn't heard her say those words since she was a girl. She had a terrible crush on Jesus when she was thirteen. Funny. It took me back.' She considered what she'd said. 'It made me happy,' she added.

Finally, she released Ray's hand. She nodded at him, her face went blank, and he left her alone with her memories and went out to sit in his car, with Bach playing soft and regretful melodies, as he wrote his report on his laptop, pausing occasionally to gaze out of the window at the dusk slowly effacing the parkland of Fanshawe Hall.

When his phone rang, he looked at it a moment, cautiously, and answered in his most formal manner: 'DI Wilkins. Can I help?'

SEVENTEEN

And now, in Oxford, the nudging rush-hour traffic glittered in the narrow, darkened streets. The shops in the centre slowly emptied of customers, office staff turned off their lights and locked up, the grand monuments flattened into shadow, assumed their famous night-time silhouettes, became cardboard cut-outs. In busy Cornmarket and Queen Street, the crowds thinned, drained away, leaving behind the debris of homeless people, who settled into the doorways of closed stores, burrowing under blankets, or sat blankly on their bits of cardboard, thinking of all they'd lost.

In Gloucester Green, a woman crept along and went warily into the side doorway of the Odeon cinema, where two or three people lay in sleeping bags. She hesitated, looking round, licking her lips, then squatted down with them.

'Seen Waitrose?'

No answer.

Birdlike, she picked through the cartons and bags lying around her, glancing sharply from side to side.

'Hey,' she said. 'Waitrose around?'

The person in the sleeping bag next to her continued to shake quietly without speaking, and Lena waited, watching him.

'Waitrose been here?' she said, after a while.

She rubbed her mittened hands together.

'Fucking useless,' she said mildly.

A man came along and sat down at the edge of the steps, and Lena watched him as he drank from a plastic litre bottle. He had a recent gash on his forehead and blood had run into his eyebrows and congealed and darkened there, black as oil, but he didn't seem aware of this. He began to talk, perhaps not to her, to the shaking man maybe, or just to hear his own voice. 'Three months I been here. When is it? March, is it? Three months, they won't sign me off.' He drank and began to talk again, rummaging in his trousers with one hand, keeping a tight hold of his bottle with the other. 'Intentional vagrancy, three, four months. What's intentional about that? It's a joke. Steal the Horse, three weeks. That boy Keefer, two weeks, up there on Garsington with a bottle of blue. Into the Julians, hot water, hot as they want it, just turn on the taps.' He took a prescription packet from deep inside his underwear and began to crumble the pills into his cider.

Lena shuddered. 'Don't talk to me about Garsington.'

The man drank and went on, 'Night like last night, freeze the snot in your nose. Horse and Keefer in the Julian, me out there on the canal getting frostbite. Lose my fingers, one night. No residency?' he shouted suddenly. 'I was born here,' he said, 'near enough. It's like I'm not even . . . like they can't even . . . like I fallen down a . . .' He spat. 'This city,' he said, gesturing round as if to take in the whole of Oxford.

Lena nodded mildly.

He picked up a wet sheet of cardboard and suddenly, savagely poked his finger through it, staring at the damage.

After a while, he looked at Lena.

'Up Garsington for the punters, was it?'

She looked the other way.

He held out the bottle. 'Need a cure?'

She took it and started to drink, and after a moment he snatched it back, and they shouted at each other and subsided into silence.

'Wouldn't even be here, if it wasn't for her. Only reason I'm here. One little mistake, one tiny little mistake. She took the kids. Never see them, don't even know how old they are. Got cancer in the you know what, what do you call it. I can feel it. All they say is *residency*. Residency, that's all it is with them. I tell them at O'Hanlon, tell them all the time, I don't know anything about the damage. How can I? I have the blackouts, they know I have them, I told them. Ask One-Eye Jane, ask Belfast Phil about the damage.'

He drank again.

'They don't ask,' he said quietly. 'They won't.' He fell silent again.

'Know where Waitrose is?' Lena asked hopefully, after a while. 'Seen him here before. Tried down the Martyr, in Becket Street – not there.'

He didn't reply.

Another man came in, noisier, kicking his way among the bedding and detritus, and Lena and the man drinking cider edged away. This new man had a bottle of wine with him, and a packet of cigarettes, and a whole roast chicken, scalding hot, which he held with difficulty in a greasy hand, and he shouted aimlessly, as if to clear a space around himself.

After a while, he stopped shouting and began to eat, dropping chunks of the hot meat into his lap.

'Spitty?' Lena whispered.

The man ignored her.

'Spitty? Seen Waitrose?' she asked, and he turned to her at once.

The afternoon gave up and dissolved into evening. At St Aldates, Ryan worked on alone. Small developments were nudging the general picture this way and that. Justin Darling had given them the names of Zara's yacht-club friends – who had in fact admitted responsibility for the state of the apartment. Zara had given them the key so they could house-sit, they'd had a party which had lasted three days and badly got out of hand, and, when they came to their senses, they fled the scene and forgot about the dogs. Zara hadn't been there; it wasn't her drugs mess, after all. And Nadim had discovered where Zara's Rolls-Royce Phantom had been for most of the last fortnight: in the municipal underground car park at Gloucester Green. Excepting the three journeys they knew about, it seemed to have been parked there the entire fortnight. The images from the private cameras inside were clear enough: it had taken up two bays, and, though it would have attracted attention, it hadn't been damaged in any way – an almost touching testament to British respect for the private property of the very rich.

She hadn't been looking for a dealer. She'd been looking for someone else. But she'd taken care that she wouldn't be noticed as she searched.

Ryan sat alone in the shared office, remembering what Zara had looked like in that little empty attic room. Like she had nothing left, like a street beggar. It seemed almost to be the conclusion of a deliberate process – giving away her possessions, leaving her Roller where it could easily be damaged, refusing a divorce settlement, abandoning her apartment to the rich lowlife who would trash it.

But he thought also of her five thousand pounds in cash. It hadn't been found at her apartment or in the Polstead Road house. So, where was it? Who had it?

He left a voicemail for Ray, who wasn't picking up. 'We need to look at last November. Something happened to her, made her take that overdose, try to kill herself. Where the fuck are you, by the way?'

He worked on alone, labouring over paperwork, not his natural strength. It was seven o'clock. He'd called Jade earlier to tell her he wasn't going to be home for little Ryan's bath and bed, and he thought of that now with anguish.

He called Nadim, who was also still at work.

'Where's Ray? Some of this paperwork is his.'

Nadim thought he was still at Fanshawe Hall.

'Well, he ought to be back by now. I'll have to have a word.'

'Maybe think about having a bit of sensitivity around Ray, Ryan.'

'What about me? No one's had any sensitivity around me since, well, ever.'

'Just saying.'

Sighing, he turned again to his report.

But Ray was not at Fanshawe Hall, he was sitting in his car outside a house in Rose Hill. Like the other houses in the street, it was a modest thirties semi, with brickwork below and pebble-dash above – the sort of house a small tradesman might own, or a cabbie. But it was where the Deputy Chief Constable lived.

Tiny front garden, brief snippet of privet hedge and, set back at the side of the house, a little garage with an old-fashioned up-and-over metal door, slightly buckled, and a side passage to the back garden. The house next to it was under scaffolding: a sagging roof was being replaced. It was a two-minute walk one way to the Kia Motors showroom and the Rose Hill main drag – a Chinese, an Indian and so on – and a five-minute drive the other to a lock-up garage in College Lane, Littlemore, where, several years earlier, a man called Steven Walsh and known as Shocker had been shot dead by Lynch – in self-defence, she'd said. There had been no witnesses. Walsh was the alleged leader of a gang responsible for a number of armed burglaries and had been for some months the subject of an intensive investigation by Violent Crime, headed at the time by Chester Lynch, who had said on more than one occasion that her motivation to bring Walsh to justice had become 'personal'. Forensics established that Walsh had been shot with a 9-mm bullet fired from Lynch's Glock-17. There was an inquiry, which upheld Lynch's version of events but noted the lack of conclusive evidence: it was never satisfactorily established, for instance, how she had been led to the lock-up in the first place.

Shortly afterwards, Lynch was, in her own words, 'moved on' from Violent Crime – to bigger things, as it happened – and her legend had grown a little wilder.

Ray looked at the house a while longer. It wasn't what he had expected, even when Lynch had given him the address. He still had no idea why she wanted to see him; in the call she'd made to him while he was at Fanshawe Hall, she'd simply told him to come. He checked his watch, got out of the car and walked up the short concrete driveway to the front door.

Dressed as before, in jeans and leather jacket, she was shorter than Ray remembered from the awards ceremony, but more compact, more tightly sprung, and she looked at him a moment – a short, searching look – before turning and leading him down the narrow hallway. The first thing he noticed about the house was the stairlift, also grab rails on the walls. They went into a front room, where Lynch introduced Ray to her husband, who came forward in his motorised wheelchair, a frail man, still young, but bent out of shape, with large eyes, a sensual mouth and a pleasant expression. 'Walter,' she said, by way of introduction. Her terse cockney turned it into 'Wa-ter,' the gasp of a lost soul in the desert. She rested her hand on her husband's shoulder and he smiled up at her affectionately. Then she was saying that she was going to take Ray into the back room to talk, and Walter smiled again and lifted an elongated veal-pale hand, and they went out and down a short ramp, through a galley kitchen, into a back extension overlooking the garden. It was a straightforward room, plain and practical, without any of the expensive materials or design flourishes Ray was used to in north Oxford. Round wooden table and wooden chairs. Sofa with torn arm-covers. Dresser crowded with crockery. The walls were mainly bare, though Ray's attention was caught at once by a large framed photograph above the sofa, showing a group of boys standing team-like in front of a tent.

'Boot camp,' Lynch said. 'Know about that?'

A few years earlier, she'd set up a boot camp called Grade X for young offenders, a spartan place of deliberately harsh conditions, sited on a field next to the Kassam Stadium in the Leys, on the edge of the city, which put the youngsters through punitive army-style courses run by the Brize Norton paratroopers. Days were long and gruelling, rewards few, punishments brutal. Young offenders loved it; recidivism among those who completed the course was non-existent.

'They don't want it easy, Ray, don't want pity. They want it hard – harder the better. They want to prove themselves. Should see them. Take them out at night to building sites for war games. There's a site we go to at the moment – Newman Place development, at Littlemore – big, all half-built apartment blocks and excavated foundations, piles of materials, cranes, diggers everywhere. Five hours, fighting for territory. They absolutely love it.'

There were now four other boot camps in the same franchise in other parts of the country. It had become a side business.

'Get through that sort of thing, they can get through anything. Basic psychology. Don't need to tell you that, Ray. Teamwork: they'd die for each other. Self-respect.'

Again, the searching look.

There were other photos on the wall: Lynch receiving awards; Lynch with her team on assignments abroad; Lynch in the ring, a fixed, hieratic look on her face. They talked boxing for a while.

Lynch had been a pioneer of the women's sport. 'Thing is, Ray, I've fought against people all my life, in and out of the ring.'

Then she wanted to smoke, and they went outside and stood on a patio of cracked flagstones raised above the garden, an unexpectedly vast plot, at least three times the size of neighbouring gardens – one of the reasons for buying the house, Lynch said. It stretched all the way to Rose Hill Cemetery, just visible through the trees, and was now a brown February mess, an area of wilderness, a tangle of dead things and inexplicable gaps. Some targets were set up here and there. Chester came out regularly to practise her marksmanship: it calmed her, kept her sharp. As she silently rolled a cigarette, Ray listened to the surf-noise of traffic on the nearby ring road.

'Have you always lived here?'

She finished rolling her cigarette and blew out smoke, nodded.

'Since I worked the streets round about. I like the people, Ray. Got the shops close. Fair bit of extra land down there, thought about maybe developing it one day. House is okay, put in the stairlift for Walt.' She smoked, picked tobacco off her lip. 'MS, if you're wondering. Probably noticed the wheelchair, being an award-winning detective.'

Ray murmured his sympathy.

'It is what it is, Ray. We don't do self-pity. Good days, Walt can walk the length of the back room, with crutches. Medical infusions slow the illness down, a bit. Vision not great, sort of a blurring, but nothing wrong with his brain.'

She took a last drag and shot the butt off the patio, where it lay with other butts, pale scraps against the dark winter earth.

'Well. You'll want to know why you're here.'

She explained. National Uplift was looking for an 'ambassador', someone working with diverse recruitment and new recruits. A big role, salary to match. Big responsibility, too: the ambassador would liaise with Whitehall on a regular basis; the PM was personally behind the initiative. There would be national coverage, major exposure.

'The force needs change, big time – you know that, everyone knows that. Finally, I got the suits to agree. But I need people to make it happen. Good people, people I can trust. People who want to go places.'

The post was dual role: partly comms, partly policymaking. She needed someone with presence, television skills, someone with the credibility of street experience, someone with ideas. Someone young, with energy.

She looked at him. 'Just talking to people at this stage, that's all – feelers out sort of thing, asking for views.' She raised her eyebrows. 'Got any?'

Ray stood, galvanised in the instant, the way he used to be on the rugby pitch at school, the ball slung suddenly to him, too quick for him to take in the picture of the game, too sudden to calculate all the angles and options, but moving at once instinctively, as you do, taking a risk.

'It all depends,' he said, 'on the authority of this person to criticise the force and be taken seriously.'

Chester Lynch gave him a strong, fierce look. 'Fuck me, Ray – first question I asked myself when all this started. Exact same question. Okay, then – let's talk.'

They stood above the darkened garden. The different browns of the trees and dull greens of the bushes had all become the same, thickened to an impenetrable black against the pale grey sky. The birds were silent. Neighbours' lights were orange glimmers through the looming shadow lines of the scaffolding next door. Ray smoked one of Chester Lynch's roll-ups. After the first rush of excitement, he began to feel unsure. Lynch was working him hard. 'Someone I can trust,' she was saying. 'Someone I can value. Are you valued, Ray, where you are?'

She got a call and stepped inside for a moment to answer it, leaving Ray with his thoughts. Some of what Lynch was saying on the phone reached him outside: curt phrases, hard. He overheard her say something angrily – it sounded like, *Don't call again* – then she reappeared and stood there, looking at him.

'One of the things you'd have to get down, Ray – how to deal with the media, brush them off when you have to, keep them onside if necessary. You'd be fine, I know you would; they like you already. Not like the other Wilkins,' she added. 'Saw his presser the other day.' She lifted an eyebrow.

'He's just getting used to it,' Ray murmured.

Her eyebrow remained raised.

They went inside and drank tea and talked some more.

'So, Ray. What do you think? Interested?'

He left a beat before he answered. 'Yes. But.'

She nodded, shrugged. 'I get it. Felt the same, your age. You want action, the impact on the street, instant results.'

'It's not that I don't think this is a fantastic opportunity; it's just that I don't know if I'm ready for this sort of ambassadorial role.'

'Come back to what I was saying. Are you getting the opportunities where you are?'

Ray said nothing.

'Do this job, two, three years, go back to detective work on your own terms. Detective Super, if you want it. Thing is, you got it, Ray, I could see that, first time I saw you come up on that stage. Ideas, push.'

She looked at him fiercely, her face some sort of weapon pointed at him.

'Advice to you? Never let yourself get too comfy.'

Ray nodded. 'Okay. I am interested, yes. But I've got to think of my colleagues, too. I don't want to let them down.'

'Fair enough. Give it a few days, then. Not too long, though. I'm moving things on fast. Hectic schedule. Fly to Washington next week for a month. I want someone lined up by then. If it's you, I want a bunch of quick meetings, off site, away from the station – here, or in a hotel I know – be alright with you?'

'Sure.'

She said goodbye to him at the front door, and he went and sat in his car in the stillness of the dark street, not thinking of anything, belatedly feeling surprised. He smiled to himself. And at last he drove out of Rose Hill and through town, back to north Oxford.

Elsewhere, Lena was making her way cautiously up the dark towpath, the canal on one side and the stream on the other. Narrowboats were moored there, bags of charcoal and lengths of hose and other useful things piled on the verge alongside. As she passed one boat, the dark shape of a dog rose up on the flat roof snarling, and she hurried on, up the path and across the bridge at Sheepwash Pool. A fire burned low and smoky in the dark bushes there, among tents and makeshift awnings slung from the trees, and she went in warily, looking about her, ignored by the five or six people who sat on the ground drinking, and settled down, unassuming.

'Seen Steal the Horse?' she asked, after a while.

They were talking about a child's bicycle, a possession none of them had any use for, their argument swirling backwards and forwards.

'Seen Waitrose?' Lena asked hopefully.

One stood and pissed into the darkness, crying to himself. Another, on the ground, ranted about the bicycle. It had been stolen from his skip in St Ebbe's, he said; it was his. He had no children, but that wasn't the point. The point, never mentioned, was his self-respect, his inner being, his immortal soul. A kiddie bike with one stabiliser missing. The standing man pissed and wept, shouting into the darkness.

'He been here, I heard,' another man said quietly to Lena. He sat incapacitated on the wet ground, his trousers undone. He was black, older than the others, his cropped hair grey. Long ago, he had been injured in a fight and his mouth drooped at one side. He spoke with an Irish accent. He held out the cider bottle to Lena and she took it and drank, and after a moment he grabbed it back and fell in a heap, muttering.

'Where is he now?' Lena asked.

No reply.

'Everyone wants Waitrose,' he said, after a while.

'Who?'

'What's he got, people want him for?'

'Who wants him?' Lena said.

No reply.

'Belfast!'

He propped himself up with difficulty, spent a moment focusing on her.

'Who wants him, Belfast?' she said again.

'Keefer. He been here from up St Giles', asking.'

'What for? Money?'

'What money?' he said quickly.

Lena became careful. 'Keefer always wants money,' she said. 'Why'd he want Waitrose?'

But Belfast Phil had fallen asleep; he lay, grunting slightly from his lopsided mouth. Lena tugged at his trousers and he woke shouting. When he subsided, he said, 'Keefer said there's this woman.'

'What woman?'

'Been asking, said she'd pay if he found out where Waitrose was.'

'What woman? Goldy hair woman?'

'Don't know what woman.' The cider bottle had fallen over and emptied its contents and he began to weep, cursing. The argument about the bicycle continued around them, gathered intensity. One of the men hit out, a woman began to scream. Another man appeared suddenly and fought him, and stood over him, shouting. At last there was quiet. The newcomer sat down, sucking his hands, grumbling about the weather. Drizzle was coming down again, silverish in the darkness, like a haze among the trees.

'Horse,' Lena said softly to the new man. 'Horse. Seen Waitrose?'

He turned and looked at her a long time, his face pale and wet, his black hair matted, small eyes black as judgment.

'Spitty told me you seen him,' she said.

He watched her. 'How long you been in Oxford?'

'Came August. Six months.'

'You know Waitrose, then.'

Lena bit her lip. 'I didn't. I do now,' she added. 'I know who he is now,' she said softly.

'Yeah. Watch yourself with that cunt.'

She nodded, humbly, waiting.

Steal the Horse looked at her for a long time.

'What do you want him for?'

She said nothing.

'Pills, is it?'

Silence.

'Snow? What? Spice? Big Spice man – used to be, anyway.'

She didn't say anything.

'I tell you where he is, you tell him I sent you, tell him I want my cut.' He waited until she nodded. 'Up on Garsington,' he said. 'Old garage there, know where I mean?'

Her face crumpled. Belfast, still lying on the ground, made a noise like laughter. 'She knows,' he said. 'Garsington twenty-four-hour. She knows alright.' He laughed.

Lena was already on her feet.

'Tell him I sent you!' Horse shouted after her, as she walked quickly away through the silver-dark drizzle, hugging herself.

Ten o'clock, night. Ray and Diane sat side by side on the floor of their spare room with the feeding twins: a scene of north Oxford

170

domestic calm, faint street light coming through the curtains, small animal noises in their laps, a car alarm in Summertown, so distant it seemed polite. Perhaps, in Summertown, car alarms were polite. They spoke quietly.

'A big move. A position with real influence, a high profile. A chance to work with Chester, to make a difference. To be there at the start of something.'

'You sound as if you're trying to convince yourself.'

He didn't reply. They sat there, listening to the quiet, feeling the cool hush of the house around them, the quietness of the sleeping street.

'You'll miss the cases, getting results.'

He didn't say anything.

'You'll miss working with Ryan.'

He said nothing.

'Won't you?'

'No.'

They sat there.

'My father would want me to take it.'

'Of course he would.'

Outside, a car went slowly, quietly, up the street.

'When do you have to decide?'

'Within the week.'

They fell silent. The twins carried on feeding.

And at last Ryan got home. He went into the back room, where Jade sat watching television. The news was just ending: an image of the Polstead Road house, a newscaster intoning, an impression

171

of unexplained savagery, mystery, an investigation that hadn't got going.

Ryan said, 'You would not believe the fucking day.'

Jade ignored him. He shuffled about.

'Maybe go up, just take a look at him.'

'What, and wake up him like last time? That worked, didn't it?' He winced.

She turned off the television. 'Listen, Ryan. I know this is hard for you. But, if he sees you now, it'll just set him off. Think about it. Every day he's had the same thing. You promise to come home in time to see him, and you don't. He's upset. He hardly spoke to me all evening.'

'He's missing our conversations. There's stuff about time and light I want to ask him about. Maybe if I just pop up—'

'Listen, Ryan. I said to him, if he was awake when you came back, he could have a quick talk with you, and he looked at me and he said, "I don't want to talk to my daddy anymore."'

The room seemed to buckle suddenly. Ryan even put out a hand to steady himself. He stared at her. Swallowed.

'He said that?' he said at last.

She nodded.

'Don't want to speak to me?'

'Sorry, Ryan.'

He felt it in his stomach like a wave of nausea. Tears came into his eyes and he wiped his wet nose with his finger and stood there, not knowing what to do.

Jade watched him for a moment, then she put the television on again.

Ryan carried on standing there, looking at nothing, feeling sick.

EIGHTEEN

Next morning, Ray was absent from the briefing. Ryan went through developments for Barko, who sat at his desk, staring at him unpleasantly.

Incidental stuff, he said impatiently, minor things, suggestive, circumstantial hints and nudges, nothing solid, nothing to pull on. 'What do you even think happened?' he asked.

Ryan didn't know. But something had happened to Zara the previous November. As a result, she'd had a breakdown and taken an overdose, then made a slow recovery. She'd become, it seemed, a changed person, with a plan, who came to Oxford looking for someone. With five grand in her pocket.

'But also hiding from someone.'

She'd hidden her car in the municipal car park. Clever move: who would look for a Roller there? She'd hidden herself in the empty house in Polstead Road. That had taken careful planning too: none of the neighbours had even suspected she'd been there.

'But someone found out,' Wallace said.

'Yeah. Maybe the someone she'd been scared of.'

'But who?'

Ryan shrugged, prompting the expected response from Barko.

'Well, find out! Double-check the cameras, review her records, go through her contacts, ask better questions. Put the hard hours in, Wilkins.'

He bent forward, his voice a hiss.

'Have you seen the papers? Have you?' Apparently they were saying Zara had been part of a death cult that sacrificed dogs. Naturally, the police hadn't the wit to uncover such evil.

Afterwards, Livvy sat with Ryan for an hour. She reported in passing that they had reviewed the Westgate and Cornmarket CCTV footage to see if they could spot Zara picking up one of Carol's flower-shop cards, but had found nothing. Ryan said he'd ask Carol if there was anywhere else her girls had been.

'Where's Ray, by the way? Why isn't he here?'

Livvy thought perhaps he was at an off-site meeting. There was something in the matter-of-fact evenness of her tone that made him feel petulant, and he wondered if she was judging him. She'd worked closely with Ray on a previous case. She called Ray *Boss*. She'd never called Ryan *Boss*. As usual, these thoughts made him defensive, and he swung his feet on to the desk and gazed fiercely at the crazy wall. Earlier, he had taken down a photograph of Lawrence Hobhouse, added a picture of St Anne's Addiction Rehab Clinic and drawn a moustache on Justin Darling. There was another photo too, of little Ryan sitting solemnly on a playground roundabout, which he stared at in a sort of anguish.

'Remind me to go home at five tonight,' he said. 'It's important.'

Livvy looked up, nodded, carried on working.

Ten glassy-eyed minutes passed, then he spoke again.

'Postmen,' he said.

Livvy looked up again, waiting. But he said nothing else. He got up and went out of the office and down the corridor.

In his newly serviced but still barely functioning Peugeot, he went east out of St Aldates Police Station, towards the new 'trade city' off Sandy Lane, in Blackbird Leys, where Oxford's sorting office is situated, a low-slung industrial unit in brown brick and tinted glass. In reception, he made enquiries and waited by a darkened window. Neighbours in Polstead Road had seen nothing of Zara or any break-in at the house; they sat in their front rooms, staring into their cups of tea, or went discreetly to and fro without bad-mannered nosiness. But posties are always in the street, up and down the driveways, looking about them.

After a few minutes, he was joined by Tony Barrett, who covered north Oxford.

'Everything west of the Woodstock Road, from Observatory Street to Lark Hill,' he said. 'Fair old schlep.'

'Been doing it long?'

'Since I left the service, three years ago.'

He was in his late twenties, a small but tightly constructed man, with a postman's calf muscles (comprehensively tattooed on one of them with the face of a girl and some dates), dressed in a Royal Mail red sleeveless gilet over a red shirt and black shorts, and wearing a tight-fitting black beanie with a Royal Mail logo on it. Understandably, he was nervous being called to speak to a detective – tight-lipped and defensive.

'Cover Polstead Road?'

'Yeah.'

'House at the end – 1A.'

'I know it.'

'And you know why I'm asking you about it?'

'Yeah.'

'So. Tell me about it.'

'What, the house? Empty. For sale, must be two years now, I reckon. See it more and more, round there. Bought as investments. Don't think it's right. I been on a list for a flat all that time, can't get anything.'

'Circulars all piled up on the doormat.'

'Well, no one told me to stop delivering them.'

'Delivered anything else there?'

'What, in the last two years? Not that I remember. Maybe some bills, long time ago. Not since then.'

'You been up to the house, though, fairly regular, with the circulars. Notice anything?'

'Don't know what you mean. There was no one there. Until . . . Weeds getting longer, that's about it.'

'Someone broke in, smashed a window at the back.'

'Nothing to do with me; I never go round the back. Front door only. We're all timed.'

Ryan nodded. 'Relax. I just wondered if you'd seen anything out of the ordinary – say, in the last couple of weeks.'

Tony looked blank, shook his head.

'Caught sight of anyone in the house – at a window, say?'

He showed Tony a picture of Zara.

'You seen this in the papers already.'

176

Tony shook his head. 'Yeah, but I never saw her there. Must have kept herself hidden away.'

'Anyone else?'

'In the house? No.'

Ryan tried again. 'Anyone hanging round the house, then? On the driveway, down the side.'

'No.'

'Or on the street? Anyone out of place?'

Now, he hesitated. 'Well, it's funny you say that; there was a guy there, couple of times, these last few days.'

'Who?'

'Vagrant. Not doing anything. Just odd to see him. Don't usually see them round there.'

Ryan felt a prickle of interest at the back of his neck.

'Go on.'

'Well, that's it. Old guy, wild-looking, wild-haired, wrapped up in coats and dressing gowns, stumping along, boots probably two sizes too big for him, shouting to himself. Mental health, I expect. Probably didn't know where he was, just found himself there, walking along, pushing his trolley.'

'Trolley?'

'You know, one of them supermarket things. Looked like he had everything he owned in it.'

'Recognise him again?'

'I reckon.'

Ryan went back to his lousy car and called Livvy, asking her to pass on the message to the officers on the street, and in return got the contact details for the director at O'Hanlon House.

He sat a moment longer, then started up the car, listened to its engine thump for a bit, waiting for it to settle, and drove off.

O'Hanlon House, hostel for the homeless, sits at the end of unlovely Cromwell Street, at the back of the law courts, a stone's throw from St Aldates Police Station. With its high gates, metal doors and cameras, it looks like a prison, but it provides secure temporary accommodation for the dozens of people sleeping rough in the city. Ryan sat in his car looking at it while he left another voicemail for Ray.

'Ray! Man with a trolley, Ray! I'm on fire, mate. Get a name for you soon, maybe. By the way, where the fuck are you?'

Then he went up to the metal door and was buzzed in.

The director, who sat behind her desk listening to him, was an open-faced lady from Barbados, very competent and good natured. She was new in the job.

'You mean Waitrose,' she said. 'That's what people call him, I think.'

'Real name?'

She shook her head. 'We don't see him here; he's not in the system. He's quite well known in the city, but what I know is only what my staff and other homeless people tell me about him. Everyone just calls him Waitrose.'

He'd lived on the streets a long time, she knew that. He'd blown into Oxford perhaps a dozen years or more ago, irascible, unpredictable and abusive, an almost mythic troublemaker, and had become a 'local character'.

Ryan asked about drugs.

Waitrose had built up a reputation for selling, in a small-scale, chaotic sort of way, mainly to others in the homeless community. But over time he'd sold less, gradually pushed out of the market by other more organised dealers; now, he probably used more than he sold.

'He's getting old,' the director said. 'Body old, not age old. He might be still in his forties, but he has the body of a seventy-year-old. Living on the street so long will do that for you.'

'Mental-health issues?'

'Of course. But, as I understand it, he doesn't let us get close enough to help him. He's an eccentric, an oddity, a little dangerous. Most of the other homeless people are frightened of him.'

'Dangerous?'

'He can lash out, if provoked.' There had been at least one incident – it might even have been investigated by police.

'Keep records here?'

'Not what you would call records.' She explained the situation. For the past few years, they had used a national database, which systematised the information in various useful ways, but, prior to that, it had been their practice to keep 'daybooks', a sort of collective journal in which staff and volunteers – and even, occasionally, the occupants – informally jotted down a whole range of things: descriptions of events, recommendations for improvements, memos to colleagues, reminders, complaints – almost anything. Entries were not always dated; some of the books had been lost or mislaid; the handwriting was often impossible. The intention had been to gradually transfer all this information into the new database, but that hadn't happened and probably never would.

'Sounds quite similar to our records. That's a joke, though

not really. This incident happen before the database, then? Got a date? Rough date?'

She called a colleague and spoke briefly, in a different tone – brisker and more authoritative – waiting a moment, then crisply replacing the phone.

'It was 2011,' she told him. 'Not sure what time of year, but probably October.'

'Take a quick squint?'

'If I haven't put you off.'

She led him along the corridor to a storeroom, where the 'records cupboard' stood, an old wardrobe crammed with dozens, perhaps hundreds, of notebooks, of many sizes and shapes, stacked on sagging shelves, in an order that was part wishful, part fanciful and part accidental. His heart sank.

'Happy reading,' the director said.

'Reading not really my thing,' he said gloomily.

He began to take books off the shelves. He immediately despaired. The records formed a vast artwork of found objects, a jumble of lost things: a thought about the kitchen, a note about medical supplies, a report of an incident of violence, an account of a conversation. Names recurred without explanation, the same person was given different names, even the vocabulary was strange – *jake, blue, skippers, Antabuse, cuffing.* There were stories of stolen horses, rat dreams, wet beds and Lucifer, people living in unimaginable ways, characters who had lost their proper names: Bottle Curt, Hinky Jane, Pill Bill, Bubble Head, Steal the Horse. It wasn't information, it was lives. Here, the homeless existed in the same messy, partial, undone way they existed on the streets.

He read at random.

On a script. Says lithium and risperidone for depression. Wife threw him out, children don't want to see him anymore. Moved on years ago, pneumonia from being hosed, bad lungs still. Worst thing, shame of begging in your home town. Cleansed by the 'elders' of the people's church. Doesn't want to go back to a life of crime.

Came from Sudan. Says he fought against the government three years. Rocket launchers. Two years in prison. Showed marks on feet, back. No possessions, no family. Can't prove residency. Says you can't trust homeless people. Asked for Subutex to help him come off heroin – but caught selling it before. Says, if he doesn't get in, he'll be moved on by the police.

Martha, calls herself Esmé. Fifty-one. Breast cancer. Poor choice of men all her life, abusive. Boyfriend Robert married but doesn't see his wife. Brought her three cats – Snap, Crackle and Pop. Also four fish and a rat. Expelled from Julians, possession of heroin. When she's clean, the little things are too much.

He noted the many mentions of being moved on, last fear of those without a place to go, as if, once they had no home, they could be swept away entirely, pushed overboard and lost at sea. He noted the chaos, the self-pity, the outrageous lack of self-control, and felt a twinge of recognition. But at least he'd grown up in a trailer, at least he'd known where the beatings were coming from.

Still, he couldn't help feeling that some of these people were a right fucking pain.

At last, he found the book for October. He went through it quickly, entries snagging at him, and, in the middle of the book, found a mention of Waitrose.

Spitty Pete says Waitrose bothering people worse since attacking the woman at Cowley Library, wants to know when we're going to do something. Note to talk again to police officer.

He went back to the beginning of the book and found another, which he'd missed.

3 October. Visit from St Aldates to talk about W. Won't talk to them, attitude throughout 'contemptuous'. Explained he's not in our system. Asked what had happened at Cowley. Attack on woman outside library. Young woman, smart, well dressed, polite. Had approached him to offer him money, he verbally abused her ('Blonde bitch', etc.), said odd things ('You ruined my life'), pursued her down the street, striking her about the head with a metal coat hanger. She fell, broke collarbone. Delusional, perhaps intoxicated. Woman very upset, pressing charges. Discussed possibility of welfare, psych team, etc. Difficulties of that. Conviction likely. Agreed to liaise.

He went to the end of the book and found one more, very brief.

Waitrose case. Violent Crime called. No further action.

Ryan thought about all that, then put the book back in the wardrobe and went to see the director again.

'Found what you were looking for?'

'Maybe.'

He asked her some more questions about Waitrose – where he came from, where he might be found – but she was unable to help him. After a while, he got up to go. He stopped at the door.

'Why's he called Waitrose?'

'Well.' She smiled at him. 'The trolley, I imagine.'

'Why not Sainsbury's or Tesco?'

She smiled at him. 'Is it important?'

'Everything's important, until it isn't. Old copper told me that. It's bollocks, but it stuck in my mind.'

All in all, he felt perky. He had a suspect, a name – or a nick-name at least. He called Livvy, told her to put out an immediate APW, and set off for St Aldates in a good mood.

NINETEEN

Activity in the station was muted; Ryan put it down to routine business, the dutiful grind of a February afternoon, people sitting at their desks shuffling screens, going in and out of each other's offices, making their way from one meeting to the next. They turned to look at him as he ambled along the corridors in his knock-off Kappa trackie and Nike Air Max trainers, an orange and green animation in the static grey surroundings. It was funny, he thought, after all this time, how people still gave him these looks. He didn't care, he even liked it. He was feeling pleased; as usual, it made him feel defensive. He put on a little swagger.

He went to his room, but Ray wasn't there. Livvy appeared down the corridor, beckoning him, but he waved a hand at her and swaggered his way upstairs and across the open-plan, where all the desk jockeys – also a little muted, he noticed – stopped to watch him pass and breeze into the Super's office without knocking, where he found Ray with Wallace and DCC Chester Lynch, who stopped their conversation and turned together to look at him.

A moment's silence.

'Oh, yeah?' Ryan said, wary. He knew instantly from Ray's face that something was coming.

'Ah, Wilkins. You know the Deputy Chief Constable,' Wallace said. He hesitated, glancing sideways at Lynch, who stood in Barko's usual position in front of the window, gazing expressionlessly at Ryan.

'Come to lend a hand?' Ryan said to her, deadpan.

She said nothing. Took off her Aviators, carried on gazing.

Wallace made some awkward-sounding preparatory noises, said, 'Ray has just informed me he's taking up a position in the National Uplift programme, working with the DCC.'

Ryan looked at Ray. Ray held his eyes for a moment and looked away. Ryan jerked his chin at him. 'Going up in the world, is it? Big desk job?'

Wallace said, 'An ambassadorial role, as I understand.'

'Course it is,' Ryan said. 'Looks good on TV, thinking woman's copper. Got the vocab.' He shook his head. 'Ray, mate,' he said.

Wallace twitched, cleared his throat. 'Appointment with immediate effect,' he said.

Ryan started to react. 'You're shitting me. You are fucking shitting me.'

'Wilkins!' Wallace said, the slab of his jaw moving up and down, making his cheeks quiver. 'Provision is being made for a certain amount of Ray's time—'

'Talk about betrayal. We're in the middle of this Zara Fanshawe thing; you can't just pull him out of it to go sit in front of the cameras and talk shite about equal fucking opportunities.'

185

'*Wilkins!*' Wallace produced a sound of a hundred-per-cent-proof fury, and there was a momentary silence in which Lynch said calmly, in her usual east-of-Tower-Hamlets drawl, 'Use your head, son. You're only here 'cause of equal opportunity.'

'I'm at the messy end, mate. Isn't that where you started? How long before you put your feet up and pushed paper?'

Wallace was turning different colours. 'For Christ's sake, Wilkins—'

Lynch didn't move. She said, 'It's alright. Don't mind passion; I like it. But I was Detective Superintendent at your age and still working the streets. So, you need to get your thinking in order.'

'Seen some of your street work the other day,' Ryan said. 'Sloppy done. Maybe should have stuck it longer, learned how to do it right.'

Wallace moved now to physically intervene.

Lynch put her hand on his arm. 'Wait.' She looked at Ryan. 'Got the floor, go ahead.'

There was silence and, in it, Ryan made the mistake of looking at Ray, who closed his eyes and slowly, sadly, shook his head; a moment passed between them, and all the wild, irresponsible anger went out of him.

'Forget it,' he said.

'Right, now you'll apologise,' Wallace said.

Lynch shook her head. 'It's alright; he's perked me up. But I still want to hear what he's got to say. Come on, don't be bashful.'

Ryan stood there fidgeting, drenched in the feeling that he'd lost control and gone too far.

'Don't matter,' he said, standing alone in Lynch's gaze.

For a moment, she said nothing. Then she spoke: 'Dave here's a good man. Lucky break for you. Me, I don't believe in second-chances bullshit.' She pointed at Ryan with her Aviators. 'Saw your presser, couple of days ago. Sloppy done, as you put it. You've had too many chances, that's your problem.' She put on the Aviators, paused a moment. 'Some people find the strength to change. Far as I'm concerned, the others can fuck off.'

She waited a moment, as if to let Ryan respond, and, when he didn't, nodded curtly to Wallace and Ray and walked away, out of the office and through the open-plan, which fell completely silent as she went.

What was left, the aftermath, among the remains of the confrontation, might have been almost as painful, but at that moment there were rapid footsteps outside and Livvy appeared in the doorway, her usual calm disarranged.

'Incident just called in, Garsington Road. Involving a vagrant – a man with a trolley.'

Ryan and Ray ran out.

187

TWENTY

They fought their way through early rush-hour traffic on to the Garsington Road, past stationary vehicles queuing for the ring road.

They did not speak or look at each other.

They reached the old garage. It sat on the corner of St Luke's Road, opposite the business park, an empty hulk disused since the newer Shell station was built nearby. In the early days of its abandonment, anti-climb fencing had been erected round the forecourt, but over the years it had fallen, and it lay now in rusty sections along the cracked concrete and behind the old pumps. In the past, sex workers had gathered there for the kerb crawlers, and dealers still occasionally met under the canopy, but generally it was deserted. Now, a patrol car was parked on the forecourt and a small group of people stood there with the half-reluctant, half-fascinated manner of those who find themselves witness to something out of the ordinary. Even as Ray and Ryan ran from their car, they could see the body lying on the ground, like a bundle of clothing.

After a moment, they recognised her as the homeless woman they had talked to in the graveyard of St Thomas the Martyr. Lena. She lay crumpled on her side, her face cushioned on a spreading pool of blood. Next to her was an overturned shopping trolley, its contents spilled across the concrete. The young officer who had found her was in shock. 'She's going to die,' he said, every few seconds, staring hard into their faces, as if demanding to be told he was wrong. He'd arrived just after the assault, half an hour earlier, alerted by the sight of people running across the road towards the garage, and had found the woman conscious but unable to speak, lying next to the overturned shopping trolley, which a witness said belonged to the man who had assaulted her. He could say no more.

They left him shaking and went to talk to the witness, a youth in a grey hooded top, immediately identifiable as someone sleeping rough. He was frightened. He hadn't been doing anything, he said, nothing at all. He'd been resting in the doorway of the old kiosk, where he had set up a little tent. He heard the screams and saw them fighting by the old pumps, a wild old man in multiple coats and the woman. The man was shouting at her, pulling her about by her hair, hitting her with what looked like a coat hanger, and she was screeching and trying to get away. They fell together on to the ground and she was curled up like she couldn't move and the man got up holding something he'd picked up – a bar, a rod maybe – and he hit her with it, over and over, until he was tired. When he saw people coming, he limped away down St Luke's Road.

'He's fucking mental,' the youth said.

'Seen him before?'

'Yeah. Waitrose, they call him. Always got that trolley with him, collects rubbish in it or something.'

Ray nodded. 'What about her?'

'Comes round now and then.'

'Shouting at her. What was he shouting?'

The youth shrugged. '*Whore.* Used to be, what I heard. Didn't need to go on about it, though.'

'Anything else?'

'Usual shite about being moved on. He's like some sort of fucking preacher, you know.'

Ryan said, 'What about her? She say anything?'

'Screaming, mainly.'

'Nothing specific?'

'Well . . .'

'What?'

'There was something, but I can't . . .'

'Can't what?'

'Can't remember.'

'Try.'

'Yeah, but . . .' He shifted around half-heartedly. 'Got something wrong with my memory.'

'Course you have,' Ryan said. 'Too many fucking doses of Spice. How about you come down the station, or maybe you and me just go behind the garage, here, nice and quiet, and I can give your head a couple of shakes, see if we can free your memory up – alright with you?'

'Wait, wait. I've remembered.'

'Go on.'

'*She found you.* Said it over and over. *She found you, didn't she?* Kept saying it at him.'

'Interesting. And what did he say to that?'

'Nothing, just made him wilder.'

The young officer called out, his voice half a pitch too high. 'She's gone!'

They ran over and Ray moved him away, kneeled to take Lena's pulse. Briefly, he looked at Ryan and shook his head. Scraping her mouth free of blood and vomit, he hauled her on to her back and began CPR, heels of his hands on her bony chest, shoving in short thrusts – shoving, pausing, stooping to listen, shoving again – saying nothing, eyes fixed on her face. In the distance, a siren, miles and miles away. Pinching her nose, Ray bent over, glued his mouth to hers. His hand was in the pool of her blood. Then he began to shove again. Clumsy prints of her blood spread across her chest.

A few minutes went by with a sort of slow-motion uselessness. She was the colour of gravel.

'Ray. Ray, mate.'

Ray ignored him, spat out a little blood and vomit, redoubled his efforts. Shoved, blew, listened, shoved. Short sharp thrusts, hard enough to hurt, if she had been capable of being hurt. The sirens were closer.

Shoved, blew, listened.

'She's breathing,' he said.

The ambulance bumped on to the forecourt and the paramedics took over.

The young officer was sitting on the ground, receiving treatment. Lena was being loaded on to the wheeled stretcher. Ryan and Ray stood together at the edge of the crowd.

'Fuck, Ray. You did it. You fucking saved her.'

Ray said nothing.

'Thought she'd had it.'

Traffic had arrived and they were trying to move on the rubberneckers, standing in the road making old-fashioned hand gestures. The late-afternoon gloom had deepened, car lights shimmering in exhaust fumes; buildings in the business park opposite were illuminated aquariums in the twilight.

'Got blood on your jacket, though,' Ryan said, after a while. 'What is it, Hilfiger?'

Ray shrugged.

'You got to go with the medics, get checked.'

Ray wiped his mouth. 'I know that.'

They stood there awkwardly. Ryan went into a wincing dance of fidgets until he broke out again: 'Look, Ray . . . Ray, mate—'

'Forget it.'

'You'll miss saving people's lives when you've gone, you know.'

'I don't want to talk about it.'

They stood there, waiting for the ambulance to be ready.

After a while, Ray said, 'Wallace and the DCC negotiated a transition period. I can give half my hours to the case for the next fortnight. Livvy can step up.'

Ryan made a noise. 'Yeah, but . . .'

'Yeah, but what?'

'It's just . . .'

'Just what?'

'Can't do it without you.'

Ray said nothing to that.

After a while, Ryan made another noise, but, before he could speak, his phone rang: Livvy, wanting an update. He filled her in. 'Brief the APW team. . . . Yeah, down towards the shops at Templars Square and Florence Park, out by Rose Hill Cemetery. Allotments there, end of the Grates, know where I mean? . . . Yeah, I know it's been forty minutes, but he's a limping old man, how far can he get?'

The ambulance was nearly ready.

'What I came to tell you in Barko's office,' Ryan said. 'It's him Zara was looking for – Waitrose. He's the dangerous fuck she was scared of but needed to find. Few years ago, the deluded bastard mistook some other blonde woman for her and gave her a beating. When the real Zara turned up a few days ago, I reckon he tried to rip her head off. And now,' he said, 'he's had a good go at killing Lena.'

Ray nodded, turned away.

'What's he going to do next?'

Ray made no reply.

'Something to pull on, at least.'

Ray shrugged.

Ryan went on. 'Still don't add up, though. Why was she looking for him? What connection could there be between a fancy celeb like Zara Fanshawe and an old derelict like Waitrose?'

They stood there, thinking about that, and at last the ambulance was ready.

Ryan said, 'Can't get far, though, right?'

Ray looked at him a moment without speaking, then walked away and got into the ambulance, and Ryan went back to his car and headed towards St Aldates.

★

It was ten o'clock when Ryan left the station. He was tired. There had been more paperwork, the presser. At the hospital, Lena had not regained consciousness; she remained in a critical condition, prognosis gloomy. Ray had remained uncommunicative. Waitrose remained at large. Last thing, Barko had treated him to his worst dressing-down yet – he'd insulted the DCC, he'd disgraced himself, he'd let down the force, he'd betrayed the trust placed in him by Barko himself – a twenty-minute tirade in which the Super had changed colour thirteen times and had to sit down twice.

Worst of all, he had missed little Ryan's bedtime yet again.

Now, at least it was over. His tiredness filled him, weighted him down. He stood outside Carol's front door, breathing in and out, the night thick and dark overhead, though it gave him no comfort to lift his face and look at it. As always, though, his natural buoyancy worked its magic. The day had finished. Carol was waiting for him. He could ask her again about her flower-shop cards, maybe get somewhere with that, have something to eat, a sit-down, maybe later a bit of the other. He could make it up to little Ryan.

She opened the door and stood in the doorway.

'You would not fucking believe the day,' he said. 'Looking fit, by the way.'

She did not move. Folded her arms. 'Listen,' she began, as if reluctantly. 'You and me.'

Her tone caught him off guard, made him stupid.

'Yeah?' he said, stupidly.

'Come to the end. Let's not kid ourselves, Ryan. Not happening, is it?'

He stood there, cocked his head to one side as if he hadn't heard. After a while, he realised his mouth was open. As if to take advantage of that, he began to speak, though without knowing what to say. Some words came out at random.

'This is a bit sudden.'

'Time for talk's gone, Ryan. Time to move on now.'

'Is . . . is this 'cause of Ry, 'cause he don't want to—?'

'Not just that.'

She didn't elaborate. She let the silence do its work. Somewhere in the woods, an owl was calling for its mate.

'You know me. Got no patience for indecision. We're both adults. Let's get it done, eh? Clean break's best.'

He shuffled about. 'Oh. Right, then.'

'You'll thank me.'

'You reckon?'

'Take care of yourself, alright?'

He stayed where he was.

She shut the door.

For a moment, he stood there, looking at it. Weird, he thought. He'd been moved on. What was he feeling? Small, the size of something picked up and dropped again. A memory came to him of another woman shutting the door on him – Shel – only, that time, he'd been dumping her. He'd had enough, couldn't handle her anymore. He remembered the way her face bent out of shape as he turned to go, and wondered now what his own face was doing. A little jolt of delayed anger went through him and he thought briefly about kicking the door or throwing back his head and shouting at the sky, though he did neither of those things. Instead, he turned and went quietly back across the gravel, just hoping the Peugeot would start.

Night deepened, hours passed, the temperature dropped, the darkness thickened further. Over the doorways of Blue Boar Street and Cornmarket, over the pavements of Blackfriars, the churchyard camps of St Ebbe's and St Thomas the Martyr, down by the canal, under bridges and in underpasses, it curdled into freezing rain, drifting across the feckless, the sad, the inebriated, who shifted restlessly with useless anger under wet cardboard or found their way, beaten and numb, into the dirty concrete crevices of the elegant city. It thickened too over a dark scrap of waste ground in between the office blocks of Oxford's 'Knowledge Centre' next to the ring road, where, carefully staying out of the light, a wild old man was standing in the darkness, talking on a stolen phone.

'You always were a cold-hearted bastard. Don't you understand? She came to see me. Me! I've got my fucking self-respect. . . . No, I can't stay here; I need help. . . . They know me, that's why – they'll find out. . . . Where? Kassam? . . . Alright, I know it. I need money; the fuckers took it. Lost my trolley too, everything I got. . . . You better. . . . Never mind what I done. How do I know I can trust you? . . . Tomorrow, yes. I tell you, you better.'

Then he was on the move again, limping erratically, moaning to himself, occasionally stopping to curse, hurrying on again, heading for the underpass and the low, dark mass of Blackbird Leys beyond, the filthy nest of his head shaking as he looked jerkily from side to side, his bad leg slapping wide, his sloppy old Magnum Panthers kicking up the wet dirt as he went.

196

TWENTY-ONE

Lena Wójcik was thirty-five years old. Born in Racibórz, in southern Poland, she had made her way to London at the age of sixteen, after the deaths of her parents, and, two years later, in 2005, found herself in Oxford, where she was questioned twice for soliciting near the Garsington Road twenty-four-hour garage. Back in London shortly afterwards, she acquired a domestic-abuse specialist, a recovery worker, a criminal-justice support provider, an addictions counsellor and a sex-worker outreach officer, and was constantly on the move, struggling and failing, struggling again and aging fast. She had been living rough for about a year. Six months earlier, she'd returned to Oxford and was currently trying to qualify for one of the flats in sheltered accommodation.

Against the odds, she'd survived the night, but had not yet come out of her coma. The nurses were primed to alert them as soon as she regained consciousness, if she did. Nadim delivered her report in her usual brisk manner, glancing occasionally at Ryan, who was staring distractedly out of the window.

'And, the last couple of days,' Livvy added, 'she's been going round looking for Waitrose. Motive uncertain. We hear she had a fight with him in St Ebbe's churchyard a few days ago.'

Barko grunted. 'Zara knew this Waitrose, trying to find him. Lena knew this Waitrose, also trying to find him. Connection between them?'

They did not know.

'What do we know about Waitrose?'

Waitrose had vanished.

Barko said, 'But what do we *know* about him? Literally all we seem to have got's a nickname.'

There was nothing else known yet about the wild old man. There was only that incident in 2011, which had featured in Ryan's report of his visit to O'Hanlon.

'Didn't go anywhere. Violent Crime shut it down.'

Nadim had started trawling the police databases, but it was hard going without even a name. 'Waitrose' did not feature in the official records. Violent Crime did not seem to have recorded it at all – sloppiness or pragmatism, depending on your point of view. Perhaps some details would turn up in another part of the system.

Ryan stared, unfocused, out of the window as diligent Livvy rounded up loose ends to pull together. She asked Ryan if he'd gone back to ask Carol about the flower-shop card that had been found in Zara's bag.

He looked up, shook his head, mumbled something about doing it soon, seeing again in his mind Carol's face as she closed the door on him.

'You alright, son? Too much for you, is it, all this?' Barko growled.

Ryan tried to snap out of it. He talked about the shakedown of the homeless community. If Waitrose had gone to ground, chances were there was a vagrant somewhere who knew where he was. But it wouldn't be easy. They had started first thing that morning and it wasn't going well. The homeless did not want to talk to the police. Living on the streets, they were good at picking up the vibes of the city, the moods and reflexes of law enforcement; they sensed what the police were going to do before they knew it themselves. When officers arrived at the well-known churchyard sites, the usual doorways and canal sides, they often found them abandoned and had to follow the trails of migration out to hideaways in the parks and under flyovers, in the fields and around industrial units. They were moving with painful slowness through all the necessary momentary encounters, bumping, as they rarely did, into these other lives, sad or vivid, exhausting or strange.

'Could do with a hand,' Ryan said. 'I mean, where's Ray?'

Barko breathed in and out a few times, made it seem like an unusual and difficult procedure. 'We discussed all this yesterday, Wilkins. He can't be here all the time. I believe he's going to a meeting with the DCC this morning, off site.'

Ryan made a noise.

Barko made a face. 'Listen, I'm expecting you to step up,' he said. 'So, you better get used to it, and fast. Dismissed.'

Out they went.

Chester was waiting in the lounge of a hotel at Sandford-on-Thames, just outside Oxford. At that time of the day, it was deserted, and she sat alone in the corner of the room, wearing her trademark jeans and leather jacket, occasionally looking at her watch. In a few days, she was going to be on a flight to Washington. Before then, she had to move fast. All her life she'd been a fighter, the sort of person who makes things happen, who instinctively goes towards trouble. On the streets of Walthamstow, in the tutorial rooms of Exeter College, Oxford, in the boardrooms of the police force, in different ways, she'd confronted those who tried to bring her down. No different now. She was older, of course – the battles in the force, with the suits, with the politicians, had slowed her down – she couldn't deny that she occasionally got tired. But her virtues were determination, decisiveness, courage and outright aggression; and, in the end, she got what she wanted. Through the picture window, she saw the car draw up. She took off her Aviators and closed her eyes for a moment. She heard footsteps on the flagstones outside, then inside, then the scrape of the chair opposite her.

She opened her eyes and they looked at each other.

Carol said, 'You ought to be scared.' She was flustered, but defiant.

Chester carried on looking at her for a while. At last, she spoke, her usual cockney drawl, but low and fierce: 'Not as scared as you, Carol.'

They sat, looking at each other, in silence.

Morning turned to afternoon, afternoon lengthened and failed and began to disappear in turn, into the drizzle, the murk of roadside slush and slops in overworked drains, in the hidden doorways and on the slick far-distant pavements where the homeless had taken their bedding, hoping to be undisturbed.

In a concrete underpass, with ring-road traffic thundering overhead, Ryan found a man with a horse on a bit of rope, who claimed he'd 'rescued' it.

'Rescued it from what?'

'Looked like ready to cough, only reason I took a hold on it. Humanitarian.'

'Know about horses, do you?'

'Know where to find them.'

Ryan took a bag of Spice and some pills off him, and learned nothing. The guy asked for the horse back. 'It knows me, see.'

Rain had settled in after lunch, it persisted through the dusk that started to fall soon afterwards; people became shadows against walls, bundles on the ground. A day that vanished but never seemed likely to end. Three times, Ryan tried to speak to little Ryan, but each time his son would not take the phone from Auntie Jade.

'I know I've fucked up. But I wanted to tell him I'm not going to be going to Carol's no more. And this is a bit . . .'

'A bit what, Ryan?'

'A bit, I don't know, a bit unfair.'

'He's three, you knobhead – it's not about fairness, it's about promises. Listen, he thinks he's losing you. He lost his mother, remember? Kid's going to feel it.'

'Tell him I'll be home tonight, for sure.'

He carried on with the manhunt.

Towards the end of the day, Ray joined the team, after his protracted appointments with the careers people, and went with Livvy through the backstreets of Botley and on to the meadows at Hogacre, where a camp had been set up in scrubland beside

Hinksey Stream. Two women and a girl sat on tarpaulin, wrapped in duvets blotted grey with rain. They half-heartedly complained about the violation of their rights and asked for cigarettes or sweets. They knew Waitrose and hoped he would be locked up. They didn't like him; he 'talked funny'. Lena, they said, was nice but unpredictable. They told Ray the Mover was coming – she'd been seen among them, a rumour made real, like an ogre or the sandman – and suggested Ray tuck them up for the night.

They learned two things. In the days before his disappearance, Waitrose had been visited by a woman driving a big car, an elegant, well-spoken woman, who had gone round the pitches and camps asking for him: she had something to give him, she said. And, at some point, Waitrose had complained of being robbed – not of the usual things, like alcohol or bedding, but of actual cash money. But they did not learn where he was. Perhaps no one knew. Or else the homeless people were too frightened to give such hard information to the police; everywhere they went, they heard about being moved on. With his constant warnings about the coming of the Mover, Waitrose had been the prophet – and the police were the prophecy come true. If they were physically mobile – many were not – the homeless fled at the sight of them, staggering away loaded with possessions too precious to leave behind: blankets, plastic sheeting, phones, bottles.

Night fell dark and early, and the rain slowly intensified, giving senseless voice to the gutters and drains. At 5.30 p.m., Ryan got a call from one of the DSs who'd been at the McDonald's up at Headington. There had been an incident and they were back at St Aldates with a guy who had something interesting to tell them. Ryan told him to call Ray and meet him there in ten.

TWENTY-TWO

They found that, in those ten minutes, the homeless guy had managed to get himself a lawyer. They stood there gloomily, looking at the two of them waiting at a table in C3, a lady in a pencil skirt and irreproachable jacket, and a youth with a foxy, grown-old face.

'Know him,' Ryan said. 'Couple of years above me at school. Dozy little prick. He won't remember me.'

They picked up the report and went in.

LOCATION: C3, windowless subterranean lair, foul repository of other people's sweat.

INTERVIEWERS: DI Wilkins (Raymond), in Aran cable-knit zip-neck sweater and BOSS blue denims, and DI Wilkins (Ryan), in something silver and green.

INTERVIEWEE: Keefer, wet and dirty.

LAWYER: Maddy Tompkins, Wild and Crippen Associates.

WILKINS (RAY): Do you know why you're here, Keefer?

KEEFER: [silence]

WILKINS (RAY): Keefer?

KEEFER: Don't have to say nothing, what I been told.

WILKINS (RAY): When DS Holmes approached you this evening, in order to ask a few routine questions about an ongoing enquiry, you shouted to one of your companions, and I quote, 'Fuck me, it's the rozzers. Get the stash.' What did you mean by that, Keefer?

KEEFER: Like I said.

WILKINS (RAY): 'Stash', Keefer?

KEEFER: The finger, basically.

WILKINS (RAY): DS Holmes subsequently apprehended a zippered holdall which had been flung into nearby bushes, and discovered in it cash, in fifty-pound notes, to the approximate value of four thousand, six hundred pounds. Where did this money come from, Keefer?

KEEFER: Mum's the word.

WILKINS (RYAN): Fuck me, Keefer – who wasted four hundred of it?

KEEFER: That were Spitty Pete, he . . . Sorry. As before, nothing to say.

WILKINS (RYAN): You give Spitty four hundred?

KEEFER: Didn't give it him.

WILKINS (RYAN): *Spitty?* Are you fucking nuts?

KEEFER: He swiped it. I'll get him, now.

WILKINS (RYAN): What's Waitrose going to say when he finds out?

KEEFER: He can—

TOMPKINS, MADDY: Enough. You're leading my client, as

you know. Any answers to such questions will be inadmissible.

KEEFER: Yeah, actually. Thought you'd got me going, eh?

WILKINS (RYAN): Keefer, mate, you were almost there.

KEEFER: Suck on it, Fed.

WILKINS (RAY): Seriously, Keefer. We just need to know where you got the money.

KEEFER: Not happening. You're fucking well inadmissible, mate.

WILKINS (RAY): Such a large amount of cash in the possession of someone without means is quite a puzzle, Keefer. We'll obviously have to investigate that.

KEEFER: Don't bother me. Gets me out of the wet.

WILKINS (RYAN): Ray. Ray, mate. Tough guy, here. Too tough to crack. Tell you what, Keefer, take a break, have a leak, whatever; we'll get some sandwiches in, talk it over. Alright with your lawyer? Ten minutes.

TOMPKINS, MADDY: Keefer?

KEEFER: Yeah, sound. Anything with cheese, has to be gluten-free, though, 'cause I'm vegan, right. No tomatoes, can't take those love apples, man.

WILKINS (RYAN): Good enough. Toilets down there, on the left.

The St Aldates gents for visitors is a functional space containing three stalls and two cubicles, clean but somehow flimsy, with a mild, disturbing echo. Keefer was relieving himself when one of the Feds settled in at the stall next to him. The one dressed in – what was it called? – lounge wear, that was it. Fucking eyesight problems, must be. Keefer suppressed a smile.

There were a few moments of companiable silence.

Then the Fed spoke. 'Won't remember me.'

Keefer gave him a glance. 'Inside?' he hazarded. 'Did six month in Spring Hill.'

'No, Keefer. Managed to stay out of prison. School. Couple of years below you.'

Keefer shrugged, splashed a little.

'Knocked around with some of your mates, though. Mick Dick, remember him?'

Keefer gave the Fed a longer look. He began to smile. 'I remember you now.'

'There you go.'

'Skinny little cunt.'

'Well, thank you, Keeefer.'

'Fucking that funny-looking Irish whore, right?'

He didn't see the arm move. If it was the arm. Something hard connected with the side of his head; something else crashed into a tender part of his back he hadn't ever been aware of before; then, for some reason, he was doubled up and his face was in the stall, where it was being used to clean the urinal. Then he was against the wall, sort of high up, suspended by his throat. He began to make much-delayed noises.

The Fed said, 'Talking about the mother of my son, you piece of toilet slime. Just made it personal, didn't you? Bad move, Keef. Anger-management issues and I'm having a bad day. Understand what I'm saying? Give me a sign.'

Feet twitching uselessly in the air, Keefer gave a short bark, an instinctive noise from race memory. Then his scrabbling toes felt the tiled floor again, and he had the chance to gulp air, just once, before the Fed kicked his feet away, and he sat down hard in the wet. The Fed placed a foot on his knee, the bad one, and put some weight on it.

'Heard of the Mover?' he asked, in a calm voice totally inappropriate for the amount of pain and distress he was causing.

Keefer nodded violently, made mad conjuring gestures above his bending knee.

'Me and the Mover.' The Fed crossed two fingers and held them in front of Keefer's face. 'Like that. Know what I'm saying? Thing is, I say the word, you're not going to have another night's peace. Ever. You're never going to get in O'Hanlon again. All those cushy numbers in the Julians going to be shut to you. You're going to be moved on, and moved on, and moved on. And, in the end, Keefer, you're going to be found one night in the Hogacre ditch with your testicles in your pocket. Getting through to you now?'

Keefer began to weep.

'Or you can just tell us, nice and sweet, you got the money off Waitrose – which we already know, by the way – and you can go back to drinking yourself to death without any hassle whatsoever. Nod if you think that's a good plan.'

Keefer made wild movements with his head, some of which were nods. The Fed removed his foot.

'Really glad we had this chat, Keefer. Appreciate it. Best get back. Clean yourself up first, eh? Piss and pubes round the mouth, never a good look.'

★

It was late. They knew, finally, that Waitrose had recently had in his possession five thousand pounds in cash. The surprising truth was that Zara had spent the day before her murder touring the homeless camps looking for him in order to give him the money. By chance, Keefer had been one of those she talked to and, by another chance, he was also at the Becket Street camp when she finally caught up with the old man and handed over the bag. Naturally, Keefer had swiped it at the earliest opportunity, setting in train the usual comedy-capers chaos of fury and chase.

But, the reason why Zara had given Waitrose the money in the first place, they did not yet know. Why would she seek out a dangerous old vagrant to give him such a large amount of folding money? But no more could be discovered that night; the homeless had crept like animals into the nooks and crannies of the city to wait out the hours of darkness.

'Glad you turned up, by the way,' Ryan said. 'In the end.'

Ray made no comment.

'Now you're here, you can help me get the paperwork done.'

Ray looked at his watch, shook his head. 'Got another meeting.'

Ryan made a noise, half air, half moisture.

'You think I'm doing half a job, Ryan, but, the truth is, I'm doing two.'

With that, he left, and Ryan returned alone to their office, where he made a brief, bitter call to Jade, to tell her that he wouldn't be home for bath and bedtime, and reluctantly began to work his way through a series of reporting documents.

An hour passed, the building drained of staff, lights went off and he worked on; and, at nine o'clock, he got a call from the front desk: there was a guy with two children downstairs to see him.

'What guy?'

'Says his name's Gary.'

Ryan thought about that; he looked at his watch, sighed.

Waiting in reception was a thickset, round-shouldered man wearing blue overalls stained black with rain. Sitting behind him were two children, still in their school uniforms. After a moment, Ryan recognised him as Carol's ex, a man he had seen only twice and had never spoken to.

The man said, not quite aggressively, 'Do you know where she is?'

'Carol?'

'She's not at home.'

Something went through Ryan, he couldn't get hold of it, a twinge of alarm, but something else too, some other form of fear, some prickle of strangeness, disturbing and suspicious.

He buzzed open the door. 'Better come through.'

In the meeting room, the two children sat close together in silence and Gary paced in front of them while he talked. Carol hadn't picked up the kids from school, he said. At four thirty, he'd got a call from a teacher and had dropped work and driven back from Bicester to get them and take them to Carol's, but she wasn't there. He'd had no word from her, either then or later. Whenever he called her, he just got voicemail. According to a girl who worked in one of her florists, she'd left the shop at lunchtime and hadn't returned.

'Something's happened,' he said. 'She never forgets school pickup.'

'Range Rover missing?'

Gary nodded.

'Got the reg?'

Ryan put out an APW, while Gary fiddled with the straps of his overalls.

'So, what do you think's happened?' Ryan asked.

Gary had no idea. His attitude towards his ex seemed to be a mixture of resentment, respect and fear, and, like many practical, down-to-earth people, when confronted with the inexplicable, his imagination tended towards the sensational. He thought her body was in a dumpster somewhere or at the bottom of the river.

'You'll have to explain that one.'

Gary told Ryan what little he knew about Carol's money worries. 'Big ones,' he said. 'Serious.' In his opinion (in fact, in Ryan's too), if Carol was desperate, she'd fight hard – dirty, if necessary – to protect what was hers; she wouldn't hesitate to take risks, even stupid risks. Gary thought she could have got herself in trouble with the wrong sort of people.

'What people?'

He seemed to imagine loan sharks, extortionists, criminals. People who, if they didn't get their money back, took you outside, and, if you were lucky, they only broke your legs.

'Does she know anyone like that?'

He looked away. 'She could've got herself in trouble,' he repeated stubbornly.

Ryan thought about it.

Gary had to take the kids back, get them to bed, he said. He gave Ryan a look. 'Came here 'cause I thought she might have gone to yours,' he said. 'Aren't you and her—?'

'Not anymore.'

'Sorry for all this, then.'

Ryan shrugged, watched them go back out through reception into the dark rain, the two children holding hands. Nine thirty. He still had another hour filling in forms, and he turned and went back into the building. He thought of Carol dumping him the night before, her sudden coldness. *You'll thank me*, she'd said. And he thought again of the card for Carol's florists, found in Zara's bag.

Nine thirty turned into ten thirty, a much more depressing hour. He was tired. At last, he finished the paperwork and trudged up to the floor above to put a printout on Barko's desk. Barko wasn't there, his PA wasn't there, most of the lights were out, everyone had left the open-plan; it lay on either side of him, a shadowy complication of silhouetted shapes, an impression of abandoned things – things no one was ever coming back to – and he walked through it to the lift, thinking about Carol, her inexplicable abandonment of her children, and wondering why she'd gone and if she was ever coming back.

He stood in the lift, jabbing the button, suffering with mounting irritation the usual delay. He looked at his watch and groaned and jabbed again. In sober judgement, the day had been a bastard. He stared at the unmoving lift doors with fury. And then, as they finally began to close, there were footsteps outside, a hand reached round and forced the doors open again, and Chester Lynch stepped in.

A moment of mutual shock. They looked at each other mutely, faces clenched, radiating distaste. Then Ryan leaned across her and gave the *Close Doors* button an angry clout. Keeping her eyes on him, Lynch put her hand out and punched a different button. The doors, which had in fact begun to close, came open again, and Ryan made a noise with his mouth, an angry puff of air, not quite an expletive.

Lynch presented him with the blankness of her Aviators. 'Say something?'

Longing to say something, Ryan forced his mouth to stay shut, an effort that made him look cross-eyed, and Lynch remained a moment staring at him, as if in curiosity, before turning away again. Together and apart, they awaited the shutting of the doors, every second slow and heavy, until finally they were sealed in with a hiss and, after another agonising hesitation, began to descend, standing there, still and moving, in the vacuum-like silence, staring at different parts of the lift interior.

Lynch spoke to the doors: 'Hear my Wilkins got you out of trouble last night.'

Ryan said nothing.

'Sloppy work, lose a key witness. Talking about Lena Wójcik.'

Ryan bit his lip, twitched a bit.

For absolutely no fucking reason at all, the lift stopped at the floor below and the doors opened and no one got in, and, after another intolerable delay, the doors closed again and they began to descend once more.

Lynch said, 'Lucky for you, he stepped up and saved her life.'

Ryan lost the struggle with himself. 'Pull him off the case, then – not exactly an operational move of genius.'

Lynch cocked her head on one side, as if listening. 'Know what that is, son? Sound of someone out of their depth. Heard it all my life.'

Now, the lift seemed to be actually stuck. Ryan leaned over and banged the button again and again.

Lynch went on: 'Not surprised. Seen your pressers. Not even across the detail.'

Ryan couldn't help himself. 'Not across the detail? You didn't even breathalyse her.' He immediately wished he hadn't said it.

A pause, a frown, a new level of hostility. 'You taking something, son? 'Cause you're not making sense.'

Ryan willed the lift to continue. It didn't.

'Explain.'

He shuffled about a bit, feeling foolish and angry. 'New Year's Eve 2005. Stopped someone, give her a ticket, didn't breathalyse her.' His sneer was to cover his embarrassment. 'You won't remember. Just pointing it out. Get off your high horse, what I mean.'

In the silence that followed, the lift began to move again.

Lynch said nothing, stared. Then she made a noise. After a moment, Ryan realised she was laughing. She stepped in front of him, put her face up close, slowly took off her Aviators.

'That what this is about? Yeah, well, newsflash for you, son: remembered it soon as the whole Zara Fanshawe thing blew up. That's what you're talking about, right? So, I'll tell you. New Year's Eve. Short-staffed – course we were – half the team had developed slight headaches. Volunteered, went out, drove round all night, taking a look at the beautiful people getting incapable. Must've handed out seven, eight tickets – maybe you been collecting them all. Where was it? North, wasn't it? Wolvercote somewhere?'

'Godstow Road.'

'That's it. Recognised her straight away – course I did, I read the fucking papers, what do you expect? Going about ten mile an hour, both sides of the road. Something going on. Bit weepy. Some guy next to her with a face on him like he'd just stopped shouting. Didn't need to breathalyse her to know her problem wasn't drink.'

'Interesting,' Ryan said, despite himself.

The lift finally reached its destination.

'Is it?' Lynch said. 'Wouldn't know; you're the operational genius here, obviously.'

The doors opened, revealing a group of nighters waiting for the lift, who moved aside deferentially when they saw the DCC. Lynch ignored them. She was still focused on Ryan.

'Me?' she said to him. 'I was just putting the hard hours in, getting the job done. Paying attention to the detail.'

Ryan stood there sullenly, self-conscious in front of this new audience. He tried to see a way past her, but she'd blocked him in.

'Tell you something in private? Don't think you're going to make it. Seen a lot of coppers in my time – good, bad and fucking disgraceful. But you? Class of your own.'

Ryan lifted a hand and made contemptuous talking gestures with it. 'Yeah, yeah.'

A sort of startled rage came into Lynch's face and she lowered and deepened her voice. 'Don't push it with me, son.'

'Why?' Ryan said. 'What you going to do? Take me into a lock-up, shoot me in self-defence? Talk about a fucking disgrace.'

He shoved past her and through the group of bystanders, who parted, open-mouthed. Then he was swaggering away towards the entrance, his face set in a sneer, which, however, was already coming off by the time he reached reception. He hurried on down the steps to the sally port, with the feeling quickly growing – a feeling as personal and disgusting as the smell of his own shit – that, once again, he had gone too far, and this time with the worst possible person, in the worst possible way. He found his way at last to his awful Peugeot, and slammed the door and sat there, trembling. A minute passed, two minutes . . . and, as always, he began to calm down. Something took over, some adrenaline jolt of defiance, some ingrained carelessness. For his life was and always would be a mess of disappointments and contingencies, and only giving two fingers got him through it.

If he was cooked, he was cooked. Fuck it. He'd been cooked before.

He sneered at his wing mirror.

He got his breathing under control. And, almost immediately, he began to think about Zara Fanshawe – he couldn't help himself – it was that glimpse of her that had caught his interest, and now it came back, demanding attention: a young woman in a car on New Year's Eve, fragile and suffering at the thick end of some man's outburst, a detail in a pattern still noticeable seventeen years later in the attic of an abandoned house; and, for the first time, he wondered if the reason for her murder lay in the past. Men, not drugs, had been her problem. Lady Fanshawe had told Ray that. Now, unexpectedly, Lynch had confirmed it.

He drove home slowly, ignoring the banging of the engine. Little Ryan had long been asleep. Jade had gone to bed too. He checked his phone and found a message just arrived from Wallace, telling him to be in his office first thing in the morning: Lynch acting quickly. But he put the thought from his mind and stood at the upstairs window, looking across at the houses opposite, bleakly shining in the weak lamplight, thinking of the homeless camps scattered through the city, the slipshod humps and heaps of damp bedding in doorways, wondering if Waitrose was hiding under one of them. He didn't think so. Waitrose was a danger to the homeless as much as to anyone else; they would keep him out or flee from him. He was on his own now, no one to help him and nothing left but his own animal cunning.

Finally, he was tired. It had been another terrible day. He thought of his sleeping son. In his ear, he heard Jade's voice telling him not to wake him up, and he listened to it for a moment, then tiptoed into the room they shared.

He wasn't going to speak to him. Only look at him.

From the little chair next to the bed, he watched his son sleep, grinning. He listened to the boy's breaths, those small wisps of air, stared amazed at the pink blush of his cheeks, that sheen of hair, so blond and soft and sticky against his hot forehead.

He wasn't going to touch him. Only touch his hair.

He put out a careful hand.

Little Ryan opened his eyes.

Ryan kept grinning, he could feel it pulling his face open.

He wasn't going to talk to him. Only if his son wanted him to.

'Ry. It's me, Daddy.'

Little Ryan stared at him.

'It's late. I've missed you.'

Still his son stared.

'Shall we have a conversation?'

For a moment longer, little Ryan was perfectly, ideally expressionless. Then he burst into loud and violent tears.

Then Jade was in the room.

Then Ryan was out of the room. Mylee, Jade's daughter, had also started to cry.

Then Ryan was downstairs on his own, head in his hands.

Then, finally, his phone rang. He looked at his watch. It was the hospital. Lena Wójcik had regained consciousness.

TWENTY-THREE

At the John Radcliffe Hospital, the Trauma Unit stands separate in its new cladding, pale and dimly shiny now, in cold moonlight, the quiet forecourt ringed with idling ambulances. Here and there, small groups of drivers were having a night-time cigarette, and Ryan went in, along deserted corridors and up to the sixth floor, where he found a nurse, who told him that Lena had come round an hour earlier, very weak and confused. The blows to her head had caused significant swelling and leakage of blood, and she was suffering from post-traumatic amnesia and slight speech impairments. Worse, her general physical and physiological state, the result of so many years on the street and various other complications, were now combining to make her condition critical.

'Recovery chances, on a scale of one to ten?'

She just shook her head. 'Talk to her while you can.'

'Say anything since she come round?'

'Been asking for someone called Jasmine.'

'Jasmine?'

The nurse shrugged. 'Don't expect much from her. She's on a high morphine dose.'

In the small room packed with equipment, Lena lay in the classic hospital pose, unmoving, devoid of expression, wrapped in tubes, head concealed in a protective guard, arms linked to monitors and drips. Only her eyes shifted as Ryan went in, following him round to the chair, where he sat.

'Really done you up, didn't he, Lena?'

Her eyes seemed to register the comment, but she said nothing.

'Want to tell me what happened?'

Silence. Slight twitterings from the surrounding machines. Her breathing made no sound at all. Her eyes had left him and seemed to be following something moving on the ceiling.

'We're looking for him now. Any idea where he is?'

No answer. He tried a different tack.

'What I don't get, Lena, is why you were looking for him.'

Her lips moved, he leaned in.

'What's that?'

'I know what he done.'

'That's interesting. Give me a bit more.'

She gathered her strength, murmured something.

'What's that? Can't hear you, Lena.'

Her eyes closed briefly, but they opened again soon and she sighed, as if trying to rouse herself. Her voice, when it came, was a murmur, almost religious in its otherworldliness.

'Toby.'

'Toby? Is that Waitrose's name?'

Her eyes roamed around the ceiling, distracted. 'They fly to me,' she said wonderingly. 'But they never speak.'

'Lena?' He gave her a wave. 'Tell me about Toby, Lena.'

She looked at him as if surprised to find him there, smiled and closed her eyes. After a moment, she gave a little start and opened them again.

'Didn't know him. He'd changed. She did, she knew.'

Ryan leaned forward. 'Who did?'

She smiled again, the weak impersonation of a smile. 'Goldy hair.'

Ryan leaned further in. 'You talking about Zara? Zara Fanshawe? The woman we showed you in the photograph?'

Now, she lifted her head off the pillow to make a bigger effort. 'I seen him, though, before.'

'Where d'you see him? In London? Here, in Oxford?'

'In town. The Odeon,' she said, after a while.

'On the steps there? That where he hangs out?'

She dozed off for a moment and he watched her. Her eyes fluttered open towards the ceiling.

'What about Zara, Lena? Remember the photograph? Pretty. With the golden hair.'

'Famous,' she said. 'Dressed up fancy.'

She sank back. Her eyes closed again, stayed closed. Ryan got up and walked about, thinking. Twenty minutes or so passed, and she spoke again.

'We were friends.'

He went back to his seat. 'I'm all lost here, Lena. You and Toby? Or you and Zara?'

Lena's eyes shifted about, watching invisible presences on the ceiling.

'They never speak,' she murmured fearfully. 'Why have they

come? What's happening to me?' Her thin fingers clutched the blankets and she looked at Ryan in terror. 'Am I dying?'

'You'll be fine,' he said at last, awkwardly. 'But, Lena. Who was your friend? Was it Toby?'

He thought she smiled. 'Goldy hair,' she murmured. 'What we called her.'

'You mean Zara? Zara was your friend?'

'She can't hurt nobody.' There was a sudden fierce confidentiality in her whisper. 'She's dead.'

'Yeah, she is. You heard about that?'

Lena gave the slightest of nods, began to cry. 'They put her in a bag,' she said.

He frowned. 'A bag?' Something stirred in his memory – Zara on the roof of St Anne's Rehab Clinic, raving, *Kill me now, bag me up.*

Now, Lena's eyes were going wildly from side to side, staring above her. 'I know where they fly to.' Her mad eyes sought his.

'Where?'

She hissed at him: 'The twenty-four-hour.'

He thought about that. 'Up there, on the Garsington Road? Where we found you?'

A sort of terror came into her face, then; it seemed to give strength to her voice. 'Three of us,' she said, 'most nights. Where the bad things happen.' She began to tremble and gasp.

'Who? What bad things?'

With enormous effort, she lifted her head off the pillow, all the tendons in her neck standing out, like a climber reaching up the vertical cliff face above, and her voice, when it came, was a rush of pain and air: 'I was her friend and they put her in a bag!'

221

And now, her trembling got worse, spread through her body, choked off her voice. She gave an enormous shudder, her eyes went wide and she stared at him as if seeing him for the first time. Her mouth was still open and he leaned forward hopefully, but she let out a great groan and fell back. All the monitors in the room threw out alarms at the same time and the nurse ran in.

TWENTY-FOUR

At five thirty, dawn was still hours ahead. Trucks and buses went in and out of the quiet city, their lights moving through darkness. The temperature had dropped; hoar frost sugared the blankets in nooks and crannies where homeless people lay inert or stirred restlessly, trying to get their circulation going; and, in O'Hanlon House, where the more fortunate slept, there were the usual night-time noises and disturbances of nightmares. Up at Rose Hill, it was quiet. But, in his bedroom, Walter spoke from his orthopaedic adjustable bed to the shape of Chester Lynch, silently dressing by a chest of drawers.

'What's wrong, love?'

Lynch did not turn round. 'Nothing wrong. Go back to sleep, Walt.'

'I always know something's wrong when you're out practising this early.'

Lynch adjusted her holster. 'It's nothing. Just the usual bullshit, getting things straight before Washington. An hour in the garden'll sort me out.'

She turned and stood there, to Walt no more than a shadow, then she was gone.

Everything was quiet in Grove Street, too. Ray and Diane sat side by side on the carpet of the spare room, feeding their babies in the orange glow from the teddy-bear-faced night light. They were dull with lack of sleep, and their voices, when they spoke, were flat and low. Ray was exhausted and irritable.

'Anyway,' he said, 'I won't have to put up with him much longer.'

She looked at him. 'Are you sure you won't miss him?'

He snorted. 'I've never worked with anyone so irritating.'

'I thought you'd come to like him. You think he's good.'

'He is good. And I like him for a few minutes, and then I want to gag him.'

Ten minutes passed.

'He can't control himself. Who knows what he'll do next. He's going to get into trouble again.'

Another ten minutes passed.

'Not my problem anymore,' Ray said.

'What about the job, though?'

'What do you mean?'

'Are you sure about it? Are you ready to sit in meetings, do interviews?'

'After this, it'll be a relief.'

She looked sideways at him. He was doing that thing with his jaw: tightening it, pushing it forward.

'The cases, Ray, the investigations. That's what you've always liked.'

He made a dismissive noise.

They fell silent, then; there was quiet for a moment, until Ray's phone rang.

'Christ,' he said, 'it's Ryan. Six o'clock in the morning. He really knows how to pick his moments.'

He answered, listening, and his face came awake suddenly.

'Be there in ten,' he said crisply. Then he'd handed over Felix and was getting his clothes.

'What?' Diane called. 'What is it?'

'We've got him,' he said, as he ran down the stairs.

Priory Road wasn't a road but a path. At the Littlemore end was a mossed-over railway tunnel, too narrow for vehicles; at the Leys end, the ruin of the fifteenth-century Priory Inn. Along one side of the path were meadows, trees and bushes, prickly now with the litter of ice; along the other was the long multi-part block of the Vue cinema and various outbuildings and storage facilities, and, behind them, the Kassam football stadium, grey against white dawn mist. Out of the hush came crow croak and muffled car noise from the ring road.

Ryan was waiting, grinning, by a wooden fence on a patch of bent winter grass glistening with dawn frost.

'Glad you were free to join me.'

'Don't start with that. What's the news?'

'Got the call half an hour ago. Guy sleeping by the bridge down there saw him scavenging in the Littlemore streets, followed him up the path, saw him go into one of these lock-ups.'

Ray was looking around, getting his bearings.

Ryan pointed. 'Out there, just the sewage plant and agriculture.

Littlemore's back that way, where he come up from – residential, Minchery Road, Priory Road, know it?'

'Not really. Why'd he come out here?'

Ryan shrugged. 'Rat up a drainpipe. But how did he get in? Think all these lock-ups be shut up nice and tight, right?'

'You sure he's in there?'

'Well.' Ryan hitched up his trackies, sniffed, wiped with a finger. 'Let's go see.'

The wooden gates were open and they went through to a small yard. There was a white van parked there and some metal drums against the fence and the brick wall of the building, which had four big roller doors set into it, one of which was slightly open at the bottom. Creeping up to it, they waited. Faint noises came from inside: the rattle of something human, footsteps, muttering, grumbling, the odd sobbing note of desperation. They retreated to the fence and spoke in whispers.

'Talking to someone?'

'To himself, I think. He's a mad old fuck, right? By the way . . .'

'What?'

'Lena woke up last night. Had a quick chat, though her head's still all over the place, but what I gathered is his name's Toby.'

Ray looked at him.

'I know. What sort of fuck name for a vagrant is Toby? Know what I think?'

'What?'

'Posh boy fallen on hard times. Those homeless you spoke to down there by Hinksey Stream, they said he talked funny, remember? And why do you think they call him Waitrose, not Lidl or Asda? Upmarket. Makes sense, right?'

Ray thought about that.

'Interesting, though, isn't it? There's other stuff Lena told me, too. Reckon somehow that disused garage on Garsington Road's got something to do with it. Bad things happened there.'

They talked quietly for a few minutes and then fell silent, looking together at the lock-up. The doors were tall enough to get a truck through; it would be a big space inside, more like a warehouse, potentially full of stuff, complications.

'What do you want to do, then? Call in back-up?'

Ray gave a shrug. 'You're lead.'

'Call them now, if you think we got to play it by the book.'

Ray looked at him, gave a snort.

'I can play things by the book. If I feel like it.'

They waited.

'Fuck it, Ray, he's a broken-up old tramp. Think we can't take him?'

Ray shrugged again.

'Another thing. Talking to himself like that. Sounds a bit – what's the word?'

'Perturbed?'

'Nice vocab, very nice – you ought to be in one of them TV jobs. Perturbed, yeah; don't want him doing himself a mischief while we wait out here for armed response, right?'

Ray didn't have time to reply. From inside the lock-up came a different noise, a total surprise – the familiar crack of a gunshot, sudden, harsh, sharp – and, without thinking, they ran, colliding into each other, struggling with the roll-up door, shoving and heaving, rolling inside at last, going instinctively sideways to the walls, moving low. It was dark in there; the echo of the gunshot seemed to reverberate among the shadows. After a moment, they made out shapes: equipment of some sort, crates stacked above head height. Quietly, they moved forward, squirrel-fashion, scuttling a few steps, freezing motionless, scuttling again. They crept between piles of things, peering round corners, seeing nothing in the dimness but boxes, racks, equipment, shaking their heads at each other, sending signals with their hands, everything as tightly controlled and demented as ballet. Ray jabbed a finger. On the ground ahead, just in view, a different shape, something untidy – trouser legs, a pair of boots, toes pointing at the ceiling – and they ran forward together.

He lay on concrete, a bundle of nothing, rags and stink, only his face human, the emaciated face all bone and hair, eyes wide, mouth open, the back and top of his head blown apart like smashed crockery, as if he'd been dropped from a height, head first on to the hard floor, scattering bloody bits around him.

Heads up and cocked, listening, they held their breath. Nothing. They began to move forward again, more urgently now, running crouched from stack to stack, scanning the darkness. There was no one there, they could hear the emptiness, and they ran free through the lock-up to the far side, where they found a door ajar and went through it at pace and came to a halt in a small yard surrounded by a high wooden fence, totally deserted, looking round and around them, like men on a hilltop scanning the distance.

'There.'

Ryan ran forward to the fence, where there were fresh scrabble marks in the splintered wood, and they went over together and ran down the path towards Littlemore, looking about them as they ran. They went past the meadow, accelerating down the slight slope, under the railway bridge, past garages into Minchery Road and stopped there in the middle of the street, panting and looking around. It was quiet here, an ordinary scene at seven o'clock on an overcast, frost-rimmed February morning, nothing to see but a long, still view of flat-fronted houses, hedges, brick walls, fences, paved-over front gardens, pickups and taxis on verges. The common morning affair, completely at peace with itself. As they watched, a delivery van came slowly round the corner, a red post-office van moved away, a front door opened and an elderly man appeared wearing a dressing gown, and a young woman came along the pavement with a pushchair. No, she said, she'd seen no one. Why? They stood there uselessly for a few more minutes and then trudged back up the path, Ryan talking on the phone.

Back in the lock-up, they tiptoed round the body, crouching and peering, picking gently among the filthy clothing. Nothing of interest in the overcoat pockets. A little way off was a nest of cardboard where Waitrose had obviously slept the night. Eventually, the support units arrived, the ambulance and tracker dogs, the forensics team, the crime-scene specialists. Ryan talked more to Nadim and Livvy on the phone, the morning lengthened towards noon, and at last he and Ray went back to the station.

TWENTY-FIVE

Although Ryan had received several texts from Barko, by the time he got to the station Barko was no longer on site.

'Shame.'

Nadim looked at him. 'He was summoned to see the Chief Constable.'

'Oh, yeah?' He looked furtive. 'Say what it was about?'

'No. He was in a bad mood, though.'

He winced.

'Said he wants to speak to you as soon as possible.'

He winced a bit more.

For an hour, he and Ray worked through the usual immediate admin aftermath of a homicide, then the preliminary forensics report landed. Occasionally Ryan remembered what was coming to him and let out a little groan, which he immediately replaced with a sneer, in case Ray looked up.

Barko still didn't come back.

'You'll have to run the briefing,' Nadim said.

'You say that like you think I can't run briefings.'

'No comment.'

They hunkered down in the shared office and took stock. For once, they did not have to take into account any media attention; there wasn't any. The murder of an old homeless man had passed unnoticed. Nadim summarised the forensics report for them: Waitrose had been killed by a single shot to the back of the head, the bullet a 9-mm Parabellum, fired from a Glock-17.

Ray frowned.

'What?'

'Nothing,' he said. 'Just, rules out anyone from the homeless community. They don't carry firearms.'

Ryan asked about Waitrose's boots. 'Noticed he was wearing Magnum Panthers.'

But his ancient, battered Magnum Panthers did not match the prints found at Polstead Road: they were too large. 'Nothing yet to link him definitely to Zara's murder.'

Ryan said, 'Postie identified him as the vagrant he saw in Polstead Road, though.'

Nadim shuffled paper. 'Not in the file, Ryan.'

'Had a word with him day before yesterday; slipped my mind. Anything else from Forensics? Got an ID yet? A tenner says it's Toby something.'

It had just come in from Fingerprints. Waitrose's name was Toby Lewin-Mercer. Privately educated at Lancing College and Oxford University, he was an actor in early adulthood, briefly well known in the late nineties and early noughties for roles in three movies. After that, he had a short run in *Coronation Street* before completely dropping out of sight. According to his former agent, he had found the pressure of the movie

231

and television industries unendurable. It was a spectacular fall from grace: one minute, the go-to actor for nicely spoken, good-looking, floppy-haired Englishmen; the next, a wild old man with a trolley. Matching him up to records of 'Waitrose' in a number of agencies working with the homeless, including O'Hanlon House, they thought that he'd been living rough in Oxford, sometimes dealing drugs among the homeless, for more than twelve years. He'd been subject to numerous complaints about his behaviour over the years and had been interviewed once, as Ryan had found out, about an assault. That was when his prints and details had been taken. He was forty-two years old. More than that they did not yet know. But they had a contact – a friend from Toby's university days – who had already agreed to speak to them.

'Links to someone else, too,' Ryan said. 'Lena. She seemed to know him.' He explained what Lena had told him in the hospital, her confused memories of Toby, her strange comments about Zara.

'Not in the file either, Ryan.'

'Just getting to it.'

Ray said, 'It's possible Toby and Zara had a relationship in the past. Her mother said she dated actors.'

'Good shout. Reckon the same person killed them both?'

'Different MO.'

'Both cases, it was someone who knew what they were doing. Hard to break someone's neck. And Waitrose? That's a fucking execution – that's someone who really knows what they're doing.'

Ray thought about that. 'And someone who knew where they both were. Not an easy thing to find out, in either case. Who knew Zara was camping at Polstead Road? Who knew Waitrose was hiding in that lock-up?'

'Someone with training. It's a skill, that is – finding people. And the way he disappeared this morning. We were right there, Ray. Door-to-door in Minchery Road's all done: there were lots of people up and out at that time; no one saw a thing.'

Momentarily, they were on the same wavelength, thinking about it. Ryan read out loud, with some mistakes, the description of Toby's old friend.

'Already read it,' Ray said, when he'd finished.

Ryan said, 'Point is, if you go have a chat with this guy, you can find out a bit more. Sounds like your type. Posh boy working in something wanky – what was it? – publishing.'

Ray said stiffly that he had a meeting scheduled with the DCC.

'No bother. Do it myself,' Ryan said, after a small, awkward pause. He scratched in exaggeratedly relaxed fashion. 'I can get on with anyone, me,' he said to the room.

Everyone looked in a different direction. Ray and Livvy left, and Ryan sat, biting his cuticles. A few minutes passed. He looked up.

'What?'

Nadim said, 'Rumour going round.'

'Course there is. It's Ryan fucking Wilkins.'

'Argy-bargy in the lift. With the DCC, of all people.'

He snorted, opened his mouth, realised he didn't know what to say, shut it again.

Nadim watched him sympathetically.

'She started it,' he said at last.

233

She stared at him. 'Don't think any of us have got the hang of you yet.'

'Nothing in it,' he said. 'Straight up. Just a bit of banter. She'll be laughing about it today.'

He began to bite his cuticles again, gnawing down hard.

'Think she likes me, really,' he said, after a moment.

'She doesn't like anyone, Ryan.'

'I know that.'

'Ryan.'

'What?'

'It's serious. The DCC. You need to get ahead of it. Anyone you can speak to, put your side of it across?'

'Yeah, absolutely; I'll see if one of my pals on the National Police Chiefs' Council'll speak up for me.'

'You know what I mean.'

'Think I can't speak for myself? I can speak.'

She raised her eyebrows. It was more than he could stand.

'What I'm going to do is get this case cracked, go out with a bang, right?' He picked his ear, rolled something and flicked it. 'Anyway, better go see this publisher. Children's books, it said in the report. Got this book about a mouse and a mole I can talk to him about.'

A short while later, he was following Amit Kandhari out of the sleetish rain into a modest Victorian terrace of the sort favoured by Oxford's culture professionals, the fellows of the university, the publishers, writers, teachers. There were framed prints of botanical drawings on the walls of the hall, and paintings and etchings hanging in the front room, in the spaces between book-shelves, piano and harp.

'Drink, Inspector? Tea, coffee? We have Earl Grey, classic blend and smoky.'

Amit had dazzling teeth and he smiled long and hard at Ryan, who declined the offer and sat on a small sofa in the bay window, waiting for the smile to end. It was a cultured room and Amit was a cultured presence in it, pleasant, articulate and childishly open-faced, sitting smiling in a woollen pullover, corduroys and brown leather shoes decorated with perforations in understated patterns.

'Working at home?'

'In a manner of speaking.'

'Children's books, right?'

Amit said modestly that he was manging director of a small publishing company, yes.

'Heard of *Mouse and Mole*?' Ryan said. 'That's a children's book.'

Amit had heard of it, had read it, was a personal friend of the illustrator, had once tried to buy educational rights in it; he began to talk about it fluently and enthusiastically in both emotional and technical terms, adopting the slightly arch, self-deprecating tone common to publishers of children's books – 'Truly one of the great books on friendship' – and Ryan hastily shut him down.

'Toby, yes,' Amit said. 'It's so long since I last saw him, I don't suppose I'm going to be able to tell you anything useful.'

For some time, that seemed to be true. Gracefully, he sketched out his complete lack of knowledge. He didn't know where Toby had been or what he'd been doing; he didn't know if he had any relatives or other friends. He knew of no one who might have wanted to do Toby harm.

'I'm afraid I'm turning out to be a grave disappointment to you,' he said, after twenty minutes, with a brief flash of teeth.

That was also true.

'The last time I heard from him must have been ten – no, fifteen years ago. That's the way it often works, isn't it, with college friends? You probably find that. We simply went in different directions. Much later, I heard on the grapevine that he was having personal problems, but by then we weren't close and, besides, I had no idea where he was.'

Teeth again.

'Didn't know he was in Oxford, then?'

'Really? Whereabouts?'

'Becket Street churchyard, canal side, Blue Boar Street – anywhere he could get out of the rain.'

No teeth now. He looked aghast.

Ryan went on: 'Yeah, that's it, been living on the street. You might have even seen him, not knowing it – wild old man, pushing a trolley.'

Amit suddenly got hiccups and, getting to his feet, began to walk about the living room, shaking his head in distress and hiccupping, the energy of his shock coming off him like the accidental heat of a physical injury. He was one of those thin-skinned people who have no defences against the blows and disappointments of life.

'I can hardly believe it,' Amit said at last, believing it, but not wanting to. As he sat disconsolate in his chair, even his lovely shoes looked sad.

He could not usefully answer any pertinent questions, but he could at least describe the 'original' Toby, as he put it – the undergraduate. What he'd been like. They'd been students together ('years and years ago') and had kept in friendly contact in a diminishing sort of way for a few years afterwards, gradually losing touch, until finally they saw each other no more; and he began to talk – wistfully, now – about Toby as he had known him. A lovely man, sociable, popular, thoughtful. Good fun: a witty conversationalist, an entertainer with a fund of good anecdotes. Spoke well. Prominent member of OUDS, the student dramatic society.

'Good looking, too,' Amit said, 'in an English sort of way, you know, hair, chin, good nose, I remember. No surprise to anyone he broke through in film and TV.' Looking back, there was even a moment when Toby was actually, properly famous. Big parts, exotic locations, beautiful girlfriends, the whole red-carpet life.

'What happened?'

Amit didn't know. He speculated that the entertainment world was a difficult place in which to be happy: too much glamour, too much sudden wealth, too much scrutiny.

'Toby always liked a drink,' he added. 'Perhaps that was the problem.'

'Girlfriends? Remember any names?'

There had been lots, they came and went, glimpsed on Toby's arm at receptions, gala events, opening nights. 'He must have dated every eligible bachelorette going.'

'Zara Fanshawe one of them?'

Amit realised he was on the verge of giving useful information and perked up. 'I can tell you something about that. They didn't

237

just date, they were engaged for a time. Yes. I thought of it the other day, when I heard about . . .' He drifted off for a second. 'Met her myself,' he said. 'Lucky me.' The teeth reappeared, but vanished immediately. 'You don't think their deaths are connected, do you?'

'Why would they be connected?'

He squirmed. 'No reason.'

'Where did you meet her?'

'At the party when they announced their engagement. Rooms in St Hilda's College, here. A wild night, if I remember. My God. Drunken punting after midnight. Fireworks. Someone kissed a horse, I think. You know what it's like in Oxford. But I can still see them driving off together at the end of the evening, everyone waving. He was renting a little place out in Garsington village. She was a little – how shall I put it? – unsteady. He seemed very happy.' He became wistful again. 'Last time I saw him, I think. I wonder, now, how happy he really was. At any rate,' he added, 'the engagement was over almost as soon as it began – within days, I think. Toby was like that, of course. He could never seem to settle, somehow.'

Ryan watched him for a while, but Amit said no more. At last, Ryan stood to go. 'Don't suppose you could lay your hand on a photo of Toby, could you? As a young man.'

Amit didn't think he could, not easily, though he could fish one out later, probably, fingers crossed. He lived optimistically in a world of these mild contingencies. 'Oh, wait a minute – he's in my college photo. Over here.'

The photograph hung at the far end of the room, above the piano, a framed landscape-format group portrait, prominently decorated with a heraldic device and inscribed by hand in fanciful blue and gold script: *Exeter College Matriculation, 1998*. It showed several banks of teenagers, identically dressed in black gowns, ranged on a fringe of expensive lawn against a backdrop of historical masonry.

Amit pointed and Ryan leaned in. Tall Toby Lewin-Mercer sat in the centre of the front row, shoulders slightly hunched, as if surreptitiously trying to avoid contact with those sitting next to him. Like the others at the front, he was holding a mortar board over his knees. A thick strand of floppy hair bent over his left eye. His face was soft, almost feminine. He looked pleased, a little vulnerable and very young.

'And that's me,' Amit said, pointing to a figure at the end of a row, further back. 'My shoes were too tight.'

But the smile was immediately recognisable.

Ryan idly browsed the photograph.

'I'll see if I can dig out something better,' Amit said.

Ryan stayed where he was, staring, not listening, no longer looking at Toby or Amit in the photograph, but at someone else entirely.

'Her,' he said, pointing.

Amit leaned in. 'Oh, yes, I remember. Bit of a wild cat. Forget her name. She boxed, you know. Back then, that was pretty . . . out there.' He leaned in further. 'Even looks scary, don't you think? Wonder what happened to her.'

'She know Toby?'

'No. No, no. Toby and I steered well clear. She had a terrifying upper cut, I heard.' He stared at Ryan, puzzled. 'Do you know her?' he asked, after a while.

239

Ryan ignored him. A call came in from Livvy and he said goodbye to Amit and went out into the street.

She said, 'Ryan? Thought you should know: a Range Rover's been found.'

He left a beat. 'Carol's?'

'Yes.' There was a pause. 'I'm sorry.'

'Where?'

She hesitated. 'Near Sandford Lock.'

It was a well-known suicide spot. He breathed a little. What came to mind were those two kids holding hands as they left the station the night before.

'No damage to it,' Livvy said. 'Forensics haven't found anything yet.'

'Got the divers in?'

'Frogmen have started searching the area below the lock.'

He thought about that. 'I'll tell her ex,' he said. 'Give us a bell if you find out any more.'

He stood there for a moment longer, the drizzle blowing around him in tiny, almost playful specks; then he walked back to his terrible Peugeot.

TWENTY-SIX

Still the drizzle drifted as the mid-afternoon dusk fell, and Ray and Chester sat in Chester's back room, talking, looking out at shadows shifting sluggishly to and fro in the vast and ragged garden. The purpose of the meeting was to agree priorities while Chester was in Washington, but Ray was distracted, his mind still running on the shooting in the lock-up. By now, he'd heard the rumour about the bust-up between the DCC and Ryan, and he wondered how bad it had been. For her part, Chester also seemed distracted. She was short with Ray, picking him up on things he said, demanding more input, asking him to go much further in his thinking, though sometimes she seemed not to listen to his answers. The tone of flattery had gone from her conversation; what remained was cold and dismissive. The role itself seemed more political than before, more communications than strategy.

'Like I said, one of the things you got to get down, Ray – how to deal with the media.'

He nodded.

She was silent a moment. When she spoke again, her voice was tighter: 'Quick heads-up.'

'Yes?'

'The other Wilkins.'

Ray waited.

'Last days, I know, but don't get too close to him, Ray. He's not going to make it. People think Dave got it wrong, bringing him back.'

She held his eyes.

'Now, it come to the attention of the CC.'

Belatedly, Ray nodded.

'You got a relationship with him, of course – normal, working streets together, facing situations, I get it. But it's time to choose sides, now.'

After a while, Ray realised that she needed a response. 'I've chosen,' he said belatedly. 'I'm in.'

There was another, more searching, silence from Lynch.

'But not really on it today, are you, Ray? Where are you? I need you here, with me.'

'Just tired. The shooting this morning . . .' He trailed away.

She raised her eyebrows and left a little pause, as if to put a space round his words and show off their insincerity. 'Fuck off, Ray. First thing, we're straight with each other – got it? None of this soft-option shit. Something on your mind, fucking well tell me.'

Nettled, Ray said, 'Just the case.'

'What about the case?'

He began to describe how he'd been called out to the Kassam, and, for the first time that afternoon, Chester seemed to be listening to him.

'Lock-ups, back of the Vue?'

'Yes.'

'Know them. Know them very well.'

Something in the way she said it made Ray look at her.

'Boot camp used to rent a couple. What bay?'

'Number three.'

'Used to be one of ours.'

Ray couldn't keep the surprise out of his voice. 'The same bay?'

Chester shrugged. 'Had problems with vagrants ourselves. Burglaries, too. Roller doors not secure, why we ended the lease. Shame – it was handy. Camp's set up on the meadow by Littlemore Brook, there, and the Newman Place construction site, like I said. So, what's the killing look like? Homeless on homeless?'

'No. He was shot.'

Chester seemed unsurprised by this. She nodded. 'Drugs gangs – all tooled up, these days. Take out anyone dealing on their patch. That what was happening?'

'We don't know yet. It's possible. He would have been defenceless, though,' he said.

'Bad old world, Ray. Can't save everyone. Got to save yourself, right? Vagrants, they need to get off the street. Deaths down sixty per cent, when I was involved. But you know what happened with that.'

She was looking at him hard, her face so still and intent, it seemed a test of some sort – of loyalty, perhaps. He found himself thinking of the people he'd talked to, still scared of being moved on – telling him, in fact, that the Mover had been seen on the streets again. But he put it from his mind, held Chester's eyes a moment, and began to pack up his papers.

'Push on tomorrow,' Chester said, 'make up for lost time today – alright with you? I'm flying tomorrow evening, lots still to do.'

Ray nodded.

'Ray?'

'Yes?'

'Time comes to move on.'

He nodded once more, thinking of the homeless again, and went out of the house into the wet night, feeling uneasy.

Rain fell on Oxford as the temperature fell further, air congealing, gathering in damp haloes round street lamps, freezing on faces as the first commuters began their journey home, deserting the city centre, leaving behind the wet streets, the illuminated offices, people lying on cardboard in doorways and under fire escapes. Rain fell on O'Hanlon House, where they began to prepare for the usual migratory arrival of those hopeful of finding a bed out of the wet, their voices at the gates soft with a beaten quietness or loudly desperate. Rain fell on the northbound carriageway of the A34, where Ryan drove with difficulty through the dark murk (windscreen wipers had failed), making his way to a new housing development, checking his watch, thinking of his son's bath time. Rain fell on St Swithun's School, in Kennington, the end-of-school hubbub of children's cries growing, then receding, as Jade walked homeward down the road with her daughter Mylee and a subdued little Ryan in tow. And it fell up at Headington, on the John Radcliffe Hospital, where, in her bed in the Trauma Unit, Lena Wójcik opened her eyes.

She had been unconscious for eighteen hours, and she looked

about her now with surprise, not remembering where she was or how she had got there. In amazement, she lifted her arms and stared at the tubes trailing from them, and, turning her head, gazed at the machines surrounding her and felt neither alive nor dead, but in some other unreal state of disconnection, suspended in the harsh electric light. She tried to speak, but her mouth seemed unsure of itself and, anyway, after a while, she realised there was no one in the room but her. Something like panic seized her then and she made efforts to escape the bed, twisting feebly from side to side, bleating, occasionally fainting with the effort, coming round every few minutes to find herself still chained with the looping tubes that seemed to throw themselves around her.

Then someone was in the room, after all: a big woman in a hospital smock.

'What you been doing, Lena? You're all crooked. Lie still a minute.'

Lena found her voice: 'I got something to say.'

The nurse loomed over her, busying herself with the bedding.

'Something I saw,' Lena whispered.

The nurse made clucking noises as she untangled the tubes.

'Years ago,' Lena whispered. 'Up at the twenty-four-hour.'

The nurse finished settling her. 'You been asleep a long time. It's good you woke up, though; your welfare officer's arrived to see you.'

She turned away to read the monitors and then she was going.

'But I haven't got a welfare officer,' Lena whispered after her, unheard.

*

Fifteen miles away, Ryan arrived at a half-decorated new-build in an estate off Wretchwick Way and sat with Gary on camping chairs in the pink plaster shell of an unfinished living room smelling of paint and shavings, talking. Gary's overalls were a little dirtier than before, his stubble a little heavier. He was thick-faced with lack of sleep, a sullen dullness in his eyes. With fingers whitened by dust, he smoked as Ryan talked, staring at the floorboards, picking specs of tobacco from his lip.

'Sandford Lock?' he said. His eyes met Ryan's and he gave a little grimace. 'Never thought she was the sort to do herself in.'

Ryan took one of his cigarettes and sat smoking with him. He couldn't get a thought out of his head: Carol's business card in Zara Fanshawe's bag.

'Ask you a question?'

'Go on.'

'Heard of Zara Fanshawe?'

'Woman murdered in north Oxford.'

'Carol ever mention her?'

Gary looked at him in surprise, shook his head. 'No. Why would she?'

'Don't know.'

'Saw her car once, though,' Gary said, after a while.

'Really?'

'Must've been a couple of days before she was killed. Phantom, seventh generation, right? Extended wheelbase. Got an interest in cars; caught my eye.'

'Where'd you see it?'

'Bagley Wood Road – just past Carol's, in fact – crawling along, about five mile an hour. I was dropping the kids back.

Listen,' he said, distracted, 'I got something I want to say to you.' He began to smoke furiously. 'What I said about money, Carol getting into trouble with certain people.' He glanced at Ryan and quickly away. 'Well, there's other people, too.'

Ryan waited, watching him smoke.

'Don't know how much Carol told you about herself. When she was young.'

'Stuff about her flower shops.'

'All that came later. Before that, though, she had a . . . different life. Didn't like to talk about it.'

Ryan waited a bit longer.

'Worked the streets,' he said suddenly. 'She was just a kid. Grew up in care – you probably knew that. Bad, very bad, lots of drugs around. Sort of lost her way. Anyway, seventeen, eighteen, she was all messed up, turning tricks.'

Ryan felt a prickle of something. 'Go on.'

Gary hadn't known about it when he met her; they'd been going out for nearly a year before she said anything. First, she told him about the years in care, the abuse. Then, later, about the years on the street with the pimps and the punters and the police. 'Lot of dangerous people in that sort of life. Get a beating from your pimp, some john gets carried away. Girls she knew on the street were murdered, about that time – could easy have been her. Next five minutes is all you think about, she said. Get the money, get the fix, get out of the pimp's way, talk the police out of it. Every five minutes, stay alive or don't.' He lit another cigarette with trembling fingers.

Ryan said, 'How'd she get out?'

He shrugged. 'Guess you know how tough she is. Always

247

dreamed of being a businesswoman, running her own company. Stupid dream, for a hooker. Reckon it saved her.'

At any rate, it had given her the strength to break free, get help. She was still young, healthy, good looking. She ran. A church group found a room for her, she got a job in a florist's in Abingdon, learned the business, had the idea of the pop-up stalls, took out a loan.

'Doing well, by the time you met.'

'Better than well. Only been off the street a couple of years when we met – she already had all these pop-ups round Oxfordshire. Gigs at functions, shops in Summertown, the covered market.'

Ryan thought about that. 'Fast work.'

Gary shrugged. 'Got that skill with money. She'd bought the farmhouse on Bagley Wood Road and was doing it up. But, look, what I worry is, those people make bad enemies, they don't forgive, maybe they don't forget. What if she tried to touch one of them for money now?'

'Names you can give me? Pimps? Punters? Police?'

He shook his head. 'She never mentioned anyone, not even the other girls. To protect me, maybe. But she also kept herself apart from them, I don't know, always felt she was different.'

He lit another cigarette from the butt of the old one, and Ryan sat smoking with him, thinking. After a while, he said, carefully, 'Where was her patch?'

Gary thought about it, blew out his cheeks. 'Different places, I think. Mentioned Magdalen Bridge to me once or twice.' He thought about it. 'Down by the rail station, too.' He finished his cigarette, looked at his watch and stood. 'Got to finish up.'

Ryan gave him his number. 'Anything else you remember, give me a bell.'

And, when Ryan was at the door, Gary called out, 'Oh, yeah, another place she used to work – that disused garage, up on the Garsington Road.'

For the first time in days, he was home for bath time, but the house was silent when he went in and Jade was in the kitchen on her own.

'What's up?'

She wiped her hands at the sink and turned and pointed her nose at him. They hadn't spoken since the noise and distress of the night before.

She left a long, withering pause before she spoke. She was good at pauses. Pauses with intent. Also good at saying unexpected things. 'Doctor's just been.'

Something lurched sideways inside him, a feeling of major organs colliding with each other, and, when he spoke, his voice was bright with fear. 'What's happened to him?'

'Calm down. Just a fever. Some bug going round. They've both got it. Reckon it's made him a bit weepy, these last few days.'

'What bug?'

'Don't worry about what bug.'

'What about medicine? What medicine does he need? Has he got it? Shall I go and get it?'

'Ryan! Stop panicking. The doctor give him some medicine, now he's asleep.' She gave him a look. 'And don't go waking him.'

'Course not. I'll just go take a look at him.'

'You'll just sit down there and listen to me. We've had enough of this, Ryan.'

He wasn't listening. His mind was full of his son – his son ill and restless in bed, his son's face flushed on the pillow, his son weeping, his son shouting at him. 'I upset him,' he said.

'And, when he's better, you can make it up to him. Honestly, Ryan. Who's the child, here? You got to calm down and grow up.' She looked at him. 'Funny how you're clever and stupid at the same time. It's not like that ought to happen, really.'

He got up.

'Where are you going?'

'Just upstairs. I won't go in.'

'Ryan.'

'What?'

'You know he loves you, right?'

He shrugged, shuffled around a bit inside his puffa; he felt his face start to grin, his nose prickle. He made a damp, modest noise, felt his eyes film over.

'What you got to learn,' Jade said, 'is how to stop making things worse.'

Upstairs, he waited outside the bedroom door to see if he could hear his son's breathing inside, but he couldn't, and he moved away and stood at the landing window, looking out at the familiar scene. Housefronts shone in the dark wet, flickering with wind-driven shadows, halos of drizzle round the street lamps. He thought of his conversation with Gary, his other conversations with Lena and Amit. He brought into his mind the various parts of a picture that didn't yet make sense.

The old twenty-four-hour garage on Garsington Road.

Zara Fanshawe, lying twisted on a camp bed, with a broken neck.

Toby Lewin-Mercer's head blown apart in a lock-up.

Lena Wójcik, raving in the Trauma Unit.

Carol's Range Rover, abandoned at Sandford Lock.

A young Chester Lynch, standing in a college photograph, one row behind a young Toby Lewin-Mercer.

And he had a feeling that something had happened a long time ago to link all these things together.

He put on his headphones, cranked up the music, stopped thinking, let the thoughts come to him. He watched his reflection moving in the window pane. Blur of puffa. Baseball cap pecking left and right. Shoplifter hands appearing, disappearing. No recognition in his blank face; he was elsewhere, in the swirl of moving parts of a picture that made no sense.

And then he was standing, mouth open. The music had gone, the headphones were on the floor.

He found the number in his phone and called.

Amit Kandhari said, 'Hello.'

Ryan said, 'Last time you saw him, that party when he was engaged.'

'Hello?' Amit said. 'Is that DI Wilkins?'

Ryan said impatiently, 'That party, last time you saw him. Was it New Year's Eve?'

There was a silence.

Ryan began again, louder and faster.

Amit said, 'Sorry, sorry, you just caught me by surprise. Yes, you're quite right. Very jolly. Fireworks, some rather unsteady punting after midnight. Did I tell you someone kissed a horse? And then—'

'Shut up. What year?'

'What year? Gosh. Long time ago. Let's see . . . It must have been . . . Yes, that's it – 2005. Yes, I remember because . . . Hello? Hello?'

TWENTY-SEVEN

Crack of an eight o'clock February dawn in Kidlington, land of beige brick and caravans. Ryan pulled up at an address in Maple Avenue, switched off the ignition, listened to the engine run on haphazardly for twenty, thirty seconds. Fucking mind of its own.

Through the smeary windscreen, he looked at the pleasant estate: neat, boxy houses with raked gravel front gardens and hand-washed Toyotas and Kias on block-paving driveways. Handy for the nursery up the street, the playing fields at the back, the main road to Oxford, and not half a mile from the local police station where former PC Colin Redmond had served out his final years after a twenty-five-year stretch in north Oxford, where he had patrolled a sizeable beat extending from Wolvercote in the west to Sunnymead in the east.

He shouldn't really be here.

He got out of the car, slammed the door, gave it a look.

Redmond was a dumpy sixty-five-year-old with snowy-white hair and a pock-marked face, a slow mover and slower talker, and he stood in the doorway a moment, looking at Ryan, slowly nodding.

'On time, anyway. Catch me before fishing.'

'Canal?'

'Got a forty-eight pass at the Swan Valley Lakes.'

'Nice, out there.'

He turned slowly and led Ryan into a front room, settling himself laboriously into an armchair worn to a faint sheen.

'Remember you when you were twelve, thirteen. Yeah. Your dad used to bring you up here to watch Kidlington Town.' He didn't make it sound like a pleasant memory.

Ryan remembered those Saturday afternoons, the coaches arriving from Swindon, Hendon, Beaconsfield, bringing old men and children, the aimless spectacle, the boredom, the anxiety as his father drank his way through the second half.

'Pilfering from the canteen there,' Redmond said. 'Yeah. Sort of surprised you stayed out of prison. How's your father?'

'He *is* in prison.'

Redmond's expression didn't change. 'Funny how things turn out,' he said, at last. 'What is it you want to ask?'

Ryan asked, and Redmond thought about it, moving his mouth around silently.

'Well, let's see.' Long pause. 'Not unusual for those of us who drew the short straw to help out in other districts, that's true. Always short-staffed on a New Year, that's true too. It's just, I don't remember anyone ever helping me. Used to joke it was too far north. Course,' he said, with the same blank expression, 'if it's the great Chester Lynch saying she did, maybe I have to go along with it.'

He talked for a while about her, the impact she'd made, the reforms, the new ideas. 'She had to fight. Lots of racism around then. Good cop, no doubt about it. Clever. No one liked her.'

'So, you reckon it's possible she was up in the Godstow Road, two o'clock?'

Redmond spent some time thinking about that.

'Godstow Road?'

'That's it.'

'Two o'clock in the morning, New Year's Eve 2005?'

'Yeah.'

He chewed it over.

'No,' he said at last.

'Really? You sure?'

'In 2005?' He shook his head.

Ryan waited.

'You'd be able to check the date yourself,' Redmond said at last, 'but, as I remember it, 2005 was the year the Godstow Road was flooded. We had to close it both ends.'

'That's interesting,' Ryan said.

Detective Superintendent Wallace paced up and down in his office. Ray had never seen him pace before. It looked, in fact, as if he wasn't used to it, or hadn't got the hang of it, or perhaps his uniform was too restrictive; his trousers creaked, or else his neck. He moved his head backwards and forwards like a pigeon.

'Where is he?' he repeated. 'What the fuck's he up to?'

Ray did not know where Ryan was, or what he was up to. Not knowing did not impress Barko, who scowled at him as he went past on his way to the other side of the office. Occasionally, he moved his small, angry eyes towards a folder on his desk, which, Ray could see, had come from the Chief Constable's office. Ray was uneasy, not just because of Ryan. His thoughts ran on his own recent meeting with Chester. The developing relationship between them suddenly seemed less clear to him. He'd been unsettled, too, by the strange coincidence that Chester had once used the lock-up in which Toby had been murdered; in fact, he'd asked Nadim to run a check on the lock-up's lease and had discovered that it was still formally registered to Grade X Boot Camps. It seemed some sort of sublease was in place. Now, everything had been further complicated by the incident between the DCC and Ryan, which had forced him to choose sides. He was uneasy in these thoughts.

Barko at last sat down and abruptly started their meeting. The only new thing Ray had to offer was the possibility that Toby's murder was connected to ongoing rivalry between drugs gangs operating in the city. Barko wasn't listening; he shut him down. He didn't like the way the case was growing. It was like bacteria, he said, taking on new life, putting out tendrils, roots, limbs, whatever it was bacteria put out. He wanted it over, uprooted, killed off.

'It's like you two are fucking nurturing it,' he said.

He wanted a result, something clean, logical, definitive – something the paps would understand.

'Now, you're spinning me nonsense about drugs gangs.' He wanted proper lines of enquiry. 'And where the fuck is the other Wilkins?' he said.

At that moment, the other Wilkins arrived. The door kicked open and he came in at speed, followed a second later by most of his puffa, shouting, 'Ticket's bogus!' He stood there in the echo of his own making, trackies still quivering, face bent into an inappropriate grin. He nodded casually at Ray. 'Shocking,' he said, in his normal voice, confiding and nasal. 'I'm shocked, aren't you shocked?'

Ray was staring. Barko was on his feet.

'Sorry I'm late, by the way,' Ryan said. 'But, straight up, it's bogus, it's—'

'*Wilkins!*'

The noise was extreme; it made Ryan pause, ever so slightly. 'Course, yeah, got it.' He couldn't stop grinning. 'I can explain, though. That ticket she filled in, New Year's Eve 2005? One hundred per cent bogus. Made it up. Completely fucking well made it up.'

'Who?'

'Lynch.'

Barko's eyes bulged. There was a small silence in the office, like an intake of breath or the instant between the blow and the pain. A flush rose out of Barko's over-tight collar like a rash.

'Oh, no,' he said in a low but already rising voice. 'No, no, no, no. Please, God, no.' The flush completed the rapid seizure of his face. 'You've got to be fucking joking me, Wilkins.'

'Reckon she's involved. Something happened that night, something bad, involves them all somehow – Zara, Toby, Lena, Carol. Now, Lynch.'

Barko groaned. 'Make it stop.'

But Ryan would not stop. What he had to say came out in headlong garble, in flyaway bits and pieces, but gradually they understood that, on the night in question, Chester Lynch, then a junior constable, had falsely claimed to have stopped Zara Fanshawe and Toby Lewin-Mercer for careless driving in the Godstow Road.

Ray and Barko looked at him.

'Why?' Ray said at last.

Ryan shook his head impatiently. 'Don't know yet – not the point – the point is, there's a reason. Now all we have to do is find it out. Easy bit, really.' He grinned. 'Get Lynch in, for a start – give her the old grilling in C3.'

Barko lost it. He took off his hat and threw it against the wall. He took off his jacket and shook it at Ryan and threw it on the floor. Neither Ryan nor Ray had ever seen him in his shirtsleeves before; it awed them. He picked up the folder on his desk and threw it back down again. He began to talk – a relentless, unstoppable outpouring. The day before, he had spent forty-five extremely uncomfortable minutes listening to the Chief Constable – a man who, everyone knew, had no appreciation of his abilities – describe in appalling detail Wilkins' behaviour towards the Deputy Chief Constable in the lift, an act of gross abuse, almost certainly the single most shameful act perpetrated by an officer under his command in a career long enough to have seen many. Disrespectful, amateurish, useless, offensive – my God, what in Christ's name did he think he was doing, abusing a Deputy Chief Constable with such witless conjecture? What else could he call it? Innuendo, insult, playground stuff. Sweet Jesus, he was ashamed. What had happened to respect? What had happened to basic intelligence, to evidence, to reasonable deductions, to the minimum threshold of relevance? Did Wilkins even know what these things were? Was he, CDS David Wallace, the only officer left with a sense of basic fucking procedure? Had Wilkins taken leave of his senses, accosting the DCC with this pathetic piece of trivia?

'Didn't bother me,' Ryan said. 'Rattled her, anyway.'

'Oh, yes, oh yes – bright boy – rattled her, rattled the Deputy Chief Constable – the smart move, the right move – tell her a driving ticket from seventeen years ago's filled in incorrectly, tell her to shut up, insinuate she murdered a suspect in a lock-up, call her – and I quote – *a fucking disgrace*. Oh, yes, definitely the way to go. Why didn't you fucking nut her, while you were at it? I worked with her five years – I was there, you fucking dolt, I was a part of Violent Crime – I saw her every single fucking day during the investigation, I could've told you to ignore those imbecile rumours – that is, if you'd have thought to mention what you were going to say to her – but, no, why bother? Why not go solo, see what falls out?'

They thought, for a horrific moment, he was going to take his shirt off too, but he abruptly stopped talking and stood there, trying to control his breathing.

He said, at last, in a calmer but strangled voice, 'And now this. Let's see what we've got, here. She filled in the wrong name of a street on a driving ticket, when she was new in the job, working in an area unfamiliar to her, on a night when she'd volunteered to help out. Is that it? Is that the extent of it?'

Ryan sniffed. 'Reckon there's more to it than that.'

'Why? Why would she deliberately falsify a driving ticket?'

'Don't know. It's just . . . just stuff about her starting to look weird.'

Barko coughed up a dry laugh, jerked his chin at him. 'Go on.'

'She was at college with Toby, for a start – saw her in a photograph.'

'So, they knew each other?'

'No, but . . .'

'Go on.'

'She might've recognised him in the car.'

'And if she did, so what?'

'I don't know.'

'Go on. What else have you got? Links to Zara Fanshawe?'

'No, but—'

'Links to Lena Wójcik?'

'Not yet, but—'

'Links to Carol Hart?'

'No.'

'Links to anything at all?'

Ryan shuffled about. 'There's those Magnum Panthers.'

'What?'

'Prints of Magnums in the Polstead Road place. Size six – small, for a bloke. Lynch wears Magnums, spotted them in the lift that night.'

'I wear Magnums. *Literally thousands of people* wear Magnums.'

'Reckon we should find out what size she takes.'

'Don't be fucking stupid.'

Ryan stood there, frustrated. A note of desperation came into his voice: 'According to Lynch, they were arguing that night in the car, Zara and Toby.'

'You just told us she was making it all up.'

'No. Think she saw them. Just not in the Godstow Road. Something happened that night, something bad. They'd just announced their engagement, then suddenly it was all over. Think about the date. Couple of months later, Zara goes into rehab for the first time, Toby's career crashes and burns. And Lynch has got something to do with it all.'

Barko had had enough.

'Going to stop you before you embarrass yourself further, Wilkins. It's fancy cake of nothing and you know it. It's obvious to everyone but you that you've let your childish, stupid dislike of the DCC scramble your fucking brain.'

As he talked, Ryan kept throwing glances at Ray.

'Come on, Ray. Back me up.'

Ray said nothing, looked the other way.

Barko said, 'There are no links, here, only fantasies. I'm shutting it down.'

Ryan made a noise and Barko looked at him scornfully.

'Son, I thought you'd be better than this.'

Ryan caught the tone of pity and was nettled. 'Thing is, you don't even want to think about it.'

'Excuse me? *Excuse me?*'

'Closed your mind.'

Ray watched Barko disintegrate. His face flushed an unnatural shade of beet, he bellowed phrases to beat Ryan with, his accent slipping further, like air returning to earth, words thickening into the non-verbal, a muddy anger. Ryan – of course – began to shout back: he was fed up with not being taken seriously, not being trusted, not being respected. He was panting with the strain of indignation. And Ray watched helplessly. Something in what Ryan was saying in his garbled way aggravated his sense of unease with Chester Lynch. But Ryan's loutish display repelled him.

'Ryan,' he said. 'Ryan!'

And Ryan turned on him. 'You,' he said. 'You're just as bad. Both of you got this crush on her, this grovelling, slobbering crush.'

There was an immediate sense that he had gone too far. In the room, there was the sound only of breathing.

In desperation, Ryan made an appeal. 'Ray! Ray, mate. Starting to get it, aren't you? Come on, be honest.'

There was silence, then – or, not silence, but whatever imitates it after violent commotion.

After a moment, Barko said, 'Go ahead, then, Ray. Anything to say, now's your chance.'

There was another long pause. Certain thoughts Ray pushed out of his mind. Then he spoke, looking away. 'You're being ridiculous, Ryan. There's nothing here but coincidences.'

Barko said, 'So. End of. To be clear, there's to be no line of enquiry opened into DCC Lynch or this so-called suspicious driving ticket. None. The very thought is farcical. Any attempt to do so will trigger immediate suspension. To be absolutely crystal fucking clear, I'll be monitoring everything you do.'

The meeting was at an end. Just as well. Ray really could not bear it anymore, and, face deadpan, moving carefully and deliberately, as if he'd only just learned how, he buttoned his black wool peacoat, turned from both of them and walked out of the office.

And, a few seconds later, Ryan flung himself out after him, not at all careful, not in any way deadpan, but like a large piece of brightly coloured litter blowing violently with noise effects across the open-plan area, where he caught up with Ray and grabbed his arm and pulled him back, and they stood, face to face and close up, with all the men and women at the surrounding work stations suddenly watching them.

'Seriously?' A bellow.

'Let it go, Ryan.' A hiss.

Ray was a couple of inches taller and more than fifty pounds heavier, and he stood there, photogenic as ever in black cords and peacoat, balanced on the balls of his feet, hands flexed, moving instinctively into the classical boxing pose, and Ryan sneered at him.

'Not going to back me up?'

'Can't.'

'Pick your side and that's the end of it?'

'You've got nothing, Ryan, and you know it.' Ray kept his voice low and steady.

Ryan didn't: his voice was high and nasal and loud. 'Still got my self-respect. You got a crush so bad, you can't fucking see straight.'

Ray glanced slowly round and back to Ryan. He said, quietly, 'You know what this is? She called you out and you can't take it. Now, you're just making stuff up. It's pathetic.'

'Tell you what's pathetic, Ray. Lying to yourself. You know something's not right.'

'I'm not even interested anymore. Work it on your own.'

Ray tried to turn away, but Ryan pulled him back.

'When did you stop caring about the truth? I'll tell you when. When you started thinking about your next promotion.'

Ray stepped forward then, put his face into Ryan's, said in a low voice, 'Get your hand off me.'

There was a moment when they stood there, face to face, in anger and embarrassment, in front of everyone, on the verge of something never to be forgiven; then Ryan's phone went. He removed his hand from Ray's arm and fumbled his phone from the depths of his trackies' pocket and looked at it a moment before answering.

'What?'

He listened intently.

'Yeah, yeah. No, I'll come now.'

He said to Ray, in a completely normal voice, 'Got to go. Ry's ill. Jade's got her shift at the Co-op and the girl from down the road's not turned up.' He looked as if he was going to say something else, and then he didn't; and then, grimacing, he turned without saying anything at all and jogged towards the stairs, a swish of brightly coloured, overlarge polyester, and Ray stayed where he was, forcing himself to stare down the people at their desks until they returned to their screens; then, finally, adjusting the hang of his coat, he turned and slowly walked away, stomach churning.

TWENTY-EIGHT

His stomach was still churning when he met his father for lunch in Vincent's, the private club for Oxford alumni of notable sporting achievement, to which, as a boxing blue, Ray had been elected some years earlier. He didn't go there often, but his father liked it when he was in town. It was quiet. Ray managed to eat the sole, and his father had the oxtail soup, steak and kidney pudding, and spotted dick and custard. The club's menu took its cue from the boarding schools of the late Victorian period. After they'd finished, Ray and his father took their coffees into the club lounge and sat on the dimpled chesterfields. Hung on the wood-panelled walls around them were framed photographs of varsity teams dating back to the 1860s, mainly rowing and rugger. Other sports were represented elsewhere, and the pictures included, at the unfrequented end of the bar, a small black-and-white photograph of Ray in the ring, which, as always, his father would insist on seeing before they left. In the meantime, they sat with their coffees, looking out of the tall sash windows at the rain cascading into King Edward Street.

His father had a habit of glancing round every few seconds at the other members, as if expecting to recognise someone or be recognised, though he knew no one there; it was an aspect of his feeling that he belonged, that he took his place naturally here. Ray, on the other hand, had never felt this sense of belonging.

The lunch had been his father's idea: he wanted to congratulate his son on his promotion to Lynch's National Uplift team. It was an inconvenient time, but that issue had not cropped up when his father called to tell him of the booking. He was in a jovial, celebratory mood.

'Knew you'd move fast, Ray. Like in the ring, eh? You give this Wallace a bloody nose – biff, bang! The jab, the upper cut. Let him keep the other Wilkins. Now, we see what you can do.'

Ray was quiet. He was often quiet with his father. But the altercation with Ryan had shaken him, and Chester Lynch was still on his mind – not just the coincidence of the lock-up, other unsettling little things too. The way the homeless had insisted to him that the Mover – Chester – had been seen at their camps at a time when they'd been looking for Toby. The coincidence that Chester had been at college with Toby. The oddity of the driving ticket, for which there was no doubt a simple explanation, and yet . . .

Another thought came to him suddenly. Was it a coincidence that Lynch had approached him at the beginning of the case, as soon as he began working on Zara's disappearance?

It was Lynch his father wanted to talk about, as it happened. He approved. A woman, of course, but the country had known many strong women – Mrs Thatcher, for example, or Mrs Beeton! He frequently made such jokes that weren't really jokes.

He approved of Lynch's attitude, her resolve; he liked what he'd heard about her street vagrancy policy.

'Riff-raff,' he said. 'Everywhere – even in Oxford, now – I saw them on my way here.' He drained his coffee cup and peered round enquiringly at the other members.

'A question of loyalty, Ray,' he said. 'A Deputy Chief Constable is a person who deserves loyalty. Wallace, no. No, no.' He rose to his feet expectantly as one of the other members came towards them in greeting, a quaveringly tall septuagenarian, a Balliol man and authority on British industrial relations, who, a decade earlier, had taught Ray political theory and, forty years before that, in the 1970s, somewhere between Ted Heath's surprise victory in the general election and the beginning of the dockers' strike, had won a boxing blue himself.

Ray stood, too. 'Professor Ogilvy.'

He peered at Ray with wet eyes as he offered a pale and boneless hand. His voice was pale and boneless too: 'Good to see you, Ray. We don't often see you here.'

Ray introduced his father, who began to explain to Professor Ogilvy that they were celebrating Ray's promotion to a post he described as 'National Police Ambassador', working with the Deputy Chief Constable.

'That would be the famous Chester Lynch,' Ogilvy said. 'Interesting.' He turned to Ray. 'Good luck.'

Ray caught something in his tone. 'You know her?'

'I taught her, many years ago. You probably know she was an undergraduate here. Exeter College.'

'Remember her well?'

'Oh, yes. She's a very memorable lady.'

267

Ogilvy may have been doddery, but his memory was acute. Chester had written a dissertation for him on British fascism and underground far-right movements: even then, she had been interested in criminality.

'Of course, no one finds such subjects so fascinating anymore; all those sorts of views are mainstream, now.'

Unlike some of his colleagues, Ogilvy had liked Chester Lynch; he'd found her a sharp, abrasive young woman, unafraid to challenge orthodoxy, even if it exposed her ignorance. And a boxer, which was really quite a sensational thing, in those days. 'And also,' he said. 'How shall I put it? Personally controversial.'

A member of staff was at his elbow: Ogilvy's table was ready. He lifted that boneless hand again and took his leave of them.

Ray touched his father's arm. '*Baba*, I have to go, too.'

'Yes, yes, duty calls.'

First, they walked together through the bar to where his father's favourite photograph was hanging. The boy in the picture held his gloved hands above his head and smiled at nothing, handsome and uncomplicated, a person simplified to a photogenic image, a child. And now his father took hold of his grown-up son's hand, as he always did when they stood together here, and raised it above their heads. 'Champion!'

People at the bar turned briefly their way.

'*Baba, please.*'

They parted on the corner of the High Street, his father pulling him into an enormous clinch and away at last, laughing. 'Too strong for me!' He slapped Ray playfully on the arm. People in the street were looking at them. 'I know, I know – go back to the station; they need you.' He turned heavily, raising a hand,

and crossed the road. Ray watched him until he was out of sight, then turned and went back into the club.

Ogilvy was eating alone and had no objection to Ray joining him.

'Controversial?' Ray said.

Ogilvy smiled. 'I thought I'd piqued your interest. I remember the look you used to give me in tutorials when you thought I'd said something you could challenge.' In between his faggots and his syllabub, he talked about the controversy involving the undergraduate Chester. It had taken place in the Trinity term of her second year – June, hot and dry. Chester and two other students took a college punt and went up the Cherwell. One of them was a young man called George Hoxton. Hoxton had a reputation. Shortly after matriculating, he'd been accused by another undergraduate of date rape, a charge that collapsed after he uncovered a video of the girl engaging in S and M. Later, he achieved more notoriety in the student union by proposing the motion that 'this house believes racism is a hoax'.

'What was the controversy?'

'Hoxton drowned.'

Ray felt something shift inside him, a stirring, a memory. 'Go on.'

The verdict had been death by misadventure. Significant traces of cocaine were found in Hoxton's blood. Although he was known to be a strong swimmer, he had been incapacitated by the large amount of toxic chemicals in his system, it was assumed.

'But?'

But Hoxton's parents didn't believe it. Two bystanders in University Parks, on the bank of the river, testified at the inquest that, as the punt went by, Hoxton and Lynch were violently arguing. Mr and Mrs Hoxton were convinced that the argument between their son and Chester had escalated, that the famously aggressive Lynch had overreacted and, in the struggle that followed, had knocked their son overboard and drowned him.

'There were no witnesses of the actual incident, however, and the other student in the punt backed up Chester's story, which was fortunate for her.'

Ray felt the hairs go up on the back of his neck. He had remembered a conversation about an undergraduate who had abandoned her studies, never to return, traumatised after a fatal punting accident.

'The other student in the punt,' he said.

'Yes?'

'Was it Zara Fanshawe?'

Professor Ogilvy raised his water glass. 'Haven't lost it, have you, Ray, that sharpness. I saw it in you, the first tutorial we had. I don't know how you knew that, but you're quite right, it was Zara Fanshawe, poor woman.'

And now, in the middle of the afternoon, day tilted suddenly into twilight, more rain fell on the city, dropping heavily out of the depthless sky, hammering on skylights, clattering on car roofs, crashing against windows, jumping out of gutters, strange smells coming off it like cheese and soap and doormats. It fell on King Edward Street, where Ray left Vincent's and hurried towards the station, and on Kenville Road, where Ryan sat in a state of mental blankness at the kitchen table. He should have been working, or brooding on the enormous argument in

270

Barko's office, or thinking hard about how to get ahead of the repercussions now certainly coming his way. But he did none of these things. He drifted upstairs and put his head around the bedroom door and stood for nearly an hour, mouth open, watching little Ryan sleep, the boy's flushed face damp on his pillow. He did not dare go into the room, in case Jade came back and caught him there. On the floor, under the bed, he could see their bent and creased copy of *Mouse and Mole*, unread for many days; it seemed to him a relic of a different time, vanished now, not coming back, and he remembered with sickening nostalgia the two of them lying on the bed together only the week before, remembered too the grating sound of his own reading voice, the suckling noises little Ryan made with his beaker, the careful, somehow solemn way he took the beaker out of his mouth to say, *But, Daddy, they're* friends, *Daddy.*

Jade came back and caught him just outside the bedroom.

'Honestly don't know what's wrong with you.'

He shuffled about, offered to fetch medicines, suggested waking little Ryan up to feed him and was ordered out of the house. Almost at once, it jolted his mind into a different direction. It was five thirty when he arrived back at the station, but Nadim was still there, and he was making his way towards COMINT when he got a call from Livvy. She was out at Littlemore, she said, near the road to Nuneham Courtenay. There had been a development in the search for Carol.

He stood in the stairwell, listening.

The frogmen at Sandford Lock had completed their search: nothing had been found. But night security at a nearby construction site had reported a break-in overnight. Oddly, there was no

271

sign of a forced entry at the perimeter, but footage from a safety camera showed a rogue car driving inside the site at three o'clock in the morning, in the vicinity of some recently dug foundations.

It wasn't a good sign. Everyone knows building sites make good dumping grounds. And it was less than a mile from Sandford Lock, where Carol's Range Rover had been found.

'What site?'

'Newman Place. There's a boot camp for young offenders does night activities there from time to time and they thought at first the car was something to do with that. But it turns out it wasn't. You don't need to come. I'm here. The guys are just doing their stuff. I'll give you a call as soon as there's anything definite.'

He stood on the stairs a moment, thinking. After a moment, he continued up the stairs and on to COMINT, where he brought a chair up close to Nadim's desk and cleared his throat, a messy and protracted procedure, and looked around conspiratorially, and said in a low voice, 'There's a way to search the databases without leaving a trail, right?'

She gave him a long, cool look. 'For me, yes; not for you.'

'So, someone can't tell what you've been looking at.'

'*Someone*, Ryan?'

'Like, I don't know . . . Barko?'

She shook her head slowly from side to side. 'Oh, Ryan. What are we going to do with you?'

They separated; it seemed safer. Back in his own office, he talked to her on the phone, explaining what he wanted. He'd talk, then wait, listening to the sound of her fingers on the keyboard, then she'd talk back to him, tell him what she was looking at.

There had been numerous crimes committed in Oxford during the night of New Year's Eve 2005. Ryan was interested in those occurring at the disused twenty-four-hour garage on the Garsington Road, at the end of St Luke's Road, around two o'clock.

'Nothing.'

'Any time before two o'clock.'

'Nothing.'

He thought about that.

'Anything in the streets nearby?'

Drunk and disorderly in a house in Phipps Road, two streets along. Robbery of an electrical store in Hollow Way, opposite.

'Give me everything in a quarter-mile radius.'

Vandalism at the Premier Inn at the business park, a break-in at a shop in the Templars Square shopping precinct, and, embarrassingly, a fight in the Cowley Road police station, dealt with internally.

'Half-a-mile radius.'

Indecent exposure on the ring road, near the Mini Plant.

'That it?'

'Nothing else.'

'Fuck. Mile radius, then.'

Tapping of the fingers. Then silence.

'Nadim? What you got?'

'A murder.'

His pulse quickened.

'Last of the Underpass Murders. Remember them? Big news, at the time. Hospital porter at the JR killed three sex workers in the space of six months, stoved their heads in, bagged them up and dumped them in that underpass at Littlemore.'

Ryan frowned. 'Bagged them up?'

'Body bags from the hospital. Stupid, it's how they got him.'

'All of them sex workers?'

'All three.'

'And that last one?'

'Seventeen years old, Oxford girl, still at school.'

He paused. 'First name?'

He waited. Heard the fingers tapping.

'Jasmine.'

It rang a bell. He drifted.

After a while, he heard her say, 'Ryan? Ryan?'

He said quickly, 'Can you print it out for me?'

'Printing now. Pick it up in Facilities, soon as you can. That it? Can I go, now? Or do you want me to break any other regs?'

'Course not. Oh, wait. Don't suppose you can get into Admin, staff travel itineraries?'

She hesitated. 'I shouldn't. What for?'

'Time of Chester Lynch's flight to the States.'

'Oh, Ryan. Really?'

'Come on, Nadim. Do the right thing.'

'It's not the right thing; it's the opposite of the right thing.'

'I'll bring Ry in, promise – you can stroke his hair and everything.'

She said nothing, but he heard the tapping of her fingers. When she spoke, her voice was low and conspiratorial.

'She's catching the red eye to Washington tonight. Leaves Heathrow at eleven thirty.'

'Limo service?'

More tapping.

'Car's picking her up, seven thirty.'

'Nadim, I owe you.'

'You owe almost everyone, Ryan. Especially Ray. Just so you know.'

She hung up and he waited there a moment longer, in thought, then jogged out of his office towards Facilities.

TWENTY-NINE

In Grove Street, Ray and Diane were sitting over the remains of an early supper in their knocked-through front room. Diane had Ollie over her shoulder, making murmuring noises to him as Ray talked. He'd been talking for roughly an hour, frequently repeating himself, though neither he nor Diane noticed. He had described Ryan's extraordinary meltdown in Barko's office, and Barko's own corresponding meltdown, and his confrontation with Ryan in the open-plan afterwards, but it was understood by both of them that he was not speaking to Diane so much as expressing his own sense of injury, and exposing, for his own sense of injustice, the unforgivable behaviour of others. He had dwelt particularly on Ryan, his hysteria, the way he'd jeered at him, the accusations he'd made. But he had not talked about Chester Lynch. He did not know what to say about her and fell instead into a troubled silence. After talking to Professor Ogilvy, he'd gone back to the station and, with Nadim's help, had done some digging. Reports in the archive corroborated what Ogilvy had told him. Zara and Chester had known each other through

276

sport: both had competed for the university – Chester in boxing, Zara in equestrian events – though neither had won a blue – Chester because of a dispute with the selection committee, Zara out of general unreliability. Perhaps, in a strange way, it made them both outsiders. Ray had a sense that Chester had been protective of Zara. It made sense that she'd join Zara when she went punting with the predatory Hoxton, just as it made sense that she'd intervene, with her usual ferocity, if Hoxton started harassing Zara. He could picture it. And, if Lynch had protected Zara, he could imagine Zara covering for Lynch in the questioning that followed.

He felt more uneasy than ever. After a while, he got up and paced about the room. He felt as he used to as a child when he knew he was going to be sick, fighting against it, knowing he couldn't prevent it, only delay it. Thinking this, he realised for the first time that he was going to have to do something with what he had learned from Professor Ogilvy. But what, he did not know. It was easier to feel angrier with Ryan.

'Don't take it to heart,' Diane said absently. It was not clear what she was responding to.

'What?'

'Ryan. I think you'll miss him when you start working full-time with the DCC.'

Ray moved about the room in agitated silence.

'I don't know what I'm going to tell *Baba*,' he blurted out suddenly.

She looked at him, puzzled. 'About what?'

He didn't reply. He was trying to put off the thinking he needed to do. He relapsed into complaints against Ryan. 'I'm only surprised Wallace didn't suspend him straight away. He was out of control. He was . . .' He lost his train of thought, remembering again the moment when Ogilvy told him about the fatal punting accident.

There was a knock on the door.

'At last,' Diane said. 'The nappies delivery. They said between six and eight. Ray?'

'What?'

'The door.'

Ray began to vent again as he went across the room. 'Perhaps it's medical, something physiological, something vital missing in his brain, whatever the thing is that allows adults to control their behaviour. His three-year-old is better behaved than he is. He's completely at the mercy of his feelings. It's pitiful – pitiful and terrifying. He's a mess. I honestly think he should seek help.'

He opened the door and Ryan, standing on the doorstep, said, 'Took me fucking hours to park the car. You can tell it's posh when it's all resident parking only.'

They sat awkwardly on the sofa.

'Nice house. Pictures and that.'

There was a silence. Ryan said, 'Know a book called *Mouse and Mole*? It's good, think you'd like it.' He hesitated. 'Ry explained it to me. Kid's a fucking genius.'

Ray waited, baffled, while Ryan twitched and gurned.

'Anyway,' he said abruptly, 'thought I'd come round.'

'Yes?'

'Say sorry.'

Ray and Diane both stared at him.

278

'There. Said it. Don't usually. Can't. Like it's physical, gets stuck, back of my throat. Thing is,' he said, 'I'm a knobhead. You know that, everyone knows that. Don't know what's wrong with me. Maybe it's medical – what do you think?'

Ray opened his mouth. Diane said quickly, 'Don't be silly – it's stress. Everyone messes up when they're stressed. You should see Ray when he can't cope. Can't stop talking, round and round, same thing over and over, making no sense.'

Ray frowned at her.

Ryan said, 'Really? Cheered me up, Diane – thanks.'

Diane was still looking at Ray. After a moment, he said, tight-lipped, 'Yes. We've all been stressed.'

Diane continued to look at him.

'And I'm sorry too,' he said at last.

Ryan looked surprised, dismissed it as an irrelevance.

'In fact,' Ray said – and, as he said it, he realised there was no going back – 'there's something I have to talk to you about. About the DCC.'

Ryan took a rolled-up printout from his trackie pocket. 'Hang on to it till you read this.'

Ray read.

The murder of Jasmine Barrett. There was a grainy colour picture of her: she was petite, a little pinched in the face, with gold-coloured hair cut short like Zara's. Her body had been found in the Littlemore underpass in a bag: an official, zippered, anti-leakage, waterproof cadaver bag, standard issue to hospitals and other emergency services, such as the police. Her skull had been split open by a heavy, edged instrument, like a spade, her body battered and traumatised by multiple internal injuries. A

279

week later, John Simpkins, a porter at the John Radcliffe Hospital, was taken into custody after a tip-off from one of his colleagues and subsequently charged with the murders of Jasmine and two other sex workers, whose bodies had previously been found bagged in the Littlemore underpass. He was convicted on all three counts, began a whole-life sentence in Grendon Prison and died less than a year later.

'Jasmine Barrett. Friend of Lena's,' Ryan said. 'Lena spoke about her in the hospital – "Goldy hair" – but I couldn't make head nor tail of it. There were three of them turning tricks up at the garage, most nights. But look at the time of death.'

Ray looked.

'Two o'clock in the morning, New Years Eve 2005. Ring a bell? Read the rest.'

Although Simpkins had confessed to the earlier two murders, he always denied responsibility for Jasmine's death. Indeed, her own family questioned the jury's verdict; they campaigned long and hard against it. Because the body was bagged and dumped, the location of the actual murder couldn't be determined. The autopsy report stated that the injuries to Jasmine's head were post-mortem; actual cause of death was massive internal haemorrhaging, the result of a violent blow to the body consistent with falling from a height – or being hit by a car.

If Simpkins didn't kill her, who did?

They exchanged looks. Then began to talk, rapidly, instinctively, sometimes across each other.

'That night.'

'Toby and Zara, at a party at St Hilda's.'

'Left a bit before two.'

'Zara, drunk.'

'Heading for Toby's place in Garsington.'

'Obvious which way they'd go. Nowhere near the Godstow Road, complete opposite direction. Up the Cowley Road, into the Garsington Road.'

'Past the twenty-four-hour.'

'Where Jasmine's waiting for johns at the edge of the forecourt.'

'And Zara's all over the road.'

'And loses control of the car.'

They thought about that.

Ray said, 'Picture it. Two o'clock in the morning, Zara and Toby standing there, Jasmine in a heap on the ground. The unbelievable's happened. What's Zara's first thought?'

'Make it all go away.'

'Right.'

'Rich girls don't go to jail.'

'No. They get help; they know people.

'Like Lynch.'

'Yes. Lynch knows what to do. Bag up the body, take it off site, dump it in Littlemore, make it look like one of the Underpass Murders. Clever.'

'And the ticket she gives Zara?'

'Their alibi.'

'Means and opportunity, Ray.'

'Yes.'

'But motive? That's what I don't get. *Why* would Lynch step in, help out Zara? I just don't know.'

Ray cleared his throat, left a beat. 'But I do.'

He explained about Zara covering for Lynch after Hoxton's death in the punt. 'Lynch owed Zara, big time. New Year's Eve was payback.'

They sat there.

Ryan said, 'Alright, then. They get away with it, go their separate ways, never have nothing to do with each other again. Pact of silence, whatever. Seventeen years later, though, Zara comes to Oxford, looking for Toby. Why?'

They thought about that.

Ray said, 'The book.'

'Book?'

'In her car. Remember?'

'That little religious book? *The Catholic Confessional and the Sacrament of Penance.*'

'She couldn't keep the secret anymore. Remember where Justin saw her for the last time? Outside Brompton Oratory, early in the morning. Remember what he said? She was having some sort of spiritual development. Think of those other books we saw in the mess at Hyde Park, all about enlightenment, the soul, the conscience. She'd got off drugs, faced up to what she'd done. She'd made up her mind to finally do something about her life, just like her mother suspected.'

'She was going to confess.'

'And she came here to tell Lynch and Toby. Toby, she sweetened with five grand.'

'But Lynch?'

Ray said, 'Lynch would never let Zara go public. Never. She's DCC. She wouldn't just go to jail; it would be a disgrace, a national scandal. Lynch would stop it. Lynch would do whatever it took to make sure it never happened.'

They looked at each other.

'Shit, Ray, it's her, then.'

'Zara in the attic, Waitrose in the lock-up.'

'Got the training to find them, got the skills, got the Glock.'

They sat there.

'What do we do now?'

'Can't touch Lynch, not yet. Needs to be absolutely water-tight. If Lena was up there with Jasmine that night, if she saw anything, she's our witness. We need to talk to her.'

Ryan winced. 'First thing I did was give the hospital a call. Lena Wójcik died last night.'

'No witnesses, then. No way to prove any of it. Wait. You said three of them were up there most nights. Who's the third?'

Ryan looked awkward.

Ray said, 'You're joking.'

'Turns out Carol worked the streets when she was young, up at the twenty-four-hour, too. Zara went to see her as well, so I reckon she at least knows something about it. Which means she's got something on Lynch. Which means she's at risk. She started acting funny, soon as Zara got killed. Then she disappears.'

Ray took that in. 'Any updates?'

'Latest is, they're searching a construction site. Someone broke in. Signs of digging. We both know what that could mean.'

Ray was looking at him. 'What site?'

'Newman Place, near Sandford. Why?'

Ray said, 'Lynch's boot camp runs night activities there. She'd have access.'

There was a moment before Ryan reacted – a moment of calm, never to be retrieved.

He was on his feet. 'Fuck it. Let's go grab Lynch.'

'Wait. Wait a minute.'

'We haven't got a minute. She's being picked up from the airport in, like –' he glanced at his watch – 'like, now.'

He was at the front door.

'We'll call Wallace, explain the situation.'

'Wallace? Lynch's biggest fan?'

'Ryan! We can't do this. Wait.'

But he didn't. 'Do it myself, if you don't fancy it.' He looked back once, waited a second, sniffed aggressively, then he was gone, flapping away down the street.

And now the fucking Peugeot wouldn't start.

And now he was pummelling the steering wheel with his fist.

And now, at last, the stupid lousy engine caught.

And suddenly Ray was in the passenger seat, trying to untangle the safety belt that never seemed to work properly.

'Just don't drive like an idiot,' he said.

'Course not.'

They lurched abruptly forward, fairground-style, Ray's head snapped back and they screeched down the road.

In the small, square front room of the house at Rose Hill, Chester Lynch and her husband sat waiting for the limo to pick Chester up. Everything was packed. A delivery of power adaptors hadn't arrived, but Chester could pick some up at the airport. Now, there were just empty minutes with nothing to do but look at

284

each other, look around. There was a time when they'd thought of knocking through to the back room, but somehow they'd never got round to it. Life had got in the way: Chester's work, Walt's illness. Besides, the front room was comfortable enough; they liked its plain furniture, sensible carpet, lampshades. Pictures hung on the walls: photographs of their wedding, holiday scenes. They sat there quietly now, Chester on the small sofa, Walt in his wheelchair, waiting, looking out of the window into the darkness of the street, where the long month continued, cold, soiled, crusted with evening frost, empty, as if it had no will of its own.

'You know,' Chester said, 'I sometimes wonder about leaving all this behind, picking up over there.'

'Really?'

'Open offer of an interesting post at Quantico. Better than fighting the suits over the National Uplift thing all of the time, maybe. Health insurance gold-plated, tell you that? We talked about those new techniques over there.'

Walter said nothing.

'Check it out when I'm away, maybe.'

Motorbike noise came from the Rose Hill strip at the end of the street and faded away, and they were quiet.

Chester said, 'We been happy here, though, haven't we, Walt?'

'Always.'

They were quiet again, nothing else to say.

The driver of the limo called: he was minutes away. Walter decided to go upstairs. Chester said she'd smoke a last cigarette in the garden. They said their goodbyes. Chester settled Walter in the chairlift and watched him go up.

★

The Peugeot picked up speed down the Banbury Road and suddenly encountered stationary traffic at the Summertown shops. Roadworks, southbound lane closed. Darkness steamed above the cars, lit in the red and white streaks of their lights.

Ryan said, 'Fuck this – I'll put the disco on.'

He lowered the window.

Ray, feeling the delicacy of their mission, began to talk about a need to be discreet.

Ryan, not listening, slapped the sound and vision on the car roof.

It didn't work.

Ray breathed a sigh of relief.

'Fuck it.' Ryan swung out into the opposite lane and accelerated towards oncoming traffic. Ray made noises.

'Flash your badge at them, if it makes you feel any better.'

Ray began to make large and desperate hand gestures out of the window at the approaching cars.

Driving one-handed, Ryan said, in a conversational tone, 'Thing is, this car's a piece of shit; it's only when it's going more than seventy the engine don't bang. It's funny,' he went on, as cars ahead swerved aside to avoid them, 'but this sort of caper's pretty much the only time I feel I'm really in control of it. I tell you, took me so many times to pass my test, 'cause I had to keep going so fucking slow. See,' he said, pointing casually, 'people getting the hang of it now, shifting out of the way.'

In this sickening fashion, they cleared the roadworks, sped down the Banbury Road, through a red light at Norham Gardens, and swung with a mighty squeal of rubber into Parks Road.

'Please,' Ray said. 'Oh, please.'

'Yeah, but, get there too late, we're going to feel like dipsticks, right?'

Making good use of both narrow lanes and giving cyclists fair warning, or at least warning, or at least making themselves (alarmingly) visible, they took the High Street traffic by surprise and rushed past and through it, over Magdalen Bridge and along the Iffley Road, accelerating all the time, upwards to Rose Hill, and arrived less than three minutes later at Westbury Crescent, where they pulled up, with some whiplash, at the corner of the street. The engine banged twice and died.

When he could, Ray said, 'You're a fucking idiot.'

Ryan looked shamefaced for a moment. 'Overriding need for speed, mate.'

'Overriding idiocy.'

'Let's go get her.'

They began to argue about what should happen next. Ray pointed out that they needed to act with complete and scrupulous correctness. Otherwise, Lynch would find a hundred ways to invalidate the process. What came after the arrest, they did not know. Ryan wasn't bothered.

'Thing is, Ray, once we done it, everyone else has to work with it, right? Be their problem, not ours.'

'Just let me do the talking, okay?'

'Mate, I think I can handle it.'

'I know for an absolute fact, you can't.'

They left the car and crossed the road. Light from a street lamp rotated their shadows around them as they went. Otherwise, nothing moved in the street. There was a little traffic noise from the Rose Hill strip, no other sound.

'Funny she lives in such a small house,' Ryan said.

'Keep your voice down.'

They went up the little driveway and Ray knocked.

No answer. The front room was dark.

'Fuck it, she's gone already. The limo must have arrived.'

'Wait a minute.'

'Ray, we have to go to the airport.'

'I'm not getting back in that car with you.'

Several minutes passed. They heard a noise deep in the house. Ryan took his Glock out of his trackie pocket.

Ray said, 'You shouldn't be armed; I bet you didn't do the paperwork.'

'Just thought it might come in handy.'

He put it into his waistband, and after a moment moved it back again, and after another moment took it out and held it at his side.

'At least stop doing that.'

He put it back in his waistband.

No lights came on in the house, but the noise grew louder – something mechanical, a whirring; they saw the shimmer of a shadow through the frosted-glass panel and stepped back as the door opened and showed the shape of Walter in his wheelchair. He recognised Ray.

'Sorry to be slow, I was upstairs.' He waved a hand behind him at the chairlift.

Ryan said, 'Has she gone?'

Walter looked curiously at Ryan for a moment, 'Not yet,' he said. 'She's waiting for the car.'

Ray said something about needing to speak to Chester as a

matter of urgency. Walter turned the wheelchair with difficulty in the narrow hallway and they followed him into the front room, where he turned on the lights with a remote. The house was quiet.

'Out the back,' Walter said. 'She was going to smoke a last cigarette while she waited for the car to take her to the airport.' He turned to Ray. 'You know the way, don't you? You won't have long, though; the car's due literally any moment.'

Ray thanked him and led Ryan into the back room. Through the windows, they could see the edge of the patio and the darkness of the garden beyond – black, mobile shadows of bushes and trees, a dim turbulence of clouded sky, mauve-grey, like the reflection of some distant conflagration.

Ray said, under his breath, 'She'll be out there on the patio. Can't you put your Glock somewhere she won't see it?' He opened the back door and they stepped out. There was no one there. Beyond the patio, the garden was jungle, a depthless sprawl of darkness, shapes of trees and bushes, wells of shadow; they couldn't see the end of it, and they stood there, at a loss.

'Goes all the way down to the cemetery,' Ray said.

'And you reckon she's down there somewhere? Like, what? Doing a bit of gardening? Give her a shout, Ray.'

Ray ignored him. They listened. The garden was perfectly, ideally silent. They peered around uncertainly. There were cigarette butts on the ground.

'She comes on to the patio to smoke,' Ray said in a low voice. 'And into the garden to practise shooting.' He gestured.

Ryan frowned. 'Oh, that's reassuring.' He suddenly shouted, 'Lynch!'

Ray hissed at him, fell silent, and they stood there in stiff, silhouetted postures, listening. In the darkness, there was a creak somewhere, an unmistakable scuffle of movement, then a sudden thud, like boot on wood, and instinct kicked in and they went sideways in different directions, low down and fast.

'Chester!' Ray shouted. 'It's Ray.'

No answer.

'We just need to talk to you.'

Nothing from the darkness.

Ryan said, 'Don't think she wants to talk to us. Going off the idea of talking myself, to be honest.'

They moved cautiously, low down, away from the light of the windows behind them, into shadow. One by one, they dropped down to the garden. Now, they could see almost nothing.

'Gig's up, Lynch!' Ryan called out. 'Stop fucking about!' He heard Ray hiss at him again from the other side of the patio, then there was another noise ahead of them, further off – footsteps, the sound of someone moving quickly through undergrowth. Then silence. After a moment, invisible to each other in the darkness, they began to move forward, creeping round bushes, pushing their way through mounds of weeds. They came to gaps – not lawn, but open areas of earth and grass – and crept round the edges, weaving themselves into the shadows. They had no torches and went blindly, seeing nothing, listening, hearing only themselves, the loud crack of winter twigs and constant paper-bag rustle of leaves, the louder beating of their hearts. Every few seconds, they paused, listening. The silence in the rest of the garden seemed to be the silence of hidden presences. Overhead, the moon appeared from behind a cloud and showed them dim glimpses of what lay ahead – a shadow-play of shapes that made no sense except to demonstrate the anarchy of nature. And then, by a full-grown tree, the shape of a person, waiting for them.

'Lynch!' Ryan called again.

Ray called out, too: 'Chester? It's me, Ray. We have to talk.' The figure by the tree made no reply. 'Chester,' Ray said again. After a moment, he stepped out from behind bushes and stood there, fully visible in the weak moonlight. Ryan made alarmed noises, but Ray took no notice. Very slowly, he began to walk forward, hands in front of him, empty palms up, talking, or not talking, but giving voice to disconnected bits of talk – *Chester? I'm not armed, Chester. Chester, we have to talk*, things like that – hardly aware of what he was saying, trying only to capture a tone, the trusting and trusted tone of someone reasonable and unthreatening, whom it would be a mistake to shoot, and, in this lulling manner, he went across the open space, all the way up to the silent, unmoving figure, and found that it was one of Lynch's targets.

Ryan had come out behind him, by then, and they went together, bolder now, between mature trees, more and more certain there was no one in the garden anymore, until they came at last to a tumble-down stone wall and saw, beyond, the Rose Hill Cemetery, crowded with the usual funerary monuments and tombstones, spectral in the moonlight, and deserted. An asphalt path ran away to the left and right, under an avenue of trees.

'She's fucked off,' Ryan said. 'At least Barko'll believe us, now.'

They stood there a moment.

'What does she think she's doing? Where's she going to go?'

They were baffled.

Ray said, 'We should get back, get the APW out.'

They jogged back up the garden, urgent again, stumbling in and out of darkness. Ryan tripped and fell heavily, and lay there.

'You alright? Ryan?'

Ryan got to his feet. 'Yeah.' He stood there. 'But I think I've found Lynch.'

They stared at the dark shape on the ground.

THIRTY

The shooting of a Deputy Chief Constable, gunned down in her own back garden, was the only front-page story next morning. Like the report of Zara Fanshawe's death a week earlier, but even louder, angrier, more serious, it swamped everything – no cautionary tale, this time, but an act of evil carried out, it was assumed, by organised crime against an iconic defender of the rule of law. In fact, Chester Lynch, not always trusted by the media in the past, was suddenly the champion of civil society, a black woman in a white man's world, a feared enemy of criminals, a fighter of noble causes, a reformer as necessary and sacrificial as Martin Luther King, her controversial interventions recycled now as visionary experiments, her abrasive manner as refreshing plain-speaking. Her personal story was everywhere – Walthamstow to Oxford University, police constable to National Uplift director – a narrative illustrated with snapshots of the girl at the street market stall, the Oxford graduate in cap and gown, the bobble-headed copper on the beat and the leather-jacketed icon impressively grim behind Aviators, her face at every stage that distinctive carved oddity so expressive of strength, vigilance and bloody-mindedness; and what else, indeed, do we look for in our law enforcement?

The law-enforcement community was naturally the hardest hit, those who hadn't liked her as outraged as her supporters. Ray and Ryan's investigation was as yet unknown; there was no impediment to the outpouring of anguish and rage in the ranks, no qualification to the grief felt by Lynch's colleagues – of whom no one was more thunderstruck than long-time associate Dave 'Barko' Wallace. Briefed by Ray, finally accepting that Lynch had been in some way involved in the events they had been investigating, he had passed with maximum discomfort through various stages of suspicion, bewilderment, fury and helplessness, and, in his office the next morning, he seemed actually, physically changed, not deflated so much as somehow insubstantial, taking up the same space, but with radically reduced density.

'Worked with her for twenty years,' he said in a new, thinned voice. 'She made my life hell. She was the best I ever worked with. She changed me,' he said fiercely.

Ray and Ryan shifted uneasily, wondering what he'd been like before.

'This whole thing,' he said, in helpless despair. 'This whole fucking thing, ever since the beginning.' He looked accusingly at them, as if they were to blame.

Nadim and Livvy joined them for the briefing. An initial forensics report had been completed. Lynch had been killed with a single shot, fired at point-blank range to the back of the head.

'Guess we can rule out suicide,' Ryan said, and in the dead silence wished he hadn't.

The recovered bullet was a 9-mm Parabellum, fired from a Glock-17, as in the murder of Toby Lewin-Mercer. In addition, a number of excellent boot prints had been captured in the soft ground of the garden – Magnum Panthers, size six (Lynch, incidentally, had taken size four) – and they concluded that they were looking for the killer of all three murder victims: Zara, Toby and Chester.

'All linked, nice and neat,' Ryan said, 'just as we run out of suspects.'

The murder of Lynch had been as unexpected as it was sensational, and it left their investigation in complete uncertainty.

From Newman Place, there was one piece of new information: a team had now begun excavating one of the foundations after finding signs of what they called 'interference'.

Ryan said nothing; the others looked away.

Barko informed them that he was taking personal charge of the investigation. Politically, it was unavoidable. As one of Lynch's closest colleagues, he was the focus of the media's attention and the obvious point of contact with the Chief Constable, who had demanded daily briefings going forward. Under his direction, there was to be no more unorthodoxy, no more off-piste, fly-by-night foolery, but absolutely correct procedure at all times, with no exceptions. The honour of the police was now under the spotlight.

'And that includes *your* honour,' he said to Ray and Ryan. 'People are dead, including our own. People are grieving. From now on, it's due process, complete probity, maximum sensitivity.' He looked particularly at Ryan. The proper and logical focus was the murder of the Deputy Chief Constable, but this should in no way impede the continuing investigation into the other two murders and the disappearance of Carol Hart. He had accepted that they were all linked. Additionally, a new inquiry had to be opened into the murder of Jasmine Barrett; after campaigning so fiercely against the original verdict, her family's reaction was likely to be emotional in the extreme. But first, strictly chaperoned by Barko, Ray and Ryan had to return to Rose Hill to talk to Walter – without revealing to him their suspicions of Lynch's involvement in the cover-up of the death of Jasmine Barrett.

He had looked pale before, but now he seemed almost transparent, a papery-frail figure in his wheelchair, with feverishly live eyes. He was less calm than numb, and the controlled quietness of his voice gave everything he said an air of almost desperate vulnerability. No, he told them, there had been nothing recently to suggest danger, nothing like in the past, when Chester had worked in Violent Crime, or before that, even, when patrolling the streets. As Deputy Chief Constable, directing policy, she had spent most of her time in an office, and the National Uplift role had taken her even further away from the action, into boardrooms and conference centres. Her battles lately had been with bureaucracy, not organised crime; she complained not about danger, but a lack of it. And so, he said, her murder now seemed a terrible disconnect. His eyes went glassy and Barko reached over and put a hand on his shoulder, and Ray and Ryan looked round at the framed photographs on the wall: Chester and Walter standing outside a church; sitting on a balcony overlooking some hot, foreign beach; scenes from domestic life, unexpectedly tranquil. Unbidden, Walter told them how he'd met Chester. Before his diagnosis, he'd been a forensic psychologist, working at the Hub, and, in 2006, he'd worked as a profiler on one of the cases Chester had taken on as the new head of Violent Crime.

'She had a reputation. Aggressive. Impatient. Arrogant. That was my own profile of her, in fact. She had all those traits, she didn't attempt to hide them or excuse them. She used them to get results. Dave will tell you. She has the best case-completion rate of any head of Violent Crime. Not a single young offender to go through her boot camp ever reoffended. For the people she cared about, she'd do anything – including, of course, give them hell. Anything that worked. She cared. The truth is, that's what she was really all about.'

The strangeness of that hushed them. At last, Barko began to say something, failed, sat there unspeaking, holding Walter's hand.

Ray began, delicately. There was never a good time. The right to grieve must be respected. Yet, as Walter knew better than most, an investigation depends so much on early information. The previous evening, they had hoped to ask Chester some urgent questions. Now, with his permission, they'd like to ask Walter some.

Walter nodded.

'Did Chester ever mention the name Zara Fanshawe to you?'

'The celebrity who was found dead? No, never.'

'Toby Lewin-Mercer?'

He shook his head.

'A man nicknamed Waitrose?'

Again, a shake of the head.

'Lena Wójcik?'

'No. None of those names mean anything at all.'

297

'Carol Hart?'

Walter hesitated, frowned. 'No, but Chester had one or two calls in the last week from someone called Carol. I heard her say her name.'

'Do you know what the calls were about?'

'No. It sounded like she wanted Chester to do something for her. Who is she?'

'She's missing,' Ryan said.

Walter turned and looked at him for the first time. 'You think Chester had something to do with her disappearance? Is that why you came here last night? Is this an investigation into Chester?'

Barko said, 'No, no. We're still trying to see the shape of the thing. We just think Chester knew some of the people we've been looking into. These calls Chester got from Carol – did you hear anything of them?'

'Well, I wasn't eavesdropping. I just had the impression they were difficult. Not unusual. Chester had many difficult calls. But I remember her saying things like, *No*, *Not happening*, *Don't call again*.'

'She was angry?'

He paused. 'Well, now I think about it, she sounded frustrated, perhaps even a little desperate. At the time, I put it down to the usual stresses.'

Ryan asked him to try to remember everything that happened in the hour before he and Ray had arrived at the house. But Walter remembered nothing of interest. They were just waiting for the car to take Chester to the airport; they talked trivia, the time of arrival in DC, the hotel she was booked into, the items Chester had packed in her carry-on.

'She didn't have any power adaptors. She'd ordered them, but they hadn't arrived. She was irritated. Anyway, the driver of the limo called to say he was just a few minutes away. We said goodbye. I went upstairs; she said she was going out for a last smoke. As I was going into the bathroom, I heard a knock on the door downstairs; I thought it was the limo, but Chester shouted up to tell me the power adaptors had arrived, after all. Then, five minutes later, you arrived. By then, she'd gone into the garden.'

Ryan said, 'Can we see the power adaptors?'

Walter looked surprised. 'I guess Chester put them somewhere; perhaps she packed them straight into her carry-on.'

'Can we look?'

They looked. There was no sign of power adaptors, or of any package, anywhere.

Walter explained again. He'd been upstairs. He'd heard the knock on the door. He'd heard Chester call up, *Delivery's here*, *Delivery's arrived*, something like that.

'Hear the door opening, closing, any conversation?'

'No.'

'How would Chester know it was the delivery?'

Walter thought about that. 'Well, we were expecting it. Probably, she also saw the delivery van through the pane in the door: they usually pull up on the driveway so they can turn around. You think she made a mistake?'

There would be time later for further questions; now, they made their excuses and went out on to the driveway, standing there a moment, looking about them – at the short, wide drive, the barren plot of front garden, the lattice-work shadows of the scaffolding next door – listening to the low-grade chuntering of traffic on the ring road. By the side of the house, there was wooden gate leading to a passage.

Ryan said what they were all thinking: 'Once he gets Lynch to the door, easy enough to get her down the passage, there, into the garden, where it's nice and quiet. He's a planner.'

'Or she is,' Ray said.

Ryan looked at him. 'Whoever. But they act like a pro. Finds the victim, plans it out, executes it, disappears. Every time, it's the same: Polstead Road, Minchery Road, here. Nobody sees a thing.'

'Someone who knows how to be invisible.'

'Like I said before, touch of the professional.'

After a moment, Ray said, 'But there's absolutely no one like that in the frame.'

They stood there, thinking about that.

'What now? The only person who knows something we don't is Carol. And we don't know where she is, or even if she's alive.'

Ryan said, 'Lena Wójcik had a social worker and a welfare officer. Worth talking to, maybe.'

Barko said, 'Do it.' To Ray, he said, 'Jasmine Barrett's family needs talking to. They'll be vocal. We need some tact, there.' He looked at his watch. 'In a couple of hours, they'll have completed this new dig at Newman Place. I want you both back at the station by then, for next steps.' His face underwent a spasm. 'I hate this case. I fucking detest it. Longer it goes on, the more nonsense we know and the less actual information. Needs to change.' He looked at them. 'You two. Change it.'

THIRTY-ONE

There was more nonsense up at the hospital, in fact, when Ryan got there. The staff in the Trauma Unit had no name or contact for Lena's welfare officer. They were sure, however, that a welfare officer had been to see her, and Ryan eventually found a nurse who'd been on duty at the time – though she found it difficult providing what might be called information.

'Didn't speak to him or nothing, no. Too busy doing my job. To be honest, I assumed he'd already talked to one of the other nurses. . . . Twice, I think. . . . Quite a long time with her, yeah. . . . Comforted? Well, I think so; hard to tell, though, she was that poorly, specially at the end. . . . No, I didn't. Well, just the once, as he left, down at the end of the corridor, there – that's the only time. . . . Thing is, he had a coat on, hood up, so it was hard to tell. On the small side, I remember that. . . . Well, yeah,' she said, 'I never thought of that somehow; I suppose it could have been a woman, yeah.'

She handed him the contacts for Lena's social worker. 'Maybe he knows something. He came too, had some nice long chats

301

with Lena.' She smiled. 'Catch him down at O'Hanlon – that's where he has his office. He works with all the homeless there.'

Ray was at the station, picking up the Barrett file. Reading through the testimonies of Jasmine's parents, he noted their persistent efforts to challenge the verdict of their daughter's death, continuing for months after Simpkins had been convicted. They'd refused to believe that Jasmine had been killed by him: the idea of it turned her, in the public mind, into just another sex worker. Their truth was that seventeen-year-old Jasmine Barrett was a ordinary girl with a good education who had temporarily lost her way, a victim of the groomers and drug pushers who target the vulnerable outside school. If she occasionally sold sex, it was only because she was troubled and confused. They had repeatedly drawn the attention of their legal counsel to the nature of her injuries, to the denials of Simpkins himself. Later, they demanded an appeal, wrote to the Home Office; they accused the judiciary, the police and the social services of shocking institutional failings; they made themselves as aggravating as possible, and, in the end, no one listened to them anymore.

It had, in fact, destroyed them. Ray read the postscript. Two years after Jasmine's death, her mother died of cancer. A year after that, her father committed suicide. Jasmine's only sibling – her younger brother, Anthony – suffered a breakdown. It was Anthony whom Ray now had to inform that the investigation into his big sister's death was being reopened and all the details of it re-examined.

'I don't even know if I can do this,' he said.

302

Nadim said, 'Think Ryan should do it instead?'

Ray took a breath and buttoned his coat.

Ryan was met at O'Hanlon House and taken to see senior homeless prevention officer Josh Rigsby. As soon as he spoke, it was obvious he was a local man.

'That's it. Grew up in Cowley Marsh. Started out in construction, but had mates who went off the rails; got interested in social work pretty much straight away, did my training, ended up here. Been here now, feels like, all my life. Homelessness's such a big issue. We do what we can, with not very much. Counselling, therapy, medical stuff. Basic practical advice. Sometimes, just a sympathetic ear. You hope something works. To be honest, though, give them all a thousand quid when they most need it and half of them wouldn't end up on the street in the first place.'

They began to talk about Lena Wójcik. Josh had never heard of her welfare officer; he thought the hospital had confused things. So far as he was aware, he'd been Lena's only visitor at the Trauma Unit. He'd worked with her since the previous autumn, when she'd reappeared in Oxford: she'd come to O'Hanlon when the weather started to get bad, and had stayed overnight from time to time.

'She wanted to get into the Julians, but her addiction issues were a problem there. She had a health worker – you could talk to her, too, though I don't think Lena saw her too often.'

Ryan asked about Josh's own visits to the Trauma Unit.

He had been three times, but Lena was not always communicative; she'd been confused, he said, often relapsing into unconsciousness. She'd hallucinated, seen things flying above her head – spirits, or angels, she called them sometimes. And she'd been frightened. 'I think she knew she was going to die.'

Ryan nodded. Lena had told him the same thing. 'What else did she say to you? Mention bags at all? Put her in a bag, bag her up, that sort of thing?'

He nodded. 'Weird. I used to take a bag in with me; I wondered if it was that which set her off, but it didn't seem to make any difference when I put it outside.'

'Anything about the old twenty-four-hour garage on the Garsington Road?'

'Yes. Lena solicited up there, for a while. Not recently – way back, when she was much younger. But it still frightened her. Something happened there, something to upset her.'

'Did she tell you what it was?'

'No. But it was something she mentioned to me when we had our first session, about three months ago, and I could tell it must have been very bad.'

Ryan thought about that.

'Any more questions? I've got a client session, in a moment.'

'Ever mention a Jasmine?'

He nodded. 'Yes. Lena knew her from the twenty-four-hour. I don't know how well. Jasmine Barrett was her name. I say *was* because she was killed in Littlemore, must be nearly twenty years ago, now.'

'Lena tell you this, too?'

He shook his head. 'I knew it already. Jasmine was one of the first people I worked with as a trainee here. I had to testify at the trial.'

'That's interesting. What did you make of the verdict?'

304

'There was controversy, I remember. The family objected. To be honest, I thought it was probably the right decision. Thing is, her mother and father hated the idea of Jasmine being labelled a sex worker – that was the reason they fought against it. I mean, can you imagine their pain?'

He sat there, imagining.

Josh went on: 'It destroyed them, the whole family. The mother died, the father killed himself. Jasmine's younger brother had a breakdown. I worked with him as well, later on. He'd absolutely adored his sister. Thing is,' he said, 'what they said was reasonable – there were genuine doubts, the judge admitted it – but they were blinded by their emotions, they became obsessed. For years, Tony wouldn't accept it. In the end, he made a recovery – not that I claim any credit; there was a lot of intensive work put in by the psychiatric team – and gradually he came to terms with it. That's the thing about this place,' he said. 'It's why I'm here – why we're all here. Because, with just a little help, people who have lost their way can find it again.'

He sat there, thinking about that.

'I still see him around,' he said. 'Tony. Saw him for a drink a while back, in fact, and I mentioned to him what Lena had told me, and he was able to talk about it quite normally.' He looked at his watch. 'Time's up. Sorry.'

Ryan didn't move. He said slowly, 'You told him what Lena had said, about seeing something at the twenty-four-hour?'

'Yes.' Josh got up. 'I'm really sorry, I'm late. I'm going to have to rush you out.'

Ryan still didn't move. 'When was this?'

Josh started to show impatience. 'Late autumn. Must have

305

been . . . beginning of November.' He looked at his watch again and grimaced. 'Look, I'm sorry.'

Ryan just looked at him. 'His name's Tony?'

'Yes.'

'Where does he live?'

'Down Wootton way, I think.'

'What does he do?'

'He's a postman. Does a round in north Oxford. That's it, I have to dash.'

THIRTY-TWO

Ray turned off the main road through Wootton, on to an unpaved, unnamed road running between the backs of bungalows and tall wooden fences. A call came in from Ryan and he let it go through to voicemail. After a while, he turned again on to another unpaved road – just the same, but narrower – a two-wheel track of cinders, with a strip of grass down the middle. Bumping slowly along, he left the bungalows behind and emerged into fields. There were stables and paddocks here, and, beyond them, nothing but raw Oxfordshire, flat and colourless. The sky opened up, also colourless. A few horses stood in rugs at the edge of a field. A buzzard sat on a fence post, watching him pass. The track turned again. He passed a caravan in a field and an old Mini, up to its headlights in weeds, and some piles of building materials greened over where the tarpaulin had fallen back, then more stables of the same warped wood, so dark it was almost black, with sagging corrugated roofs. He began to wonder if he was in the wrong place, then he rounded a final bend and saw, behind a screen of firs at the end of the track, a wooden shack in a yard of earth, and in the yard an old Land Rover, and, standing next to the Land Rover, a number of cases and trunks, and a short, wiry man with a kit bag over his shoulder, who watched him suspiciously as he approached.

Ray hadn't said that he was coming. He slowed to a halt next to a *For Sale* sign and wound down his window.

'Anthony Barrett?'

The man looked at him a long time. 'What's happened?' he said, broad Oxfordshire vowels plain and untrusting.

'Know a Fed when I see one,' Anthony Barrett said. 'Is it bad?'

The cabin-like room where they sat was a flimsy box, long and straight, with timber walls and small windows and bare floorboards. The furniture was flimsy too: wooden chairs, a wooden table with a television on it, two old electric fires, a lampshade hanging low. A frontier shack – and Anthony Barrett looked to Ray like some sort of frontiersman, weathered and self-sufficient, wearing a cracked brown leather vest over an old crew-neck combat sweater and, despite the cold weather, Gurkha shorts. He wore Magnum Panthers too, Ray noticed, and it came to him how common they were, after all – the boot of choice for postmen, as well as police, ground crew, warehouse workers and any number of people on their feet all day. His eye was caught by a crowd of framed photographs on a chest of drawers under the window, all showing the same young woman, recognisable at once as Jasmine Barrett; and he swallowed and shifted uncomfortably on his chair as he turned back to Anthony.

His phone rang – Ryan, once more. He cut it, and Ryan immediately rang again, and Ray apologised and turned it off and put it away.

'It's about your sister,' he said, at last. 'I've come to tell you that we're reopening the inquiry into her death. I realise this will be a shock to you.'

Barrett stared at him so long, Ray wondered if he'd understood. His face was completely without expression. After a while, he put up a hand and touched the side of his head – a slow movement, very careful, as if he felt himself to be suddenly extremely fragile.

'I want you to know that we'll do all we can, going forward, to minimise your distress.'

Still, Barrett said nothing. His face was a blank. Then, when he spoke, his voice was surprisingly normal. 'Why now?'

Without going into detail, Ray began tentatively to offer an explanation. The new information. The investigation into the other deaths – of Zara, Toby and Chester.

Barrett watched him, it seemed almost without interest, strangely disconnected, his thoughts apparently elsewhere. He suddenly interrupted: 'Who killed her, then?'

Ray hesitated. 'We don't have a full picture yet.'

'Don't you?'

He stared at Ray, who glanced away to the smiling girl on the chest of drawers, and back again. So many photographs; it was like a shrine.

'You must have been very close to her,' Ray said.

Barrett made no reply.

'There was quite an age gap between you, if I remember.'

309

Barrett was sitting very still, as if any movement might shake him to pieces, watching him.

'Seven year,' he said, after a while, carefully.

Ray talked about next steps, conversations, support during the process – all the time with the same sense that Barrett wasn't listening, only watching. He remembered from the file that he'd suffered serious mental-health issues after the death of his sister, and tried to imagine the feelings he was experiencing now, and couldn't.

Barrett abruptly got to his feet. 'Want tea?'

Ray hesitated. 'If it's not a bother.'

Barrett turned without comment and went out of the room. It came to Ray that he'd gone to weep in private, though he heard nothing. There was silence in the shack. Ray sat there, trying to decide how much to tell Barrett about the case, how much to conceal. Several minutes passed. Still, there was no noise from the next room – no sound of a kettle being boiled, even – and the silence went on.

After a while, Ray got up and went over to look at the photographs on the chest of drawers. Jasmine had been a pretty child and a good-looking teenager, with dimples and blonde braids and a wide smile. Tiny even teeth, at first, then gaps and big front ones, then braces. There was no picture of her older than fifteen or sixteen. They were all school portraits: individual portraits and class photos at first; later, netball teams, school orchestra, and a graduation memorial, the student holding a rolled and ribboned certificate with a look of modest pride. There were no pictures of anyone else, here – only Jasmine.

Ray looked round at the rest of the room, peered out of the

310

window. It was a lonely spot, the silence in the shack was the silence of the countryside, as if Barrett needed the big empty sky and the dead rural hush. Again, Ray tried to imagine the damage he'd suffered as a boy when his sister had been murdered. A seven-year gap in their age was large; she would have seemed grown-up to him, someone to be adored, idolised.

'Lived here long?' he called.

After a moment, Barrett appeared in the doorway. He didn't seem to have made the tea yet.

'Five year, more or less.'

'And now it's on the market?'

'Landlord selling it for development.'

'Where will you go?'

Barrett looked at him as if trying to work out a hidden meaning in what he'd said.

'Not far.'

He turned and went back into the other room. He had a tattoo on his left calf, Ray noticed: a girl's face, with dates underneath.

There was silence in the shack again, and Ray went over to the other side of the room, where there were some more photographs on a shelf – this time of Anthony. In one, he stood in Royal Mail red and black, holding a package in front of a red post-office van parked in a leafy north Oxford avenue; it could have been Polstead Road.

Ray turned to another picture.

'I see you were in the forces,' he called out, after a moment.

There was no reply from Barrett.

Ray studied it. The caption said *42 Commando*. Above it, a younger Anthony Barrett stood unsmiling in green tee and

311

combats, against a backdrop of sand and salt-rimed rock. Ray-Bans, baseball cap, black fingerless gloves – the image of a highly trained killer. On his belt, a gun. Ray peered. It was a Glock.

He remembered a phrase from a medical report in the file: *Anthony is having difficulty moving on.*

Ray stood there, looking, his back to the room. The silence in the shack was deafening, a silence loud and dangerous and somehow, suddenly, very near and just behind him. Without turning round, Ray went sideways fast, low to the floor, and rolled, and came up ready. Barrett was staring at him, Glock in hand. They faced each other in silence.

Ray said, 'You. Delivering the post in Polstead Road. The post van pulling away in Minchery Road. A late-afternoon delivery at Rose Hill. No one notices a postman.'

After a while, Barrett spoke, though not to reply: 'They killed her and covered it up.'

'Tony,' Ray said. 'Tony.'

'She was seventeen.' He lifted the gun.

Ray found nothing else to say.

'Ten,' Tony said. 'I was ten.'

He took a step forward.

'How old are you?' he said.

Ray said, 'I've got twin boys, six months.'

The moment went on forever, Barrett standing there, gun up, staring at him; and then, imperceptibly at first, his hand began to shake, his face slowly bent out of shape, and at last he began to cry; and Ray stepped forward and carefully took the gun away.

THIRTY-THREE

There are many places where lost things end up, and the people who lost them, where the broken and the breakers, the damaged and the destroyers, come to rest. This is one of them: a windowless underground room, under harsh lights, in a police station. This is where street work ends and paperwork begins, the office of due process, the staging post between freedom and confinement, the space between moving and stopping, the confessional, the echo chamber of a last burst of shouting and weeping.

But Anthony Barrett did not shout or weep. He sat unmoving and impassive next to his lawyer, watched from behind the two-way by Superintendent Wallace and a dozen other officers curious to see the man who had killed their Deputy Chief Constable. The interview was over quickly. Barrett did not want to talk to the police. Why would he? That Deputy Chief Constable had smashed his sister's head in with a spade and shoved her in a bag and driven it away so that her killing could be covered up and the people who had killed her could get away with it.

He refused to explain what he'd done, though now they knew enough to put certain things to him, and he did not deny them.

They put to him that, at the beginning of November, in the Marsh Harrier pub in Cowley, he'd learned from Josh Rigsby, the social worker, that Lena Wójcik had seen something terrible happen at the old twenty-four-hour garage on the Garsington Road on the night of New Year's Eve 2005.

He didn't deny it.

They put it to him that he'd talked to Lena then and had learned what she'd seen: a car striking her friend and co-worker, Jasmine Barrett. How much Lena had actually seen, they did not know. Enough to recognise, as the passenger in the car, Toby Lewin-Mercer, whose face was well known from *Coronation Street* at that time. In any case, whatever she'd told Tony had been enough for him to start to trace the identities of both Toby and his fiancée, whose recent engagement was reported in the movie magazines at that time.

He didn't deny it.

They put it to him that, once he knew who Zara was, he had contacted her, in early November. It had prompted her breakdown and, in time, an urge in Zara to confess what she'd done and hidden for so long.

Tony spoke: 'But she didn't, did she? She did what she'd always done – spent a little time in rehab, came out talking about herself.'

Ray said, 'So what did you do, then?'

Tony said nothing.

Ray put it to him that he had sent her a message to meet him at the rail station car park in Becket Street, and that she came.

314

He did not deny it. He grimaced sardonically. 'And panicked, crashed the car and nearly killed me same fucking way she killed Jazz.'

They put it to him that he had taken Zara in his own car to Polstead Road, heard her confession, and had found out from her that Toby was now Waitrose; he had then killed her.

He did not deny it.

And that he had subsequently killed Toby Lewin-Mercer and DCC Chester Lynch.

He said, 'All this bullshit. You want me to talk about what's important? About my sister, beautiful like you never fucking saw in your life, helping me with my homework before she went out clubbing? Not even human to you, just a mess to clear up so two friends can carry on with their nice lives. They thought they could just make it go away, like the rich do – they always know someone with pull, get them out of trouble. Enough.'

Ryan said, 'What about Carol Hart?'

'Go fuck yourself,' Tony said. 'You know what? All that therapy I got said the same thing: I had to let her go. That's not how it works – I know that, now. What I learned in that Polstead Road attic was, if it's precious, never let it go, don't lose it, keep a hold on it – and that includes your anger, your rage, the fucking fury, 'cause you're going to need it one day, put things right. Jazz had gone, yeah, but what they'd done to her hadn't.' He stood up. 'I'm done here. Tell your boys to come in, take me away, bag me up.'

THIRTY-FOUR

Headlines over the next few days were more than usually volatile, with a high level of emotion and a low level of information. On the one hand, the media knew that a man in custody, unnamed, had been charged with the murders of Deputy Chief Constable Chester Lynch, socialite and celebrity Zara Fanshawe and the former screen actor Toby Lewin-Mercer, whose death as 'Waitrose' they now caught up with. On the other hand, they did not know why. The police were withholding the detail. Enquiries ongoing, they said. Superintendent Wallace, generally thought to be in his last days in post, gave twice-a-day press briefings, exemplary in their lack of facts. It drove the journalists wild and impressed DI Wilkins (Ryan), who sat in his scratchy uniform alongside Wallace, a little more competent at these things now, but no more relaxed. He was asked little and said less. Occasionally, he was pitched a left-field question about the disappearance of Oxford businesswoman Carol Hart, and whether there was any connection with the recent triple murder, to which he had learned to answer, 'Enquiries ongoing,' in a variety of different ways.

In fact, the inquiry into Carol's disappearance was making zero progress. The excavations at Newman Place, ongoing, had led so far only to the discovery of a stash of homemade weapons thought to have been used a few days earlier in a burglary in Headington. A number of sightings, including one at the ferry port of Fishguard, had proved to be false. Though it was clear that she'd been known to Anthony Barrett, he was still refusing to say anything about her.

Ryan and Ray spent most of their days in discussions with the Crown Prosecution Service, busy with the usual administrative tasks of bringing charges, and in the evenings went back to homes that sometimes seemed the same and sometimes different. In Grove Street, Ray settled back to childcare duties with Diane. They did not talk about Chester Lynch. Fortunately, Ray's father could not complain about his son not joining someone who was no longer alive to be joined; and he was cheered, in fact, by news of Wallace's likely removal, and spent his evenings calling his son to encourage him to apply for the vacant post. In general, however, there was a new sort of calm in the house. Ryan, on the other hand, experienced no such calm, but went home every evening in an agony of apprehension about little Ryan, who remained ill, and was forbidden from seeing his son.

About a week later, as he arrived home, he got a call from Ray to tell him that the team had stopped digging at Newman Place. Lack of results.

Ryan stood outside his front door, phone crooked against his shoulder, fumbling for his house keys. 'Fair enough.'

Ray hesitated. 'They're proposing to start excavating Lynch's garden.'

Ryan stopped fumbling. 'Routine, right?'

Ray made some mumbling noises. 'Nadim's been trawling CCTV. She's just got hold of footage from the private cameras at that hotel in Sandford. Turns out Carol met Lynch there the day she went missing.'

Ryan stood there, keys forgotten in his hand.

Ray said, 'Doesn't make anything more likely. Might mean nothing, right?'

'Right.'

There was no sound between them for a moment but the sound of their breathing.

'Alright,' Ryan said. 'Got to go.'

Ray said quickly, 'How's little Ryan, by the way?'

'Still poorly, I think. Just got home; I'm about to find out. Haven't seen him for, like, a week. Not allowed.'

'I'm sorry.' He cleared his throat. 'Listen, Ryan.'

'Make it quick, mate. Like I say, I just got home.'

'You know they've been inviting nominations for awards.'

'You want me to put you in for something?'

'No, no.' Ray sounded shocked. 'Absolutely not. No. I've . . . I've nominated you.'

'What?' An aggressive bark.

'I said, I've—'

'What for?'

'For the leadership award.'

'I mean, what the fuck did you do it for? You taking the piss, Ray?'

'For God's sake, Ryan!'

There was a pause.

'You mean, straight up?'

'Yes, straight up. Of course, straight up.'

There was a longer pause.

'Just a bit weird of you, that's all.'

'Well, get used to it,' Ray said crossly.

There was a very long pause.

Ryan mumbled, 'Yeah, alright. Anyway, got to go.' He didn't go. 'Oh, hey. Ray?'

'What?'

'Cheers, mate.'

The house was quiet. Upstairs, he could hear the bath running and Jade moving around. He went into the kitchen and, to his surprise, found little Ryan sitting in his chair with a beaker of juice.

'Ry! What you doing out of bed?'

His son's face was pale, his hair a little lank, but his eyes had lost that unnatural brightness. He swung his beaker away from his face and smiled, and, about three seconds later, began to talk, in an unstoppable flow, about everything he'd done that day, how he'd found a feather and been to the toilet twice and heard a helicopter and remembered that owls catch voles and things like that, and how he'd thought about the various ways in which rain falls downwards, and tomorrow, he said, he was going to nursery again, and did Daddy like mouses?

He'd done a picture for him in green crayon, which was on the table, and at last Ryan stopped gazing and grinning at him, and looked at it.

'You did this? Serious?'

Little Ryan nodded solemnly.

Ryan brought the drawing close to his face. 'Tell you what, mate. Best fucking mouse I ever seen.'

'Daddy!'

'Talking of mouses, shall I get our book? Feels like it's been about a month since we had a read.'

Little Ryan began to chant, 'Mouse and mole, mouse and mole.'

Upstairs, the bath had stopped running, and Jade appeared in the doorway and looked at Ryan funny.

'He's alright,' Ryan said to her. 'Look. He's better. He's talking again, just like normal.'

'I'm aware of that. Listen.'

'Not now. We're going to have a read.'

'Not just yet.'

'Why not?'

'Someone come to see you.' She nodded in the direction of the front room.

'Can't it wait?'

She just looked at him.

Reluctantly, he left his son and went into the front room, and there he found Carol, waiting for him with a mug of tea.

'Hello, Ryan.'

She was wearing a coat and had a suitcase with her. Ryan remembered the last time he'd seen her, that cold little smile as she shut the door on him.

He gave a half-smile, a little snort. He shook his head. 'Not buried in Lynch's garden, then.'

'Decided against it.' She gave a smile that wasn't really a smile. 'Got a minute?'

'Where've you been?'

'Nice little guest house, just off the Abingdon Road.'

'You're shitting me. What, all this time?'

'That's it.'

'You look alright, for someone who's been in hiding for a week.'

She did. She had that sort of face that doesn't fall to pieces and wouldn't ever. Great bones. Only her eyes showed strain.

'On my way to the station.' She indicated her suitcase. 'Thought I owed it you to come here first. Bit of explaining.'

The reason she'd dumped him, she said, was because she knew what was coming. It didn't really matter how it played out, it would have been bad for him.

'Didn't want to lose you, though.' She smiled.

It lifted him, despite himself.

'Course,' she added, 'not going to see you for a while, now. So. You'll want to know what happened, being a detective and that.' She took a breath. 'Here goes.'

In 2005, she'd been twenty years old, a runaway, an addict, a sex worker pimped by a number of different men, none of whom called her by her name, living hand to mouth, surviving between fixes on nothing but youth. The next five minutes was all she thought about. Days, she was kept at a place in Barton; nights, she worked various streets, including the Garsington Road, soliciting at first beyond the ring road, in the shadow of the Cowley works, and later, as the pimps demanded more profits, pushing down towards town, as far as St Luke's Road and the

321

abandoned twenty-four-hour garage. There was a group of girls she saw there regularly – Lena Wójcik was one, Jasmine Barrett another. They were all losers, every last one of them – fuck-ups, addicts, rejects, mentals, sickos. Her, most of all. Worthless, and they knew it – they just didn't think about it, couldn't.

'Except, sometimes I did. I'd tell myself I wasn't really kept in a room in Barton, that I didn't need the next fix, that I was going to get lucky and get out. I had this fantasy: running my own business, getting rich, living in a big house. Truth was, I was in that room in Barton and I needed that fix and there was no way out, none, and, though I never thought it, I knew somewhere deep inside that I was going to die, and soon – I could feel it was going to happen. All I had was the next five minutes, no more than that.'

In fact, come to think of it, death didn't scare any of the girls too much; perhaps they'd lost too much already. They used to joke about the girls who'd been murdered by the Spade Killer, even as they got into another punter's car.

She took another breath.

'Anyway, that night. Reckon you know something about it, by now.'

'Go on.'

'New Year's Eve, loneliest time of the year, good for business; our pimp had us out early and working late.'

She was at the garage. Earlier, she'd been with a couple of punters in their cars, over at the business park; now, she was back, and had gone behind the building to get a small hit to help her through the rest of the night when she heard the car coming along the Garsington Road, throwing out these strange noises – engine

322

roar, wild slippage of gears, then a long tearing scream of rubber. She looked round the side of the building in time to see a sleek, sporty thing veer across the road, very fast, one side low, the other high up, bouncing on to the forecourt, where Jasmine was adjusting her skirt. Then, the dull thumping crunch of metal on body, a shadow flung sideways like an old mat, slithering across the concrete. Too late, the car came to an abrupt stop, engine dead. There was that after-noise of no sound, sudden absence of uproar, and, in it, a moment when nothing happened, as if everyone was on pause before going on with what they should have been doing, as if Jasmine was about to get up and smooth down her skirt and go over to the car and lean in the window and give the driver a couple of prices. But there was no Jasmine anymore, just this thing dumped on the ground, starting to leak across the concrete. Then, two people got out of the car. Elegant, beautifully dressed, but pale and shaky, acting as people do in emergencies, hanging back, as if embarrassed, or irritated, as if they were waiting for time to roll backwards and return them to where they were thirty seconds earlier. Occasionally, they looked, astonished, at the body, as if amazed to find it still there. At last, the woman spoke: 'This can't be happening.' It was the woman who had been driving. The man was suddenly sick down the side of the car. After the rapidity of the crash, everything was happening in slow motion. Not knowing what to do, the two people began to argue. Then, another car came past. It slowed down, the two people on the forecourt froze, the driver shouted out of the window, 'Zara! Get a room!' and drove off again, laughing. It seemed that Jasmine's body, behind the sports car, hadn't been visible to them. But now Zara and her companion were prompted

323

into action. Zara made a call. Ten minutes later, another car drew up, a Fiesta, and this black woman got out. She was wearing a police uniform and she was carrying a bag and a spade.

'You know the rest, I think,' Carol said.

Ryan said, 'But what were you doing, all that time?'

She paused. 'Never thought me an angel, did you, Ryan? I was taking pictures.'

He looked at her.

She'd had with her a new Nokia that took photographs. Her pimp didn't allow the girls to have phones, but a punter had carelessly left it behind and she'd kept it, learned how to use it. From behind the garage, she took photos, dozens of them, and kept taking them, even when Lynch was using the spade on Jasmine. Once they'd bagged the body and put it in the boot of Lynch's car, she came out from behind the building and confronted them.

'Jazz was dead, nothing to be done about that. I was still alive. Truth is, I didn't think twice. This was my chance, Ryan. What was the most precious thing to me, at that moment? Me. My life. Saving it. Getting it back. Grabbing more than the next five minutes of it. So, I came out on to the forecourt, gave them the biggest shock of their fucking lives, told them I had the pictures to send them all to jail for a long, long time. All of them. I knew there was money in them – it was obvious from the car, the clothes they wore, the way they spoke. I didn't even have to prompt them. It was Zara's first thought: she'd just had an inheritance. "What do you want? Do you want money? I've got money. I can give you a lot of money." She ended up giving me five times as much as she offered at first; I made sure she had a good picture of what fifteen years inside would do to her. Do you understand, Ryan?

I was lost. My life, worthless. With that money, I bought my life back, bought a future. Two years later, I'd set up my businesses, got the farmhouse. I'd become a normal person.'

She swallowed. Ryan said nothing for a while and the silence went on.

'What do you think of me, now?' she asked, at last.

Ryan didn't answer, shrugged, winced. 'Five of you,' he said eventually. 'Five of you kept that secret, all this time.'

In fact, she'd hardly ever thought of the others. Lives are separate, even in a small city like Oxford. Then, suddenly, they were thrown together again. Zara appeared one night, like someone out of a dream. In fact, Carol didn't believe Zara was going to go through with it, but her own finances were shot to pieces by then and she wondered mainly if she could get any money out of her. Then there was the second shock of Chester Lynch on stage at the police ball, seeing how famous she was getting, how important; but, again, what Carol thought of first was money.

'Then Zara was killed. Changed my priorities, as they say.' She'd gone to Lynch, then; she had that instinct, more valuable than cleverness, that things were about to go bad. But Lynch was difficult, suspicious, even threatening. So, she acted alone, at once. Disappeared.

'Self-protection kicked in. Like it did at the twenty-four-hour, that night. Survive it, come out ahead – that's me.' She looked at him. 'Difference this time is the kids. Can't live without them. So.' She got to her feet. 'If I don't want to lose them completely, this way's the only way.'

She looked down at him. 'It was good with you, Ryan.' She smiled. 'Want to take me in? Might as well get the credit for it.'

Little Ryan appeared in the doorway holding a copy of *Mouse and Mole*, which he must have retrieved from under his bed.

'Daddy, I found it!'

Ryan thought of lost things. Carol, Jasmine, the lives of the innocent and the not so innocent. Zara, Waitrose with his trolley, men and women sleeping in doorways. Lena, beaten to death two ways – first gradually, then all at once. A book in the hand of a three-year-old boy with startling blond hair and an expression still damp from a week's illness. Precious things. Hold them close for fear of losing them.

Ryan said to Carol, 'You're alright. Thing is, it's time for his bedtime story. Do you mind getting an Uber?'

After she'd gone, they finally settled together on the sofa with the book.

'This is good, isn't it?'

'It is good, Daddy.'

'Been a long time, mate.'

'Years and years,' little Ryan said, conversationally.

Ryan opened the book at the beginning.

The doorbell rang.

'You're fucking shitting me.'

'Daddy!'

'Let's wait a bit. Maybe they'll go away.'

The doorbell rang again.

He got up, crossed the room at speed and jerked open the front door.

'What?' he shouted into the dark.

Chief Detective Superintendent Dave Barko Wallace stepped

into the light, wearing full uniform, a little grim around the eyes. 'Bad night, eh, son?'

Ryan shrugged and gurned.

'You're alright. Won't keep you. Just an update about the search for Carol—'

'You just missed her,' Ryan said.

Barko's expression didn't change, but an eyebrow twitched. 'Say it again, son. I didn't quite catch it.'

Ryan began to explain and petered out.

Barko's voice remained low, but with undercurrents of instability. 'So, you're telling me you just let her go?'

Ryan said something half-witted about bedtime reads and fell silent again, and stood there, enduring Barko's prolonged and unfathomable stare.

'Of course,' the Super said, at last. 'Of course you did; it's exactly what I would've expected you to do. Missing person of material interest, vital to the ongoing prosecution of a triple murderer. Why not let them make their own way to the station, see if they get there?' He looked at Ryan, nodded. 'Okay, then.'

He went a few paces down the drive and stopped and turned back.

'It's funny, you know,' he said. 'You're probably the worst policeman I ever worked with. And, at the same time, maybe the best. Doesn't usually happen like that.'

He turned away.

Ryan shouted after him, 'See you tomorrow, then. Sir.'

He heard Barko say, as if to himself, 'I doubt it,' then he went back into the living room, where little Ryan had fallen asleep with the book lying over him like a blanket, and he picked him up and carried him upstairs.

ACKNOWLEDGEMENTS

I'm pleased to have the opportunity to acknowledge the Royal Literary Fund for their support during the writing of this book; and it's a pleasure to thank the individuals who helped in different and important ways. My thanks, then, to Anthony Goff, my agent, for unignorable advice which I sometimes ignore; to Jon Riley, my editor, for invaluable insights and trustworthy judgements, and Jasmine Palmer, for making the editorial process so frictionless; to Penelope Price for another indispensable copy-edit; and to Ana McLaughlin, Lisa Gooding and Elizabeth Masters for totally expert PR. And, as always, more than thanks to my family, Eluned, Gwil and Eleri, who make basic functioning possible.

Read on for the newest book in
the DI Ryan Wilkins Mysteries

A VOICE IN THE NIGHT

ONE

Iffley Village, Oxford. 03.35 in the middle of a late April night.

It comes out of darkness, tearing the silence to shreds. At first it's inside her head, then outside, insistent and loud; then she catches her breath and fumbles for the phone.

GRETA EMMETT: Hello?

EMERGENCY CENTRE: Is that Greta?

GRETA EMMETT: Yes. What is it?

EMERGENCY CENTRE: I'm sorry to wake you. Do you know where your husband is?

GRETA EMMETT: Yes. Yes, of course.

EMERGENCY CENTRE: Where?

GRETA EMMETT: Here, in bed. He's . . .

EMERGENCY CENTRE: Greta?

GRETA EMMETT: No, he's not. He's not here.

EMERGENCY CENTRE: Five minutes ago his fall alarm was activated. He's not been responsive to our call back.

GRETA EMMETT: He must have got up.

EMERGENCY CENTRE: Then it may be he's fallen somewhere in the house and lost consciousness. We'd recommend you check, in the bathroom, also the foot of the stairs. Are you able to do that?

GRETA EMMETT: Yes. I'll get up and do it now.

Iffley Village, Oxford. 03.45.

GRETA EMMETT: Hello? Hello?

EMERGENCY CENTRE: Greta.

GRETA EMMETT: I can't find him.

EMERGENCY CENTRE: Where have you looked?

GRETA EMMETT: Everywhere. Bathroom, bottom of the stairs. Landing, hallway, kitchen, everywhere, I've looked everywhere, he's not here. I don't understand.

EMERGENCY CENTRE: Might he have gone outside? Elderly people sometimes wander, become confused.

GRETA EMMETT: There is nothing wrong with his mind. He doesn't wander, he has problems walking. Can't you tell where he is from the device?

EMERGENCY CENTRE: We've temporarily lost signal.

GRETA EMMETT: So you have no idea?

EMERGENCY CENTRE: Don't worry, stay calm, there will be an explanation. However . . .

GRETA EMMETT: What?

EMERGENCY CENTRE: We recommend you call the emergency services. Without delay.

Two hours later dawn rises like vapour in Iffley Village, slowly revealing the old stone houses, the famous church snug in its dripping precinct, and narrow walled lanes, where a patrol car stands idling and officers pass under damp greenery, knocking on front doors. Up the slope the mist-blurred estate of Rose Hill emerges and, further off, the sprawl of Kennington. Gradually, the dark river appears, and the dim, grey woods and the Eastern Bypass slick and wet. And now, three miles away, across fields of pylons, looping roads and distant buildings, daylight reaches the hotel at Sandford with its purposefully rustic building and wide sweep of lawn drenched after the overnight rain, in the middle of which an old man wearing pyjamas and dressing gown lies spreadeagled on his back, grey face to the sky.

TWO

By six o'clock Oxford town centre had also risen out of the mist, watery light shining on college, shopping centre and dreaming cranes. It would be a fine day at last. For now, the dim streets were still and hushed, though by Folly Bridge the geese were disturbing the peace of the night staff at nearby St Aldates police station, where they were patiently outlasting the final hour of their shift. Few people were in the building as yet, whole sections of it were still dark and empty, but on the top floor, in the senior management suite, one office was already lit – the one with the door plate bearing the name Dave Wallace, Detective Chief Superintendent.

But it was not Dave 'Barko' Wallace sitting behind the desk. Barko had gone – transferred, demoted – leaving behind only his name and the memory of his harsh Glaswegian bark. At his old desk, already an hour into her first morning as DCS, sat Rebecca Wainwright, multi-decorated hero of celebrated investigations: Cambridge-educated, ex-army, blonde and immaculate, sharp and uncompromising, the face of New

Policing at Thames Valley. The Changemaker. The Necessary Reformer.

She sat at her desk thinking about change, about reform. In front of her were two folders, one labelled *DI Ryan Wilkins*, the other *DI Raymond Wilkins*, both marked 'Confidential'; and now she opened them and gave them her coolly focused attention.

Wilkins, Ryan Earl

Born 5 February 1994, Hinksey Point Trailer Park, Oxford, England. Academic qualifications: none. Accepted on to the Inspector Level Direct Entry Programme June 2018. Fast-tracked to completion December 2019. Top attainment marks in his group.

First career posting: Wiltshire Police, terminated in dismissal after six months for Misconduct. Verdict overturned on appeal.

Second posting: Thames Valley Police, terminated in dismissal after four weeks for Gross Misconduct. Reinstated after rehabilitation training, anger management course, etc.

There was a photograph. Narrow-faced white boy wearing some sort of shell suit with a smear of shiny scar tissue down his left cheek. Mousy hair plastered against his forehead. A wide mouth with a humorous kink and an expression in his squinting eyes both wary and sharp. It looked like a photograph that might have accidentally been transferred from the file of a suspect under investigation. She flipped a page and read to the end, where there was an eventually legible handwritten note apparently made by outgoing DCS Wallace.

337

Note.
Trailer park boy. Father in prison. Mother of his infant
son deceased, OD. Problems outweighed by his abilities,
just. Sees things. Massive and constant supervision
required. Do not, repeat not, give him responsibility.
DW

DCS Wainwright absorbed this jumble of observations and turned to the other folder.

Wilkins, Raymond St-John Chidozie

*Born 17 March 1990, Ealing Broadway, London, England.
Nigerian heritage. Academic qualifications: First class honours degree in Politics, Philosophy and Economics, Balliol College, Oxford; College Essay Prize; University Debating Trophy. Other: Sporting Blue (Boxing); Queen's Commendation for Bravery (Police Silver Leaf).*

First career posting: Thames Valley Police, DI fast-track scheme. Exemplary record. Operational Command undertaken. See Silver Leaf, above.

There was another photograph, a studio portrait. Improbably handsome black guy with a face at once heroic and sensitive wearing a grey blazer with a pink box-check pattern over a sky-blue gingham shirt. He looked like a model for a fashion brochure and his expression showed that he knew it but was modest enough not to make a thing of it. Wainwright turned a few pages and again found Wallace's scrawl at the end.

In any organisation there were always problem personnel to be
dealt with. Dealt with promptly. DCS Wainwright did what she
always did: ascertained the facts at speed, evaluated, and took
a view. Then she locked the folders away in a drawer, glanced
at her watch, put on her hat and went out to join the Chief
Constable.

The CC was a big man, mountainously hulked in his decorated uniform, with the sort of head seen on old Roman coins,
massive and beaten; and when he spoke, his deep bass voice had
notes of brutality and dominance. A hugely scary figure rarely
seen at St Aldates, his presence in the building to introduce the
new Superintendent created an atmosphere of awe bordering
on terror. It was still only six thirty but the entire team had
assembled, as requested, in the open-plan area in front of the
Super's office, around a hundred people of all ranks, keen to
see their new commanding officer; and when she appeared
their conversations died away as the hush of curiosity fell over
them. Even the geese were quiet, and in the silence she stood
facing the crowd while the Chief Constable introduced her.
They were astonished. How old was she? *Thirty*-something?
And already Chief Superintendent. She had the fresh sheen
of the young and the calm implacability of the self-willed, and
no one there had ever seen a DCS like her. They had seen

sincere, grizzled superintendents, like DCS Waddington, whom everyone instinctively deferred to as 'Ma'am', and loud, bald ones like DCS Wallace, 'Sir' to his face and 'Barko' behind his back. Some had seen the legendary DCS Chester Lynch, uber-macho black female head of Violent Crime, lately disgraced (and deceased), and back in the day, a few had even seen Rebecca's own father, DCS Derek Wainwright, later Chief Constable in Yorkshire, now sitting in the House of Lords, advisor to the Home Secretary. But they had never seen a superintendent so photogenic as this Wainwright. She looked like the movie version of herself, her silky-fine blond hair an advert, her eyes a natural shade of blue that looked expensive, her chin the tense, delicate chin of heroines in English romance. Yet, as the Chief Constable now reminded them, she was also the hard-edged veteran of a string of successful high-risk operations in the worst trouble spots in the country, culminating in Firewall, when she infiltrated organised crime in Dover, briefly being held hostage with an undercover colleague, who later lost his life, before escaping to secure the uncompromised capture of everyone under suspicion. Nothing knocked her off course. Pressure simply didn't affect her. In her short, improbable career, she had won four Silver Leaves, the Queen's Commendation for Bravery, the Queen's Gallantry Medal and, rarest of all, the George Medal, awarded when the degree of risk of death is over ninety per cent. They looked at her, perfect as a photo in a magazine, and it seemed frankly wrong. They could not compute it, so they stared at her in silence, and she looked back, noting Raymond Wilkins standing a little aloof at the side of the crowd, tall and handsome in black woollen peacoat and long striped scarf. She did not see Ryan Wilkins. Ryan Wilkins was not there. She noted this too.

The Chief Constable's dark brown voice died away and she stepped forward at last to speak.

Her voice was calm and crisp and a little cold. 'Good morning. I'm pleased to see you here. You know who I am, and I'll soon get to know who you are, and I look forward to that. I'll be frank. This is a time of change in the police services. These changes are non-negotiable and it's my job to ensure that they're made, and made quickly and effectively, and I hope you'll come on that journey with me. Put simply, we have a duty of care to the public which we have not yet fulfilled. Going forward, our code of conduct will be at the heart of all we do. That's also non-negotiable. You will find me a receptive and engaged leader who will put your well-being first in terms of work-life balance and job satisfaction, and more than ready to reward outstanding work in meaningful ways.' She paused, scanning the crowd. 'Shout-out here to DI Hare for progress being made on the Pelzer investigation.'

A balding man at the back in a black leather blazer put on a smirk and took the envious glances of those around him.

'However,' DCS Wainwright went on, 'no one will find me lax. I'm willing to listen and learn, but also to guide and, when necessary, to enforce the code by which this service is required to abide.' She stood there calmly and everyone in the room felt she was looking directly at them. She spoke again. 'One last thing. I dislike the old-fashioned formality of "Ma'am". I am not that sort of person. You will please address me as "Sir". Thank you, that's all.' She hadn't smiled yet and didn't smile now. Before she turned to go, she issued a brief instruction: 'Wilkinses in my office in five minutes please.' For a moment she faced the Chief Constable; he nodded and turned away. Then she was gone, and Ray stood on his own in the emptying room looking after her.

He was still there when Ryan arrived a few moments later, a flurry of fluorescence in oversized lime-green puffa and multicoloured hip-hop joggers, and began speaking without explanation.

'Fucking nightmare, mate, Jade gets me down the Co-op first thing, bit of shoplifting going on, then Ry slips over in the chilled aisle, nearly brains himself, then the Peugeot, piece of shit, has a fucking identity crisis bottom of the Abingdon Road, I had to walk the last mile, I think I done something to my hip.'

He stood there, all fidgets as usual, looking around jerkily, the scar tissue on his cheek shiny under the panel lighting.

'Did I miss anything?' he said.

'You missed everything.'

'What's she like then?'

'You'll see now. She's called us in.'

'Oh yeah?' Ryan briefly looked worried. 'No problem,' he said at once. 'I can get on with anyone, me.' He wiped his bony nose with a finger and shuffled from side to side, while Ray watched him in disgust. 'Anyway, we can ask Blondie why we didn't get the Pelzer 'stead of that dipstick Hairless.'

The murder of a security guard at the Pelzer Institute of Egyptology and Ancient Near Eastern Studies was the highest profile case on the books. He had been stabbed by men fleeing the building after a botched attempt to steal a rare fragment of a Sappho poem on papyrus, loaned by Berlin and stored overnight in the Pelzer archive before its display at the Ashmolean Museum the following day.

Ray was shaking his head. Ryan mimed incredulity. 'What? Should've been ours.'

'Listen. We're going in there together, I'll be standing right next to you. I don't want to catch any fallout from anything you say or do, so try to restrain yourself. You can't go around calling her Blondie. She's not that type.'

Ryan shrugged, sniffed. 'Alright, Mum. We going in then or what?'

'Aren't you nervous?'

'I'm never nervous.'

'Well, maybe that's the problem, right there.'

Ryan paused outside Wainwright's door, adjusted his joggers again.

'She as hot as they say?'

'For Christ's sake, Ryan.'

Ryan was already knocking. A voice inside said, 'Come.' And they went in.

Like everyone else, Ryan had heard plenty about her. She surprised him even so. He clocked her slyly out of the corner of his eye. Her perfectly proportioned face, the mathematical hang of her hair, the unhurried voice speaking fully formed sentences, above all the eyes that saw through people and judged them. He knew such eyes, had known them all his life, headmaster's eyes, social worker's eyes, youth magistrate's eyes, and felt a panic-jangle of nerves, instantly replaced by his usual fuck-it-all carelessness, the dismissive shrug. All the time he was watching her surreptitiously, noticing details. He saw the authority, the perfect lack of self-doubt, in every little thing she did. Only, he thought, there was something not quite perfect about her hands. Or perhaps too perfect. The way she kept them so still, as if she'd taught herself to do it, as if afraid perhaps they might give herself away. That was interesting, he thought, he wondered what . . .

'You can stop staring at me, by the way,' she said.

He looked at the floor.

She addressed them both. 'I'll be frank. You're a problem. Collectively, and individually. Before, you were someone else's problem, now you're mine, so it's my job to find a solution. Tell me,' she said, 'why do you work together?'

They were silent. Wary sideways glances at each other.

'Interesting,' she said. She fixed her attention on Ryan. 'Late this morning. You missed my introduction. I spoke about our code of conduct.'

'Yeah, thing is—'

'Is the code of conduct a waste of your time?'

He shifted under her gaze. Her voice was quiet but inescapable.

'Tell me this. Do first impressions count for anything?'

He couldn't resist a small shrug.

She paused, letting her unwavering eyes judge him. 'Do you think you're making a good impression on me now?'

He opened his mouth, gave up, closed it again.

'Reflect,' she said. 'And please call me "Sir".'

There was a silence in which Ryan could hear himself breathing. Ray took the opportunity to give his view about the need for change which she had raised in her early morning address and which he enthusiastically welcomed. While he talked, Ryan watched him playing to her, doing his best to be smooth, his voice deep, his expression sincere but vaguely anxious. He sneezed, apologised and went on. He had ideas, was willing to discuss them . . . perhaps a separate conversation? His eyes were doing a lot of work.

The Super interrupted him and looked at them both. 'Perhaps you're wondering why you didn't get the Pelzer?'

Ray said nothing. His expression drooped. Ryan said, 'Crossed my mind, yeah.'

She looked at him.

'Sir.'

'Frankly, I'm surprised,' she said. 'Your last murder case, the Zara Fanshawe one, was a mess.'

He sniffed, shuffled, shrugged. 'Fair enough. Got the job done, though. In the end.'

'In the end,' she said, 'instead of performing an arrest, you suggested a suspect make her own way to the station in an Uber.'

'Thing is, I know her. I knew she'd go.'

The Super looked at him with destroying impassivity. 'This suspect disappeared earlier, is that right?'

'Yeah.'

'Did you know she was going to do that too?'

He said nothing.

'Perhaps, DI Wilkins, you didn't know her as well as you thought.'

She turned at once to Ray. 'During the case, you spent a lot of time with the former Deputy Chief Constable.'

He couldn't deny it.

'Yet didn't pick up any sign of her involvement until two murders had been committed.'

Ray knew better than to argue.

'So, in addition to your credulity,' she said, 'you associated yourself with someone now disgraced. For someone as clearly ambitious as yourself that's unfortunate.'

Perhaps she had more to say but at that moment, to their mutual relief, her desk phone rang.

'Yes?' she said. Continuing, unnervingly, to look at them, she listened to the voice in her ear without speaking. 'Yes, I see,' she said at last, 'No. I have a better idea. Assign the Wilkinses. Yes, both of them. Don't worry,' she said, 'I'll tell them.'

She replaced the receiver. 'A death at a hotel in Sandford just called in. Elderly gentleman discovered in his pyjamas on the lawn. Likely cardiac. They assume a guest though they haven't identified him yet. No particular reason to think it suspicious. I'd send a lower rank but I prefer to send you.'

They looked at her.

Ray cleared his throat. 'Who's lead?' he asked.

'Don't think about who's lead,' she said. 'Just think of it as a possible way back. 'Stressing the word *possible*.'

They said nothing. They left.